SHATTERED LIES

WEB OF LIES #3

KATHLEEN BROOKS

LAUREN PUBLISHING

Forever Concealed

Forever Devoted - coming January 30, 2018

Women of Power Series

Chosen for Power

Built for Power

Fashioned for Power

Destined for Power

Web of Lies Series

Whispered Lies

Rogue Lies

Shattered Lies

1

WHEN FACED with a table full of men armed with guns, a woman had only one shot at getting out alive. And Valeria McGregor wasn't the kind to bat her lashes.

One week was all it had taken for Valeria to get to this point, but it was all she needed. She had the information necessary to bring down *Mollia Domini*, the international group set on pulling the world's strings from the shadows. Now, if only she could get out of the middle of Manuel Hernandez's cartel headquarters to tell her group.

"Miss McGregor." Manuel, the head of the *Hermanos de Sangre* drug cartel, placed both hands on the worn farm table and stared at her from the opposite end. In between them were eleven heavily armed soldiers waiting to be the one to leap to do his boss's bidding. "Who do you work for?"

"You," Valeria replied in Spanish. She may have a Scottish last name thanks to her father, but she had the ability to speak Spanish thanks to her mother. Manuel grinned, and she was reminded that while he was handsome, he was also deadly.

"We both know that's not true," he said, giving her a look

as if she were a child telling a fib. It was a look she'd seen from someone else right before she'd crossed into Mexico through Tecate, a small town along the border between Tijuana and Mexicali. How she hated when men were condescending simply because she was female. It was like a curse at times. But she never let that look deter her. From there, she'd stolen a car and driven overnight to Hermosillo in Sonora, Mexico. On the streets there, she bought a fake Mexican ID before boarding a plane to Mazatlán, the resort town in Sinaloa, Mexico, that was headquarters of the *Hermanos de Sangre* drug cartel.

"You look like this American I've seen." Valeria looked at the ceiling fan over the table as she tapped one hand on the table as if trying to remember a name. But it was really just a distraction so she could reach for her gun with the other hand. "Sebastian Abel. That's it. He's some famous rich tech guy." And also the person funding the group led by the President of the United States. A group whose mission it was to bring down *Mollia Domini*.

Manuel preened at the compliment. Little did he know it was Sebastian Abel's bank account and private plane that brought Valeria to Manuel's headquarters, looking for a job. Sebastian was a billionaire and President Birch Stratton's best friend. He was funding the president's secret operation off the books. And his name was also showing up places it shouldn't have.

Valeria's job was to follow the money. She'd taken down plenty of drug lords when she was with the DEA. So imagine her surprise when she began to follow the money of Dan March and Phylicia Claymore, two corrupt FBI agents working for *Mollia Domini*, who used it to wreak havoc. And it all came back to a little bank here in Mazatlán, right along with some money from Sebastian Abel. The same little bank that also happened to be owned by Manuel as a way to launder his drug money. As the largest cartel in all of Mexico, *Hermanos de Sangre* wielded more power than the Mexican government. And that made the man down the table from her very dangerous.

"Flattery will get you nowhere. Now, we know you're no longer with the DEA. So who are you working for now and why are you here?" Manuel demanded. Flattery, maybe. Sebastian was wickedly handsome with black hair and dark gray eyes, but Manuel was like his mini version, standing the same height as Valeria's five feet six inches.

"I already told you I wasn't with the DEA. Didn't you believe me?" Valeria asked with annoyance. It was how she got into the compound. She'd told Manuel the truth—she'd gotten fired because he was paying off her coworkers and she tried to bust them. Since her career was ruined, why not come to the man she at least knew paid well?

"Yes, but I didn't believe you. You work at a bar owned by Elizabeth James, an FBI agent," Manuel accused.

The men at the table shifted.

"*Former* agent. Just like me, she was fired for doing nothing wrong. We jaded types are drawn to one another. Plus, you pay better than Lizzy does. Now, what is this all about?" Valeria refused to look at the ceiling fan. Instead she kept her eyes locked with Manuel's.

"It's about this." Manuel turned a tablet around as a video began to play. It was from a security camera within Manuel's desktop computer. It began with Valeria waking up the computer. She'd turned off the complex's security cameras, but she hadn't known about the one on his computer. At least he couldn't see the flash drive she'd copied to that was now safe in a waterproof compartment in the buckle of her belt.

"I can't check my email?" Valeria asked in amazement. They all knew she was lying, though.

"What did you see, Miss McGregor?" Manuel asked in a deadly serious tone that sent chills down her back.

"I see you have a thing for Kerra Ruby's sex tape."

Manuel didn't slam his hands down as she expected. Instead, he sat down and stared at her as if he could read the truth from her. "So you hack my computer, you're no longer with the DEA, your coworker was with the FBI, and your best friend is the press secretary. You and I both know that doesn't add up to you coming here for a job. Plus, it's very interesting company to keep. So I'll ask one more time. Who do you work for?"

JASON WOLSKI DIDN'T like Sebastian Abel. He stood toe to toe with him at the private airport outside DC. Jason was supposed to transport a dead body or two. What he didn't need was this man busting his balls. Dalton, his former PJ team member, certainly didn't trust Sebastian, and Jason couldn't blame Dalton. He didn't trust Sebastian either, and he'd just met him.

"Who are you?" Sebastian asked again as he stood tall, trying to intimidate Jason. It wouldn't work. As a PJ, nickname for soldiers in the U.S. Air Force Pararescue, Jason and his team were the last chance of rescue behind enemy lines, in the middle of the ocean, on the top of a mountain . . . it didn't matter where you were, a PJ would come for you. It was how Jason had lost his leg. A rescue in the middle of the ocean where a shark decided he looked like dinner.

Dalton had saved him, and Jason had retired to spend time with his wife, Michelle. They'd started a camp in the

Virginia mountains to help wounded veterans regain strength and independence while learning to deal with the inevitable PTSD. And then Dalton had called out of the blue. It was then that everything had taken a horrible turn. His wife was now dead, and maybe Sebastian didn't realize that meant Jason had nothing left to live for.

"Look, I was told you were cooperating with the president. If you're not, then maybe we need to have a little talk between us to find out who you are working with. When this was arranged, there was no mention of you being on the plane with me. You either need to tell me why you're suddenly going wherever I am, since I didn't tell you my destination, or you need to back the fuck off," Jason growled as he dropped the second cooler at the bottom of the stairs to the jet. He'd packed four—two with bodies and two with fish just in case someone wanted to see what was in them.

"What's in the coolers?" Sebastian asked instead.

Jason didn't respond.

"Where are you going?"

Sebastian was losing his temper. Jason saw the heat flushing his neck slightly. Good. Jason was losing his, too, and right now smashing his fist into Sebastian's perfect face sounded damn good. "Either you're with us or against us. Which is it?" Jason asked, setting his hand on the large hunting knife attached to his hip.

"I'm with you, if I know who you are."

Jason smiled a lethal smile. He had survived a shark attack. He'd saved more people than he could remember. He'd scaled mountains, swum through hurricanes, dug through avalanches, and run through enemy fire. If this asshole thought he could intimidate him, he was dead wrong.

Sebastian's eyes narrowed. "When the pilot called to tell

me the jet was ready, I had to check it out. How do I know you're not stealing it?"

"I guess that's a risk you have to take. Or simply call the president. I'm acting on his direct orders."

Jason turned to the back of the truck and hefted up another giant sized cooler. This one had Fitz Houlihan's dead body in it. Tate Carlisle, the press secretary and member of the band of spies the president had put together, had killed the Hollywood agent when he'd told her she had to join *Mollia Domini* or die. Too bad for him Tate was a crack shot. When Jason turned back, Sebastian was on the phone. Jason grunted as he carried the body up the small steps and into the plane. Sebastian was going to be trouble. Men like him were used to giving orders, not receiving them.

"SEBASTIAN, DID YOU SEE THE NEWS?" Birch smiled into the phone. He saw Alex's head shoot up and meet his eyes. He looked suspicious, and that reminded Birch that the team didn't fully trust Sebastian. His own best friend was now a possible suspect. It hurt. Sebastian had always been the one person Birch could always turn to.

Birch listened to Sebastian angrily mention a roughneck absconding with his plane. "Who is he, and what does he want with the plane?"

"He's with me, if that's what you're worried about. And you have many planes. I don't know why this is suddenly a problem. Is something going on, Sebastian?" Birch lowered his voice to his friend.

"No, it's fine. I need to leave for a couple days, and I haven't seen him before so how am I to know if I can turn a $50,000,000 jet over to him?"

Birch heard the frustration and something else he couldn't quite place. "Let's get together soon and discuss it. Make sure we're all on the same page."

"Don't do that, Birch. Don't use the negotiator voice with me. We'll have dinner when I get back."

The line went dead, and Birch felt the first fingers of doubt grab hold of him. What was going on with Sebastian?

2

IT HAD TAKEN a while but he was finally here. The private villa on the shores of the Black Sea outside the small town of Krapets, Bulgaria, was eerily silent. His villa was near the border of Romania, and well off the main coastal road. Here, looking out over the dark green waters on the quiet shores of the Black Sea, he had conceived of *Mollia Domini*. He had planned it perfectly. But now, he'd hit a bump in the road. A really big bump. He slid his arm over the desk and sent everything crashing to the floor. Years of developing a network of reporters and celebrities to spread his messages —gone just like that. He'd known while he was traveling to the villa that it was bad, but now the president was being hailed as some sort of hero as contact after contact of his were publicly humiliated on television, even here in Bulgaria.

Secretary of State Sandra Cummings would arrive shortly. He'd gotten in a couple hours before, thanks to his private jet, and the others were just settling in. She'd had a harder time getting away, but he'd gotten her a fake passport. He needed to refocus, and here, where it all began, was where he needed to be. The others in the inner sanctum were having a drink on the terrace. He would join them. He wouldn't betray his emotions. Instead, he'd plot. It was going to be hard to overcome, but he didn't become as powerful as he was without making hard choices. And one thing he'd discovered over the years: one could never have too much money or too much power. He straightened his tie and stepped out onto the terrace. His housekeeper hurried forward before he could join the others.

"Yes?"

"I just took this message. I tried you in your office, but your phone was busy."

Though he kept his cool in public and always stayed under control, sometimes in private he let his temper get the best of him. She handed him a piece of paper and hurried away. He opened it expecting bad news, but a smile broke out over his face instead.

ELIZABETH JAMES, or Lizzy to her friends, tried to sleep on the military plane, but it was so uncomfortable her whole body hurt. She and Dalton had flown comfortably in a Galaxy plane to Ramstein Air Base in Germany before holing up in the cargo of a smaller plane headed for Mihail Kogalniceanu Air Base near Constanta, Romania. When they landed, they would be near the Black Sea and have to make their way inland to Bucharest in order to find Sandra, who had disappeared after a suspected meeting with co-conspirators within *Mollia Domini*. She hoped Alex was able to find something on her location because right now they had very few leads.

Dalton put his arm around her and Lizzy lay back

against him. The plane was too loud to speak without yelling, but they didn't need to speak. The first time they'd had sex it had been about lust. But now, well, something had changed along the way. They understood each other on a deeper level. So deep that when Dalton felt Lizzy sigh he squeezed her hand in silent support. They both knew they were on a needle-in-a-haystack mission and could be walking in on something that could end their lives. However, it was the risk they both accepted. And for that they didn't need words.

HE SAT in the open air as the evening sun shone off the waters of the Black Sea. The note he'd received hours earlier was still in his hand. He didn't want to do it, but nothing would stop his plans.

He heard the doorbell ring deep in the house. His housekeeper would get it, but he walked inside to greet his new guest anyway. A minute later, Sandra Cummings, the United States Secretary of State, stepped into the hallway looking worried.

"Have you heard?"

"Yes. I'll handle it. You're needed in DC now more than ever. Does President Stratton have any inkling of what's going on?"

"No. He's too caught up following his dick. If Claudia hadn't gone after Tate—" Sandra let out a frustrated breath. "I don't know how some gossip rag got hold of this story. And where the fuck is Fitz? Has George said anything?" He saw her glance out to media mogul George Stanworth sitting on the terrace.

"His daughter, Helena, mentioned her wish for revenge

after Tate did a piece on law enforcement going easy on rich kids. I guess Tate said Helena's daughter, Blythe, should be in jail."

Sandra nodded. "Blythe was high and smashed her sports car into another car, killing a pregnant woman. The DA refused to prosecute."

"I should have known when I asked George to assist us that he'd bring all his family baggage with him. Now Helena is even more focused on bringing Tate down." He looked out over the sea, and it calmed him. "It's being taken care of, though. Would you like to freshen up before the meeting?"

Sandra shook her head. "No, thank you. I'm ready when you are."

He nodded to his housekeeper, who was waiting for his signal. She reached over and rang the old bell that had been in place since the house was a working farm. He escorted Sandra to the dinner table on the beach. Within minutes, the entire group was seated at the table as his housekeeper served them. It was a shame he'd have to kill her after his guests left. Loose ends could not be tolerated.

He was about to start the meeting when George's cell phone rang. He gritted his teeth. "Sorry," George apologized. He may be elderly, but there was nothing weak about George Stanworth. It was one of the reasons he'd been recruited to *Mollia Domini*, that and his ability to reach billions of people through his news outlets, TV shows, and movies. Not to mention his contacts with all of Hollywood's influencers. It's what made putting up with George's family baggage livable.

"Come on, Dad," Helena said, eyeing the phone. "Your bimbo can wait until later." Of course she'd dislike George's third—or was it fourth wife? The girl was young enough to be Helena's daughter.

George silenced the phone only to look down at it a second later. "What the fuck?"

Helena leaned over and narrowed her eyes. "Is that your front door?"

He raised his eyes with impatience, but Helena and George weren't paying attention to him. Frustration was boiling to the surface when George put the phone to his ear and made a call. He used his cane and stepped a couple feet from the table. Everyone kept their eyes on George the entire time. They all felt it. Something had happened, and it would affect them all. George finally hung up and slowly made his way back to his chair.

"What happened?" Helena asked as George threw back his wine.

George handed the phone to him. When the host looked down, he saw a picture of a dead Fitz Houlihan with his arm around another dead man. Someone he guessed had some relation to Fitz. "Who's the other guy?"

"A cleaner named Hugo. He disappeared when Jeff Sargent did," Helena answered.

"Tell me," he ordered.

"Christine found them at our front door when she was going to spin class. There was a note. She read it to me, and I told her to burn it. She did so while we were on the phone," George said, his breathing slightly heavy with anxiety. "The puppet strings have been cut. *Mollia Domini* is next."

The host sucked in a deep breath through his nose. His rage was boiling. "Ah!" he yelled, shoving back his chair, reaching behind his back and pulling his gun. In seconds, George and Helena lay on the ground, their blood turning the sand brown. The remaining two at the table sat silently, staring down at the dead bodies.

"Their usefulness has run out. And because of them, we

have to push phase three up. It's forcing me to do things I hadn't wanted to do. I've received word from a White House contact. I'm taking care of it since it appears I can't depend on any of you."

Sandra looked down at her plate. She didn't know he had someone else in the White House. It had been naïve to think she'd be the only one trusted with guiding the president from within.

"May I offer some assistance?" the person across the table from Sandra asked.

He turned to the other side of the table, letting Sandra shake in fear. "Yes, have your men in DC at the ready. I'll give you the orders in an hour. And we must get the bombs ready. Check in with your contacts and report back tomorrow with where we stand in terms of phase three readiness." He stood up and dragged the bodies one at a time over to the water's edge as Sandra and his other partner hurried inside. He kicked off his shoes, shed his clothes, and pulled the bodies into the sea. He pushed them past the waves, his anger cooling as his body thrummed under the exercise. With one big push, he shoved the bodies toward the open water and began his swim back to the beach. He should have known he couldn't depend on anyone but himself.

3

—————

BIRCH LOOKED out the window of the West Sitting Hall as he waited for Tate to finish getting ready for their first official date. They'd slept in as long as they could that morning—all the way until five o'clock. Since then, it had been nonstop. Humphrey had had way too much coffee and spent the day running from office to office handing out reports, handling media, and working with Tate on presenting the correct story to the public. The story was of George Stanworth using the media as his own way to push his agenda with no concern or respect for the actual truth. What was interesting was that George and his daughter, Helena, were nowhere to be found to answer for the shitstorm now coming down on his company.

Jason had arrived back home and reported the packages had been delivered successfully and offered his help at any time. Maybe that was why George had disappeared? The numbness in Jason's voice had reminded Birch of the pain of losing his own wife. That pain never went away. But as he turned to look at Tate walking down the hall toward him, he knew there was enough love in him for them both. He hoped that someday Jason would remember he was still alive. The pain was undoubtedly excruciating. So for now, Jason was doing what he needed to survive the tremendous loss.

"You're stunning," Birch told her as she did a little spin in the casual sundress. She looked relaxed even after the ups and downs of the past month.

"I feel great. I'm turning off my phone and going on a date with the man I love. Not only that, we don't have to hide. The newest popular story running is our love story. The hate and vile filth that had been thrown at me before has now changed to the almost idyllic President and the Press Secretary story." Tate laughed happily and Birch smiled at her pleasure.

"What's funny?" he asked, wrapping his arms around her waist and looking at her.

"The irony. Our relationship has been anything but idyllic. But if I get a couple hours to forget about the darkness we are embroiled in, that's worth smiling." Tate leaned up and placed her lips on his. Birch closed his eyes, getting lost in a kiss that was turning hotter by the second.

"We better head out for our date now, or we may forget we had plans and end up in bed," Birch said, pulling away. He wasn't entirely convinced that would be a bad thing.

"I'm starving!" Tate laughed as she swatted him on the bottom and hurried down the hall. Birch smiled and caught up to her, slipping his hand into hers as they headed down the red-carpeted stairs.

Birch met Abrams and Brock at the bottom of the stairs before they headed to the limo. "As per your request, we have trimmed the detail. We have two cars with us with agents in both. We have two agents at the restaurant now, securing the location and a table for you," Brock informed him quietly as he opened the door to limo for them.

"Thank you, Brock," Tate said, placing her hand quickly on his arm and giving it a squeeze.

Birch slid into the back seat next to Tate. They talked of their day. They talked of their worst first dates, and they laughed. For a moment Birch was simply a man nervous about making sure his date went well.

TATE LOOKED up at the gold letters on the red sign. The restaurant was small with a few bistro tables set outside. Couples laughed over large dishes of pasta. They stopped and stared as the limo and two SUVs came to a stop outside next to the already parked detail that had secured the restaurant for them.

"Ready?" Birch asked as the people pulled out their cell phones and a man in a marinara-covered apron came hurrying out, his pot belly swaying as he grinned broadly at them.

Abrams opened the door and Birch slid out, holding out his hand for Tate. The owner of Gimiagano's greeted them as the people at the table asked for pictures.

"Is it okay?" Birch asked.

Tate nodded and Brock handled the diners coming up a few at a time for a picture with them.

"Thank you all, but it's date night." He winked to the delight of the patrons gathered outside.

The owner showed them to their romantic table in the back with plenty of privacy. Tate noticed a table of two men nearby and spotted the coms systems. Abrams and Brock took up positions near the front and back doors as the limo pulled up to the back door out of sight from the front street.

Two SUVs parked out front as if they were regular diners, even though the engines were still running and agents were inside keeping active watch.

A complimentary bottle of wine was poured as patrons got their last photos in. After hearing the specials from the owner, who was also the head chef, they were finally alone. Birch raised his glass and Tate followed suit. "To many evenings together."

Tate took a sip of wine and rolled her eyes. "This is so good."

"I used to eat here all the time when I was a nobody in politics. Stephano imports all his wine from these small family wineries in Italy."

"Did you always live in Virginia?" Tate asked even though she knew the answer. Hearing the answer firsthand made it sound new.

Birch told her of growing up at the military base, and Tate couldn't stop smiling.

"Tell me about your brother," Birch said as Stephano set down a plate of fried calamari and some fresh bread.

Tate grinned as she thought of Tucker. He was her little brother, and while she hated to admit it, he was a good one. "He always pestered me, growing up. He'd spy on my sleepovers." Tate looked into Birch's smiling face before a force sent her flying from her chair. Her body slammed against the brick wall as the restaurant filled with clouds of debris and dust.

Tate's ears were ringing, and she coughed uncontrollably, trying to breathe. Her eyes stung as she groped her way toward the outline of a body. "Birch," she croaked as she crawled on hands and knees over broken glass and shattered tables.

It seemed far off in the distance, but she began to hear

pinging noises. Turning her head, she cringed in pain. The entire front of the small restaurant was gone. Bodies littered the floor where just moments before, diners sat enjoying their meals. There was so much dust in the air it was hard to see out of the windows. But the noise became clear —gunfire.

Tate felt a fear unlike anything else begin to choke her. If she had thought her car accident was bad, this fear completely shut off her ability to think. Escape was all she could think of. Tate pushed her body to crawl faster. The first body was that of Abrams. She shook him, screaming his name. His eyes were open and a shard of glass protruded from his neck.

Tate was about to leave Abrams when the gunfire came to a stop. Glancing to the hole in the front of the building, she saw figures moving toward them from across the street. There was no help coming, she realized dimly. Looking back, she saw Brock limping as he started flinging tables aside. Brock would help her. He would get her to safety out the back door, but he should be with Birch. If Brock was here, then . . . "Birch!" She had wrongly assumed the agents out back already dragged him into the limo.

Brock's eyes shot up at her and then at the men coming toward them. Tate pushed open Abrams's jacket and grabbed the gun. She tried to stand, but her leg failed her. Looking down, she saw why. Her leg was broken. She saw the bump of the wrecked bone. Tate bit down on the grip of the gun and crawled, dragging her broken leg toward Brock.

Stephano's body lay writhing on the floor. "Stay still, help is on the way," she said as she stopped. Then she saw him.

"Brock!" Tate pointed to the body partially hidden by Stephano's body.

Brock didn't look at her, but instead fired off a shot. A man fell to the floor and then Brock ran toward her.

"Stephano, you have to move. You can do it. Please," Tate was crying as she shoved at his side.

Brock stopped and fired another shot before bending over and flipping a table up to provide some cover. "I don't have contact with the limo. I don't know if the driver is still there or if he's under attack," Brock said into his intercoms being relayed to headquarters.

Tate continued to use all her strength to push Stephano as he groaned unconsciously. His eyes were closed and there was blood dripping from his ears. Brock fired again and bent down. "Push!" he yelled.

Stephano rolled off Birch, and Tate scrambled to feel for a pulse. Brock fired again in rapid succession from his spot behind the table. Bullets flew around them now as Tate almost collapsed in relief when she felt the flutter of an uneven pulse.

"He's alive!"

Brock conveyed the facts into his coms as four men stepped through the blown-out front of the building. "Can he walk?"

"He's unconscious." Tate shook Birch and got a groan out of him. "Birch, you have to wake up. Birch!"

Sirens sounded in the distance. Tate looked up at Brock, his face set in stone as he aimed at the first wave of men and fired. Tate looked to the back door. Could she drag Birch outside? Tate screamed as a man kicked in the back door, answering her question for her.

Brock turned to look and fired, missing the man, before the four men at the front sprayed them with gunfire. Brock ducked and Tate covered Birch with her body as she picked up Abrams's gun and fired. It hit his chest, but he didn't stop.

She fired again, this time at his head and the man at the back door fell down, dead.

She began to turn in order to tell Brock to aim for the head when she felt her face splashed with something warm. She wiped it from her eyes, and when she looked at her hands they were red. "Brock?"

Tate didn't have to look up to find him. Brock's body lay a foot from her knees and part of his head was missing. Tate choked back a helpless cry and with resolve reached for the gun in his hand.

The only chance they stood to survive was her own will to live and two guns. Tate pulled the table closer to cover herself and Birch before lying flat on the ground and crawling to the edge of the table. She took a deep breath like she did during target competition and cleared her mind. She ignored the sounds of sirens. She couldn't count on them. She ignored Brock's body and the blood pooling around his head inches from her. She ignored the warmth and stickiness of that blood on her bare arm as she laid herself into firing position.

Tate saw the targets, and she fired. Four rapid shots as if she were in competition. Two hit dead center as they fell dead, their heads blasted apart. The other two dove for cover as Tate slid back behind the table and military-crawled to the other side.

"Behind you," Birch gasped, his breathing unsteady.

In surprise, Tate spun around only to feel a bullet rip through her shoulder. She screamed, the gun in her right hand falling to the ground. The man lowered his gun at Birch, and Tate raised her left hand. She fired Brock's gun over and over. The man staggered back as she hit him in the vest, readjusted her aim and shot him in the eye. His body slammed against the back wall leaving a red mark on the wall as he slid down.

She rummaged through Brock's pockets until she found another clip. She slid it into the gun and held it awkwardly with her left hand. "Birch, hang in there, please. Help is coming."

"I love you," Birch gasped between heavy breaths. He fought to breathe as Tate leaned down and placed trembling lips to his.

"I love you too."

Then Tate did the hardest thing she'd ever done. She turned her back on Birch as his eyes slid closed. Sounds of sirens, helicopters, and men yelling surrounded her, but there were still two men inside the restaurant as federal agents and police began to surround the building. Tate knew without a doubt the two remaining men wouldn't give up without a fight.

She sat up on her knees, the pain from her broken lower leg sending a wave of dizziness through her, and scanned the area through the sight of her gun. There, at the corner of the bar the muzzle of a gun stuck out. Tate pushed everything aside as she focused on that gun. It moved slowly as the man decided to lean out. With her arms propped on the edge of the table, her knees shaking from pain and her left hand holding her injured arm steady, she pulled the trigger. She didn't wait for the best shot. She just took the shot. The shot she knew would kill him if it hit, and she knew it would. She saw the gun drop to the ground and knew she'd hit her target.

"Police! Drop your weapon!" came the command from behind her. But Tate just shook her head. There was still one more person left unaccounted for.

Tate felt them surrounding her from behind. She saw

the officers and agents storm the front. "Watch out!" she screamed, but it was too late. The last gunman opened fire. An agent fell as a hailstorm of gunfire aimed at a person she couldn't see erupted. Then all was quiet.

"It's the president!" Tate heard someone gasp behind her. "We need an ambulance ASAP!"

Tate finally dropped the gun. Her body collapsed. Her legs gave out as she fell to Birch's side.

"Are you Tate Carlisle?" an officer asked. He seemed fuzzy as the world tilted. She blinked back the shadows as she fumbled to find Birch's hand. When she clasped his hand, she looked back up. "Yes, but you need to get Birch to a hospital now."

"I believe we need to get you there too. That was a hell of a shot, Miss Carlisle."

She didn't care. She looked down at Birch as EMTs rushed inside. Tate was pulled away, and she screamed in pain. She didn't hear the officer apologize. She only watched in absolute horror as the EMTs began CPR on Birch's lifeless body.

In minutes, they had him strapped to a spinal board as six men carried him quickly from the restaurant. "I have to go with him," she yelled as other EMTs now flooded in to help the injured.

"I'm sorry, but I can't allow that. You need to come with us." Tate looked up at the unidentified agent. He didn't offer an explanation and the officer was happy to hand her off.

"No," she said with as much power as she could. "I'm Tate Carlisle, the press secretary for the president, and I will not go with anyone I don't know. Please call Humphrey Orville, the chief of staff, for me."

"You're coming with me, ma'am," he said through gritted teeth. The officer now looked curiously between them.

"No!" Tate yelled. "I will not come with you, and I demand you contact Humphrey Orville, the chief of staff."

The man grabbed for her and the young officer, no more than twenty-two years old, pulled his gun as the EMTs froze in their progression toward her. "I'm sorry, sir, but I'll need to see some identification."

"I'll have you fired for this. I'm CIA." He flipped open his badge and the young man wilted.

"I don't give a shit who you are. I'm not going with you." There was something wrong here. The man was only looking at her. He wasn't allowing EMTs to see her, and with her broken leg and a bullet wound, he'd have to carry her screaming out of here.

There was a commotion outside as cars scrambled back to clear a space in the street. Tate had never felt such relief as when she looked out and saw Crew Dixon, pilot of Marine One and member of their secret group, landing a military helicopter. Crew glanced around, his eyes locking on hers, and then to the man in front of her. Crew leapt from the helicopter, and the man lunged for her. Crew ran, Tate screamed, and the young officer fired.

4

LIZZY AND DALTON were outside the embassy in Bucharest in the middle of the night when her phone rang. Lizzy looked down and saw it was Humphrey. In the span of one minute, everything changed.

"We have to get home now," Lizzy said, hanging up the phone.

"What's going on?" Dalton asked as he lowered his binoculars.

"Tate and Birch were injured in a bombing. Birch wasn't breathing when they took him away, and then a supposed CIA agent tried to grab Tate."

Dalton was already turning the car on. "Is she okay?"

"Humphrey said Crew has her. That's all I know. He's ordered us back to DC via the military again. He's afraid our covers have been blown. He's assessing and will call with any updates. Everything is on complete lockdown."

The drive back to the airbase seemed to take forever instead of the few hours it really was. When they arrived, the sun was rising across the sleepy base. Dalton parked the borrowed car and stopped when they heard an alarm sound. Military personnel ran from the buildings in various stages of dress toward the water. With a questionable glances at each other, they followed the crowd.

"What is it?" Lizzy asked the medical team as they ran by.

"Bodies in the water!"

Lizzy and Dalton followed the crowd and stopped at the shore. Men and women were coming out of the Black Sea dragging two life preservers that lifeguards used. Slung over the long red foam were what looked to be the bodies of an elderly man and a middle-aged woman.

Dalton narrowed his eyes as his hand grabbed her arm. "Does that man look familiar?"

"No . . . wait," Lizzy felt her breath come quickly as she pulled up her phone and searched for a name. "It's George Stanworth," she gasped.

VALERIA HEARD THEM COMING. She felt the vibration of the water increase as they got closer. When she had refused to answer Manuel's questions the other day, they'd tied her arms and submerged her up to her neck in a large barrel and then put the lid on over her. There were holes for air, but since no light ever shone through, she guessed she was in the basement.

She wasn't sure how long she'd been down there. Three days? Three hours? She didn't know. What Valeria did know was that she was going mad. She was disoriented, exhausted, and only talking to herself had gotten her through it. But now was not the time to let one's brain take the lead. It was time to let her instincts loose. It was time to make her move.

The lid was pried off as light flooded the room with a single flick of a light switch. Valeria went limp as the man struggled to pull her fully soaked from the water. Good. She didn't want to use any energy, and she wanted them to use plenty of it.

"*Ayuadame!*" The guard yelled to the other to come help. It took them both to carry her limp body from the barrel. They were breathing heavily by the time they dumped her in the chair at the end of the long kitchen table.

Valeria's gun was gone, but the knife strapped to her calf was still there under her waterlogged jeans. Valeria let her head fall back as she stared at the aged bronzed metallic ceiling fan. She heard Manuel slam his hands on the table and call her name. Valeria didn't move.

"Get the bitch to sit up!" Manuel ordered. The men who had dragged her from the basement let out a sigh, but then shoved her up in her chair.

Seven men: two behind her with their hands on each of her shoulders, two on each side of the table, and Manuel at the head of the table sitting across from her.

Valeria groaned and let her head loll to the side. "Food," she barely whispered.

Manuel chuckled. "I see you're not asking for water. Get her some bread."

A hunk of dried bread was thrown on the table in front of her. Valeria clumsily picked it up using only her teeth and dropped it to the floor. With a wail of frustration she ordered the men to pick it up. "Can you either untie me or make them feed it to me?"

Valeria looked at the bread, defeated, as Manuel stared at her. All was quiet for many seconds before Valeria's hands were grabbed and the rope was cut. She devoured the bread, chewing loudly with her mouth open. Not only was she actually starving, but she had to put Manuel at ease.

"You need to start talking if you don't want to go back into the barrel," Manuel threatened.

Valeria just nodded her agreement and took a huge bite of the bread. Clumsily she dropped a piece and bent to get it. It was now or never. Manuel would never let her live. Instead, he'd gleefully torture her to death.

Valeria pushed up her pant leg, grabbed her knife, and shoved herself back in her chair so hard that it tipped over. With two quick motions she sliced the femoral arteries on both guards. She rolled backward, heels over head, and when she stood, she had one of the guard's guns in her hand.

"Kill her," Manuel said with a flick of his wrist. Men flanked him, and Valeria jumped.

Her feet landed hard on the table as bullets flew. It took two running steps to reach the middle of the table. Valeria leapt up as she fired on the soldiers below. Her hand closed around the large metal cage housing the lights for the ceiling fan as she swung through the air. Using her left hand, she fired at the men, dropping two more. The other two had moved to form a shield around Manuel.

Valeria pulled her legs up and let go of the fan. She sailed through the air, up and over Manuel and his guards. The landing hurt. She let her knees go soft as she hit the floor and rolled before springing up. Manuel was shouting for his guards as Valeria ran for all she was worth. She wanted to kill Manuel, but the information on the drive, hopefully still dry, in her belt buckle was worth more than her desire for vengeance.

Valeria could hear the alarm sound in the surrounding buildings as she ran through the compound, heading to the private garage. Men would be pouring out in seconds, armed to the teeth. She looked up as the door leading to the garage opened, and she fired. The man fell to the ground, and Valeria scooped up his AR type .223 rifle.

The garage was large, not the normal garage you found in neighborhood houses. No, Manuel's was a showcase to display his wealth. It would be tempting to go for the Ferrari, but it was the bulletproof Mercedes-Maybach SUV she headed for. It was luxury personified, but it also had big tires and a huge metal bar across the front that would be perfect for plowing people down.

Valeria didn't wait for the garage door to open. She slammed the door to the SUV closed, pushed the start button, and floored it. The giant tires spun as shots pinged off the driver side window. The tires grabbed the slick floor, and the SUV shot through the garage door, ripping the entire thing from the rails and flattening numerous soldiers who had been closing in on her.

Valeria bounced so hard she hit her head, but she kept her hands on the wheel as the $500,000 SUV took bullets from all around her. There were three gates between her and freedom. The first one would be the toughest. Men had formed a wall. SUVs were blocking the exit.

Valeria spun the car, sending dust flying and the men began to chase her. Just as she hoped, one of the SUVs from the barricade moved to follow her. She slammed on the brakes and put the car in reverse before flooring it. Val put her arm over the passenger seat and looked out the back as she drove backward past the SUV following her and right through the first solid wood gate. She hit it hard. The airbags deployed, but Valeria was ready for the hit. Driving backward, she could still see where she was going.

The SUV bounced and Valeria did all she could do to

keep her foot on the gas as she careened down the small mountaintop toward the second gate. The second fence was made of wood, not concrete blocks like the one nearest the house, which gave her more options.

The airbag began to deflate, but Valeria could see the gate quickly approaching. She didn't have time to turn around. Instead she turned the wheel sharply, veering off the dirt drive and onto the desert grass-spotted ground. The guards blocking the gate scrambled to fire off shots, but Valeria drove the back of the SUV right through the wooden privacy fence.

Valeria slammed on the brakes and spun the wheel, finally turning the SUV around before driving down the hill toward the final gate and freedom. Well, as free as she could get in a town and country owned by Manuel Hernandez. Looking in her mirror, she saw clouds of dust from SUVs and trucks coming after her. It wouldn't be easy, but she had to get away.

With her face set in determination, Valeria shot through the final fence and squealed out onto the main road. She rammed into a taxi, sending it spinning, and took off in the heavy traffic leading through the resort town.

DALTON LOOKED down at his phone. "I have a call coming in from an unknown number."

Lizzy and Dalton hurried away from the crowd and ducked behind a building. Dalton answered on speakerphone but didn't say a word.

"Dalton?"

"Val?" Lizzy asked in surprise.

"I need help," Valeria whispered.

"Where are you?" Dalton asked, taking over as Lizzy pulled out her phone and began to record the conversation.

"I'm in Sinaloa, Mexico. I'm in Mazatlán. I messed up. I need an extraction."

"What are the coordinates?" Dalton asked as Lizzy pulled up a map. Valeria read off the GPS coordinates.

"Val, listen to me," Dalton said slowly. "We are in Romania. We can't get to you quickly. Can you get a boat?"

"Yes. I'm at the shore now. I know I'm being followed. I'm hiding in a dumpster outside of the docks."

"They'll expect you to head toward the US border or the embassy. Get a boat and go west to Cabo San Lucas. If you can't make it there, then go to Parque Nacional Cabo Pulmo, it's a park in Baja. I'm sending help. Call me when you're safe on the boat."

"I can't. I stole this phone from someone at Manuel's resort. I'm sure it'll be tracked or disconnected as soon as it's reported missing."

Dalton swore, and Lizzy held her breath. Manuel must be Manuel Hernandez, and he was not someone you wanted to have after you.

"Get a boat that can hold at least eighteen gallons of gas and head for Cabo. Do you have something to write down directions with?"

"Yes," Valeria whispered.

"This is your ultimate goal for extraction. If you are not at that location, your extraction will be Point B, the park." Dalton read off the coordinates. "Hang on. Help is on the way."

"Who?" Val asked nervously.

"You won't be able to miss him. His name is Grant Macay. Stay safe."

The line went dead and Lizzy finally breathed as she blinked back tears. "It's all falling apart."

"We don't have time to think like this." Dalton dialed and waited as the line connected. "Think of it this way. We have them on the ropes, and they're so afraid they're being brazen, and we know what that means."

Lizzy nodded. "They'll mess up. Our friends—"

"I know. And we're helping them, even from halfway across the world. I'm calling Grant. You call Alex."

"Aye," a deep voice slightly accented with his Scots ancestry answered.

"Grant, Dalton."

"What's up?" Grant Macay, the pilot from Dalton's pararescue team answered.

"Where are you?"

"Edwards. Just got stationed here in sunny California two days ago for the next six months."

"We need your help."

"We who?"

"The President of the United States." Lizzy nodded to Dalton as she hung up with Alex. "Orders are coming in a minute to send you to Mexico for a classified drill. There's a woman who needs an extraction, possibly hot. She'll be at one of the following coordinates."

"Cabo is always beautiful to visit, gunfire or not. I'll find the wee lassie," Grant assured.

"I wouldn't call her that," Lizzy muttered.

"Macay! You've got orders!" was overheard from the background.

Lizzy's eyebrows rose. Alex worked fast.

"Someday you'll have to tell me what's going on. I'll get this lass back to you or die trying."

"These things I do," Dalton said seriously.

"That others may live." Grant finished the PJ motto before hanging up.

Lizzy reached her hand out and Dalton clasped it as the medical personnel walked by with the bodies from the sea. "Alex doesn't have an update yet. He can't get into the hospital. All phones are forbidden so Humphrey can't call to let him know."

Dalton nodded. "It'll be in lockdown. The entire city will be. We better go."

"Wait," Lizzy said, stopping him. "Birch sent the bodies to Stanworth, but Stanworth is here and ends up dead shortly after the bodies would have been found. Plus, Sandra flew into Bucharest but now can't be found."

"And Bucharest is only a couple hours from the Black Sea."

"It was a meeting of *Mollia Domini*!" Lizzy smacked his arm as it fell into place. "I hate leaving Tate and Birch but, Dalton, we're close. We could take out the entire organization!"

"We need to find out how long the bodies were in the water and see where they came from," Dalton said, grabbing her hand and rushing after the medics.

5

"LET ME GO," Tate ground out between her teeth. She'd had a semi-rigid splint put on her leg and a bandage over her shoulder and was now being held hostage in her secured room by the meanest nurse she'd ever met until her leg surgery at the end of the day. It had been six hours, and she hadn't been allowed to leave the room yet.

"You are recovering and getting ready for surgery tonight. You cannot get out of that bed."

"The shoulder is nothing. I am going to see the president, or so help me, I will get out of this bed and strangle you. It's been hours, and no one will tell me anything."

The nurse looked at her as if she were a child. "First, you're one of the nicer patients I've dealt with. Second, I don't have information on the status of the president. It's classified."

"Is he alive?" Tate asked softly, her voice fading as it was replaced with heart-stopping fear.

The nurse's look turned to pity. "I'm sorry. No one knows. The entire wing is closed off, and no information is coming out of it." The nurse gave her a sad look and then left the private room, closing the door after her.

Tate grabbed a pillow and covered her face. She let the tears come. Great big sobs as she cried for those who had died last night at the restaurant, all because of her. She'd taken out *Mollia Domini's* propaganda machine, embarrassing them, and innocents had died because of it. It was now clear their enemies were prepared to destroy anything they could not control.

Other federal agents had arrested the young officer who had shot the supposed CIA agent. When the agent had reached for her with his gun drawn, the officer shot. But she'd make sure he'd get out of jail by the end of the day. Crew had swooped in, picked Tate up, and had her inside the helicopter while everyone was distracted by the shooting. Tate was sure the agent was either a *Mollia Domini* plant in the CIA, or he wasn't an agent at all. Either way, the young officer had saved her, and she'd make sure he was hailed a hero.

Crew had followed the medical evacuation helicopter to Walter Reed Hospital. The military base was in complete lockdown as well as the hospital. Tate had heard the people talking as she was rushed from the helicopter pad and into a secure room. Crew had not been admitted. Instead, he was detained and was being held somewhere on the base.

"Get out of my way!"

Tate pulled the pillow from her face at the raised voice in the hall. She heard her guardian nurse calling for MPs as her door was thrown open. Standing in all of his five-foot-five-inch shining-head glory was Humphrey. He shoved the wire-rimmed glasses up his nose aggressively as he sent her a wink.

MPs ran up the hall, but Humphrey spun on them. "You

better back off, or I'll have you dishonorably discharged. Do you know who I am? I'm the fucking chief of staff, and you will listen to me. I am taking this woman, on the direct orders of President Stratton, to his bedside. Anyone who impedes me will face court martial under UCMJ Article 92."

Tate sat up and watched in awe as the men stepped back. "Sorry, sir."

"Nurse, help me get Miss Carlisle into a wheelchair," Humphrey ordered, his voice strong and sure as he directed the MPs to help the nurse.

The nurse hurried inside with a wheelchair, and the men helped pick Tate up and set her in the chair. The nurse tried to push her, but Humphrey waved her off. "I will let you know when you're needed. Thank you for your excellent care."

The nursed thanked Humphrey, and they stared after them as Humphrey walked off, pushing Tate down the hall.

"Is Birch alive?" Tate finally asked.

"I don't know. They haven't let me in yet. But they will."

By the steely determination in Humphrey's voice, she felt sorry for the wall of guards waiting in the secure ward. Tate looked back with tears in her eyes as she grabbed for his hand. "Thank you."

Humphrey patted her hand as he wound his way through the maze of corridors. "Get ready," he said, dropping her hand as they came around a corner and faced the wall of guards.

∿

LIZZY AND DALTON followed the course on the map that the military had best figured the bodies had traveled. So far, there were nothing but small houses and a few small hotels along the coast as they moved from Romania into Bulgaria.

"It shouldn't be too much farther. The medic was pretty sure about time of death and how long they'd been in the water," Lizzy said of George Stanworth and his now identified daughter, Helena.

Lizzy scanned the coast with her binoculars from her spot on the boat. "Let's go around that small bend."

Dalton revved the engine and steered around a small jetty. He slowed when he saw the coastline around the bend. A massive house sat maybe fifty yards from the shore. "I don't see anyone," Lizzy said, scanning the area.

"Let's try it. It's the first real possibility we've seen." Dalton steered the boat toward the shore. He stopped ten feet from shore and tossed the anchor into the shallow water. He hopped out of the boat, the water came up to his chest. Lizzy handed him two guns and then jumped in after him.

They walked through the water and onto the beach. Dalton held out his hand and Lizzy stopped. He pointed to the ground next to a table. Blood coated the sand. He'd seen it enough to know that dark stain anywhere. "I'll take the back. You go around front," he ordered.

They sprinted off in different directions. Lizzy hugged the side of the house as she made her way around front. She heard glass breaking in the back and used the butt of her M16 to break out the glass door.

"Clear!" she heard Dalton call as she made her way through the rooms.

"Clear!" she called back as they met in the large living room looking over the sea. "They're gone now."

Alex buzzed her, and she looked at her phone. "Alex says

Sally, the fake name Sandra is using, just boarded a plane in Bucharest."

"Dammit," Dalton cursed. "We were so close."

"Let's collect as much evidence as we can," Lizzy told him as she found the kitchen and pulled out some plastic bags.

"We'll collect the blood in the sand when we leave. Let's get some items that likely would have been touched by the people here."

THREE HOURS later Lizzy and Dalton leaned against a crate as the plane took off. They were alone in the cargo hold with a bunch of large pallets of supplies, and it was perfect. They had a duffle bag of potential evidence, a secretary of state to talk to, and the rest of an organization to bring down. But for a couple hours, they'd have peace.

"Lizzy," Dalton said against her head resting on his chest over the engine noise.

"Yes?"

"I love you."

Lizzy turned her head and looked up at Dalton's face. They hadn't slept in days, his face was scruffy, and he was still the sexiest man she'd ever seen.

"I love you, too."

HUMPHREY WOULD NEVER FOOL Tate again. He was a fierce warrior. He'd not only bullied his way into the secure ward, but also into Birch's room. He was alive—barely. Tate gasped as Humphrey pushed her to Birch's bed. He'd undergone three hours of surgery to repair a collapsed lung and internal bleeding.

As he lay on the white sheets, Tate wouldn't have known he was alive if it weren't for the beeping of the machines showing a steady pulse. "Birch," she whispered as emotion overwhelmed her. Again Humphrey was there.

He rested his hand on her shoulder. "He'll pull through. He should be waking from the anesthesia soon. And when he does we'll be right here."

Tate nodded as Humphrey parked her wheelchair next to the bed. "I'll check with the doctors," Humphrey told her, walking over to the ICU's main station that overlooked the beds.

Tate reached out and clasped her hand in his. "Birch. We're safe. We made it. Please come back to me."

Tate hoped his eyes would open, but they didn't. Instead, she rested their clasped hands against her cheek and talked. She talked about their future, about places she wanted to travel with him and things she wanted do together. Seconds turned to minutes, and minutes turned to hours.

Tate's voice had gone hoarse, but that didn't stop her. "I always wanted to spend time at a small lake in the middle of the woods. It would be just you and me there. No outside world and no responsibilities, at least for a few days. Can you imagine sitting wrapped in each other's arms on a dock overlooking the sunset?"

"I can."

Tate's eyes shot up to Birch's face at the sound of his hoarse voice. He was so pale, but his eyes were opened, and there was a slight smile on his face.

"Birch!" Tate cried, bringing his hand to her lips and kissing him as doctors and nurses rushed into the room. Humphrey fought them off long enough for Tate to whisper that she loved him, and then a nurse yanked her wheelchair out of the room.

"Stop!"

Tate's heart clenched as she heard the pain and energy it took Birch to call out. Everyone froze. "Since I am very much alive, I want you to bring my girlfriend back to my side immediately. We are not to be separated until our release. Is that understood?"

Tate was rushed back as a doctor looked down at Birch. "You're doing well. You'll be in the hospital five days or so. You lost a lot of blood. You had some internal bleeding when your rib punctured your lung. I'm sorry, but I'll have to take Miss Carlisle away in about three hours. She needs surgery to set her broken leg. After that, I will return her to your side so long as you both rest. Do we have a deal?"

Birch nodded and grabbed her hand. The room cleared, and he looked at her with such love that Tate felt her heart fill. "I want you by my side forever," Birch said, never taking his eyes from hers.

"There's no place I'd rather be," Tate smiled at him as he kissed her hand.

No matter what the next day brought, they'd all face it together. They would find Valeria, and the team would be back together. Humphrey, Lizzy, Dalton, Alex, Valeria, Crew . . . they were more than a team. They were family. *Mollia Domini* may have struck a direct hit that day, but her family would be together again soon. *Mollia Domini* would feel the full force of what they were capable of. The cracks had been made. It was time to blow them apart.

He sat looking at the videoconference screen. There were

two black squares, and he felt the rage all over again. Fucking Stanworths and their mess. Sandra and the man looked worried. And they definitely should be. He would kill them faster than he killed the Stanworths if they didn't get their jobs done.

"He survived," Sandra said with a hint of fear lacing her voice. "The vice president has already turned power back over to Stratton."

Rage erupted. He threw his glass against the wall, sending shards exploding into the air. His secretary knew better than to come in when he was like that, but he almost dared her. He wanted to lash out, but instead he took a calming breath.

"We have to move up phase three," his other partner said. "How soon can it be done?"

He leaned back in his chair and looked at the list of locations he'd stolen bombs from. "It's already begun."

6

VALERIA PUT her lips to the hose and sucked. She coughed as the mild tasting gasoline filled her mouth, but then spat at the aftertaste coating her mouth. She shoved the hose into an old gas can she found at the marina as she tried to act as casually as she could next to the large speedboat. She'd love to steal this one, but Val knew it would be missed all too quickly. However, the smaller, older speedboat next to it wouldn't be. The amount of debris on the cover led her to believe no one had touched the boat in a month.

Valeria put a kink in the hose and set a large stone on it, holding it in place as she carried the now full gas can to the older boat and filled up the tank to the top. Then she went back and filled the can the rest of the way up before pulling the hose and tossing it in the back of her boat in case she needed to steal more gas.

Val pulled the ball cap she'd stolen from a beach chair low over her eyes, hopped onto the boat, stored the gas can, and hotwired the boat. Without looking back, she pulled out of the local marina down a way from the resort and headed out to sea.

GRANT MACAY LANDED the Pave Hawk HH-60G at the Coronado naval base. Whoever this Valeria was, she must be important. And whoever was sending the orders had major talent for getting things done. The second Grant landed, fuel was being pumped full into his helo. A Navy man hit the side of the helicopter and Grant was off again, this time to a naval ship in the Pacific Ocean halfway down the Baja Peninsula.

Dalton Cage had been Grant's pararescue leader before. They'd been stationed all over the world together. But things got interesting when they were at an undisclosed location in the Middle East and a helicopter with some SEALs, CIA Special Operations Group members, and one state department greenhorn went down. Their four-man team was prepped and ready to go into the line of fire to rescue the helo when orders came down grounding them. When Dalton came out ready to steal the helicopter and go himself, it was a no-brainer the team would go with him.

They rescued the helicopter and most of the people in it and had then been thrown behind bars at the Lakenheath Air Base in England immediately upon landing. Three weeks they had been left sitting there, until one day a little man with a bald head and glasses claiming to be the new chief of staff to the new president showed up. The team was divided up and each sent their separate ways while Dalton, as team leader, took the fall and was discharged for disregarding a direct order. Then out of nowhere Dalton and some women showed up on the air base Grant had been stationed at in the Philippines. They were using fake names but had the power to commandeer a helo and Grant, blow up a boat, and kill the man on it.

Shortly after his mission with Dalton, Grant had been restationed at Edwards. He hadn't even gotten in trouble for sinking a Seahawk helicopter. Instead, it was as if it never happened. Grant had been left in the dark, but he was smart enough to put two and two together. Dalton was in some secret shit, and evidently the orders were coming from very high up the chain of command. Whoever Dalton was with was powerful enough to send Grant alone with a $50,000,000 plus helicopter and support from the Air Force and Navy. All to get one woman—a woman possibly under fire. But Grant found interrupting a shitstorm fun. It was his Scots ancestry. His parents were academics, but growing up, Grant had been more interested in the Highland games. So instead of becoming a professor or author, Grant had joined the Air Force. He wanted to fly high and fast. His ability to fly with nerves of steel was why he was recruited for the PJs. No one had more dangerous operations than the PJs, which is what made this lassie very interesting. Who was she, and what had she done to need his rescue? One thing was for sure, though Grant would get to this woman. He just hoped she was alive by the time he reached her.

VALERIA PUSHED the boat across the choppy waters. A storm had rolled in and slowed her down while using up more of her gas than she'd liked. But it also made her harder to find. Valeria pushed the boat faster as the rain fell. Her skin was waterlogged. Her eyes stung from the rain hitting them as if each drop were a tiny needle. She was really starting to hate water, but she was six hours into a nine- to ten-hour trip. A trip that couldn't end soon enough.

HUMPHREY ORVILLE RUBBED his hand over his face and bald head before putting his round wire-rimmed glasses back on. He sat in the empty parking lot of the closed restaurant, waiting. It had shut down last week, and all the security cameras had been disabled, which was why he'd chosen the place to have his meeting.

He took a sip of his coffee to help him stay awake. Tate had come out of her surgery with a steel plate and pins in her leg, but she was awake and resting with Birch. Birch had not trusted the vice president any more than he trusted anyone outside of their small group, so he'd insisted Humphrey stick to the VP's side until the doctors cleared Birch to resume the presidency. That occurred the night before, close to two in the morning. The VP had handed power back and happily went home to sleep while Humphrey got everything Birch would need to run the country from his hospital room before heading to this meeting. And now he sat waiting for Thurmond Culpepper.

The power-hungry lackey of the traitorous Secretary of State Sandra Cummings pulled into the parking lot and drew up next to Humphrey. Humphrey opened the car door at the same time Thurmond did.

"Looks like it closed," Thurmond called out instead of a greeting.

Humphrey shrugged. "Yeah. I didn't know. Oh well. This won't take long and then we can grab breakfast on the way into the office."

Thurmond walked around the car and followed Humphrey to a rotting picnic table on the side of the building. Humphrey took a seat with his back to the restaurant and waited as Thurmond looked with disgust at the wooden seat. He was probably afraid he'd get his expensive slacks or bright pink shirt dirty. Humphrey waited as Thurmond reluctantly took a seat. His hair was perfectly fluffed and sprayed, so it didn't move in the gentle summer breeze.

"I'm guessing this is about Sandra's family emergency? Well, let me assure you, she called me as soon as she heard what happened to President Stratton and is on her way back." Thurmond pursed his lips in what Humphrey guessed was a thoughtfully worried look. "How is President Stratton? When Sandra called she wanted to know if he was still in power or if she should report to the vice president."

"The president is in control of the country. He's doing well and just needs some rest." Humphrey leaned forward. "It's all such a shock. I hope Sandra is safe. I worry if it's an attack on the government that she may be in danger."

Thurmond looked surprised, but he took a second too long to look it. The prick knew. "I'm sure she's safe. But maybe I should talk to the Secret Service?"

Humphrey nodded. "That's a good idea. After all, I'd hate to have *Mollia Domini* come after her too."

Thurmond froze and then cleared his throat. "Who?"

"Silly me. I get things messed up easily with so much going on," Humphrey laughed at himself. "*Mollia Domini* wouldn't go after Sandra. Not when she's one of them."

"I . . . I . . . I'm sorry," Thurmond stuttered shaking his head. "I don't understand. Who is *Mollia Domini* and why would they be or not be after Sandra?"

"You're not sorry, Thurmond. You know all about them. The question is, did you pass intel along to them so they could attack the president? Did you know they were trying to kill him? Were you helping them do it?"

Thurmond's fake tanned skin paled. "No! I don't even know—"

"Cut the bullshit you're famous for spewing. We both know who and what *Mollia Domini* is, and we both know Sandra is up to her eyeballs in it. You always wanted to make a name for yourself, Thurmond. Now you'll be remembered as the first person executed for treason since the Civil War. The history of treason is actually very interesting, but that's for another time. The question is: do you want to die now or serve life in prison?"

"There's no evidence such a group even exists and certainly none that shows I helped," Thurmond sputtered.

"That's where you're wrong. Does the name Branson Ames ring a bell?"

Thurmond looked ready to faint. "But Branson is gone .. . um, car crash I think."

"You mean helicopter crash in Syria and he's gone because Sandra put a hit on him? Luckily we got to him first, and he had a lot of things to say about you and Sandra." Humphrey paused. "Oh! I forgot the second witness who saw you and Sandra putting cash in the locked briefcase for Branson to take. Cash that would be used to fund terror on behalf of *Mollia Domini*. Cash I am betting we can prove came from a small bank in Mexico owned by Manuel Hernandez."

Thurmond froze for one second before leaping up. His eyes were wild. He turned to run but smacked into a solid growling wall that was Jason Wolski. Thurmond screamed as Jason wrapped his fingers around Thurmond's thin arms and squeezed. Jason shook him like a ragdoll as Humphrey waited for Thurmond to stop screaming.

"Do shut up, Thurmond," Humphrey snapped. Thurmond immediately shut his mouth. "Thurmond, look at the man holding you. *Mollia Domini* killed his wife. Do you believe he'll kill you?"

Jason sneered and Thurmond pissed his pants.

"Good. Now, I advise you to start talking and I won't let Jason kill you and leave your dead body in the alley here." Humphrey waited as Thurmond began to cry. It was always the bullies who broke the fastest. Hidden within every bully was nothing but a coward. "Are you going to talk?"

Thurmond nodded and Jason turned him around and shoved him onto the bench. "Talk," Jason growled.

Thurmond wiped his hand across his nose, smearing snot across his cheek. "Sandra recruited me. She knew I wanted to climb the ladder and dangled that in front of me. One day she caught me doing something slightly unethical to get some information so I could impress her and called me into the office. She talked to me for hours about my beliefs and thoughts on politics, political leaders, and the state of the world. Over the course of months, she asked me to do little things here and there that were off the books and I knew were wrong. I was rewarded after doing each one. I was promoted. I began to have a staff of my own."

"You were given what you craved—power," Humphrey said with understanding.

Thurmond nodded.

"Tell me about George Stanworth."

Thurmond's brow creased. "The media mogul? I don't know much about him besides he has a young wife, his daughter runs a lot of the empire, and his granddaughter, Blythe, is popular in the gossip columns. What does he . . .? Oh."

"You didn't know he was part of it?"

"No. I didn't know anyone but Sandra. She told me it was better that way. Sometimes she'd give me orders and I would leave them in a fake rock and someone would pick them up. I guessed that Phylicia Claymore was one of those people after her death."

"How did you make that connection?" Humphrey asked.

"Sandra was supportive of the rebel leader Phylicia was found dead with."

"Where has Sandra been?"

Thurmond shook his head. "I don't know. She said she had a meeting and would be off the grid for a couple days. She told me if anyone needed her to say it was a family emergency. I got her fake identification—"

"Sally, yes, we know."

"How?" Thurmond asked, wide-eyed.

Humphrey just smiled. "Was it Sandra who ordered the bombing of the president?"

"I don't know. I just know I knew nothing about it. I didn't pass any notes, any intelligence, nothing dealing with the bombing."

"What has Sandra had you looking into recently?"

"Nothing about the president," Thurmond defended. "Mostly she had me researching catastrophic regulations for various departments."

Humphrey felt a chill go down his back. "Which departments?"

"The securities and exchange, the energy commission, the environmental protection agency, and the transportation department. Sandra had me compile their regulations and protocols in case of a major disaster. I assumed she had evidence of a terror attack and wanted to be prepared just in case."

"You're an idiot," Jason said, smacking Thurmond's head hard with his hand.

"Where's the research you did for her?" Humphrey asked, hardly able to sit still. He had to act quickly.

"On my computer." Thurmond glanced at his car.

"Give me the keys." Humphrey snatched them and headed straight for the car. Oh God, this was bad, very bad. Humphrey opened the car and reached for the messenger bag on the passenger seat. Rushing back to Thurmond, he opened the laptop. "What's the password?"

"I'll—"

Humphrey slapped Thurmond's hand away. "No, I'll do it. What's the password?"

Thurmond pouted before mumbling, "President Thurmond, all one word."

Humphrey typed it in and the computer lit up. "Is that your SOS password, too?"

"Yes," Thurmond sighed. "Look, I told you everything. I swear, I didn't know—"

"But you knew what *Mollia Domini* is. It's a group set on overthrowing the government. That's treason. Jason, take him away, but don't kill him. I'm sure the president will want to deal with him publicly."

Thurmond began to struggle, but Jason used one hand to hold him and another to stab a needle into Thurmond's neck. Thurmond collapsed in the blink of an eye.

"He won't remember a thing. Where do you want me to take him?"

"We need a secret jail. I have a feeling we are going to be filling it."

"Here in DC?" Jason asked.

"Yes. We need these people quickly accessible. Do you have any ideas?"

"I do. I have a buddy who's a CIA SOG. He'd know where the US black sites are, or were. Usually they're visible and easy to get to—a home, an office park, something like that. Something you drive by every day and never think anything of it. If we can find an old one, maybe it's still set up to hold prisoners."

Humphrey nodded. "Good idea. But you can't tell them why."

"Nah, I'll buy him a beer and shoot the shit with him. I'll call you when I have more information. In the meantime, I'll keep this asshole unconscious."

"And I have to warn the president we are looking at potential attacks to the very foundation of America."

Humphrey took off with the laptop as Jason stuffed Thurmond in the trunk of Thurmond's car. Sleep was going to have to wait. With Jason's delivery of Fitz and Hugo's bodies via coolers to Stanworth's front door, *Mollia Domini* was ready to make a statement. Humphrey just hoped Lizzy and Dalton could stop them before it was too late.

7

IT WAS QUICKLY APPROACHING nighttime when Valeria noticed land. She also noticed she was running out of gas. She looked down at the plastic-coated map. "*Madre de hijo de la chingada!*" Valeria cursed as she looked at the map. She wasn't going to make it to Cabo San Lucas. She turned the boat toward the heavily tree-lined Parque Nacional Cabo Pulmo.

It was the flash of light that caught her attention first. Valeria looked over her shoulder at the lone spotlight a good distance back. The light was on a very fast speedboat and was scanning the water. Valeria watched as it swung to the right and to the left before landing right on her and freezing. "*Mierda!*"

She heard their engines roar to full throttle as she pushed her old boat to the limit. Their light grew brighter as the faster, more powerful boat rushed toward her. The shore was growing nearer. The national park seemed dark just a short ways from the beachside resort. Valeria angled the boat away from the lights. Darkness was her friend tonight as the sky turned from blue to black as the sun sank deeper from the horizon.

Val cut the engine a second before the boat careened onto the beach. She already had her limited supplies of weapons, a compass, and a map stuffed in her pockets and waistband as she leapt from the boat. Her boots hit the soft sand as she took off for the woods. She looked at her watch. She was supposed to be meeting her extraction at this time. She hoped whoever he was, he would quickly figure out she wasn't there and make his way to the secondary location. Val looked up at the mountaintop that would be her extraction point, if she made it there alive. There was only so much hiding she could do, and come morning, she feared her time would be over.

GRANT LOOKED down at the extraction location. Nothing. No one. Not even some drunk kids on summer vacation. He hovered low and used night vision to see if the woman he was supposed to be rescuing was in hiding. Nothing. Grant felt it in the pit of his stomach. She'd never made it there.

As a PJ, decisions were made in a split second. That was the difference between life and death. And in that one split second, Grant was heading full speed to the second extraction site sixty miles away. He'd be there in under twenty minutes.

Grant flew low over the ocean and just far enough out that people from shore wouldn't be able to see or hear him. He wouldn't show on the Mexican radar, but it also meant his extraction target had no idea he was coming. Grant followed the coastline keeping an eye on the GPS tracker that showed him the exact extraction point on the top of a small mountain two-thirds of a mile from the beach. Fifteen minutes. His target just needed to hold on for fifteen more minutes.

VALERIA SPRINTED across the road with the map in one hand and her compass in the other. Her only weapon left with ammunition in it was slung over her shoulder as she raced across the empty street and into the wild. The ground was hard and slippery with dirt and sand. The vegetation was tough and dry as it attacked her jean-clad legs.

The light from the boat was scanning the area as Valeria pushed her way through the low vegetation and into the trees. Calmly, she listened to the boat come to a stop as she read the map and compass. Looking out into the darkness, she envisioned where her extraction was. It was a run into the woods and then up a mountain. At the sound of men jumping off the boat and into the shallow water, Valeria took off in a sprint into the night.

"*Ahí!*" one of the men shouted a second before a gunshot exploded from the beach. She'd been seen.

Valeria looked down at her white long-sleeved shirt. While it had been a lifesaver in the sun, it was like a glowing neon target in the dark. Not bothering to slow down, Valeria ripped the shirt off and left it behind. She tucked the compass and map into her pocket and moved the gun to her hand as she pushed herself faster in the navy blue tank top she had underneath her shirt.

Not being able to risk leading the men straight to the extraction point, Valeria began to zigzag her path to the meeting point. The trees began to get thicker and the vegetation more lush as she reached the bottom of the mountain. She heard the men after her. They hadn't been thrown off her trail. Checking her gun, Val turned off the safety and began the climb upward.

Her quads throbbed and burned and her back felt as if it were breaking as she kept bent over to better hide herself in the woods. She darted from palm tree to palm tree, making her way upward as her feet slipped and her calves cramped. The tree line began to thin as she worked her way to the top. Bullets ripped into the palm tree next to her, sending spears of palms flying.

Valeria leapt behind the tree, turned, aimed, and fired down the hill before taking off again. She was breathing hard, her body crying out from the torture it had gone through as she pushed forward. Her lungs burned and her head pounded, but she was still aware of the sound of the men closing in on her.

Valeria burst through the tree line and into the open mountaintop. Instead of stopping, she sprinted across the open area. As bullets dug into the ground around her, Valeria dove for the cover of the tree line on the other side of the clearing. She groaned as she landed partially on a rock before rolling to a stop. She didn't have time to feel sorry for herself. She didn't have time to think about the pain. She had to move.

Lying on the ground with a rock and a tree as her cover, Valeria steadied her gun and took aim. She didn't have bullets to waste. She needed a clear shot every time. She slowed her breathing and cleared her head as she took the first shot. The man running across the clearing dropped.

Valeria rolled behind the rock, only slightly higher than

her head, as a hail of gunfire rained down on her. She heard shouts as the men began to fan out. She listened as she lay on her back, staring up at the stars and the bullet-riddled palms. The second the gunfire stopped, she rolled to her left and returned fire. If she was going down, she wasn't going to go down without a fight.

GRANT SAW THE GUNFIRE. The flashes from the muzzles of the guns were as bright to him as a flare. He didn't even need to rely on the Pave Hawk's night vision. One gun from the far side of the clearing, six or so guns from the other side. Trained to protect his target, Grant turned the helo sharply, putting himself between her and the men firing. He saw the men clearly on his screen as he opened fire.

Grant hovered low and noticed on his night vision display that the lone person had begun to move on the far side of the clearing. He watched as the figure sprinted toward him and laid cover for her. He shot continuously into the woods as he saw his target firing behind her. "Come on, lass," Grant muttered as the men began to shoot back.

VALERIA TIGHTENED her jaw and ran. The helo was right there. She just needed to reach the door. Pain ripped across her arm, sending her slamming face first into the side of the Pave Hawk. Letting out a string of cusswords in multiple languages, Valeria spun and fired with one hand as she used the other to open the copilot's door.

"Be a good girl and duck, will you?"

Valeria almost argued with the pilot, but when she saw the handgun he was holding out she decided to listen. The man was a freaking mountain and looked like some of the pictures her father had shown her of her distant relatives in the Highlands. He was all wide shoulders, strong neck, and bearded Highlander with a wicked gleam of amusement as he fired three shots over her head.

"There we go. Can you get the door shut?"

"*Pòg mo thòin*," Valeria muttered as she shut and locked the door.

Grant laughed a big deep laugh as he pulled the helo up into the air. "I'll gladly kiss that ass of yours, lass. Bend over."

Val blinked as she stared at the man hidden behind the helmet and beard. "You speak Scottish Gaelic?"

"Aye. My parents are both from Scotland. What's more surprising is a Latina speaking it." Valeria strapped in and really looked at the man who had rescued her. He handled the helicopter expertly even without a copilot. He wasn't nervous of landing in the middle of a gunfight. There were no signs of the normal adrenaline rush. Shit, she was feeling that rush as she bounced her legs up and down in the red glow of the cockpit. Instead, he calmly flew out over the ocean nice and low. He turned and saw her looking at him and sent her a wink.

Valeria rolled her eyes. Great, another cocky helicopter pilot who thought he was God's gift. "My father is Scottish. My mother is from Puerto Rico."

"And what brings you to the lovely Mexican beach tonight?"

Valeria looked him over again. He rescued her, but what exactly did he know? "Can I borrow a phone?"

The man reached down with one hand and tapped the satellite phone plugged into a helicopter adapter so that she could hear through her headset. "Dalton's number is already in it."

"Thanks, but I need to call someone else."

"Boyfriend?" Grant teased.

"No." Valeria punched in the numbers she had memorized and waited as the phone rang.

"Hello."

Relief washed over Valeria as she heard her team leader's voice. Dalton may have put together this rescue, but Lizzy was whom she reported to. It was hard not to sag with relief, knowing she was going back to her team. "It's me."

"Val? Are you okay?"

"I'm fine."

"You're not fine. You're shot," Grant spoke as Val snapped her head in his direction to glare at him.

"Get off my call," she growled.

"You're shot?" Lizzy asked instead of yelling at the pilot.

"It's a flesh wound," Val muttered as she looked for a way to disconnect Grant from the call.

"That it is. But it'll need stitches. I'll sew her up right for you."

Valeria shot daggers at the pilot as she looked to switch off his headphones.

"Val," Lizzy said, getting her attention, "let Grant take care of you, and it's okay if he listens. There was a bombing. Birch was the target. He's been in the hospital, and I don't know much except he has resumed control of the country after getting medical clearance. We've just arrived in DC and will be meeting with Humphrey soon. You need to get to DC now."

Val saw Grant look over at her with curiosity but didn't say anything before looking back over the endless black ocean. "I'm sure Tate can step up to take care of things until I get there."

"Val, Tate's in the hospital bed right next to Birch." Val felt her blood drain. She might give Tate shit for being a girly girl, but when the cards were on the table and Val needed someone to vouch for her, she'd sent Manuel's man to Tate to verify that Val was no longer with the DEA.

"What?" Valeria asked, making sure she heard Lizzy correctly.

"Tate and Birch were on a date. *Mollia Domini* blew up the restaurant. Birch suffered a collapsed lung and internal bleeding. He was unconscious through most of it. Tate suffered a shattered tibia. Humphrey said it was horrendous. With a broken leg, Tate dragged herself over to Birch and protected him. She was shot once as well before agents and police arrived. She saved them both," Lizzy explained as Val let her head fall back and took a deep breath.

"It's okay, lassie. Your friends are alive and safe," Grant said softly through the headphones.

"They are," Lizzy confirmed. "But we need boots on the ground so we're having Grant fly you to Laughlin Air Force Base in Texas before catching a plane to Andrews Air Base here in DC."

"I'll need to refuel," Grant said simply, not even blinking as he was already changing the direction of the helo.

"When?" Lizzy asked.

"An hour from now."

"We'll take care of it. The Pave has the ability to refuel in air, correct?" Lizzy asked as Val heard Dalton telling her it could. "Dalton says we'll have a refueling crew out to you by the end of the hour. Alex will be setting up fake identifications. Just go along with whatever they say when you land. You'll both immediately be transported to a plane headed home."

"Excuse me, did you say both of us?" Grant asked with something close to surprise.

"Yes. Valeria, fill Grant in and see if he wants to help. If he doesn't, then kill him."

Grant rolled his eyes. "As if this wee lassie—"

Valeria had her knife to his throat before he could finish the sentence. "Don't call me that."

"I told you you shouldn't call her that," Valeria heard Lizzy chuckle over the headphones.

Grant didn't look fazed at having a knife at his throat, and Valeria wondered if a gunfight in the middle of the night with a drug cartel and having a knife to his throat didn't faze him, what did?

"Does this have to do with Dalton and the South Seas?" Grant asked instead of shoving her knife away.

"Yes."

"I'm in."

"Good," Lizzy said. "See you both at the bar. Get home safe."

The call disconnected and Valeria stared at the man who rescued her. "You're in and you haven't even heard what's going on."

Grant smirked. "I may have an accent, but that doesn't make me stupid. The only person with enough power to send Dalton and Elizabeth to the South China Sea and to send me to rescue you, all off the books, is the president. That was confirmed when you all called him Birch. I'm guessing he's figured out some weird shit is going on and doesn't know who he can trust, so he somehow found Elizabeth to look into it. When she needed help, Dalton came on board. After all, we were all locked up ready to be tried for disobeying an order."

"How do you know Dalton wasn't called in first?" Val asked, raising one eyebrow challenging him.

"Simple, you didn't call Dalton. You called Elizabeth, your team leader. Now, why don't you put your knife away and tell me about the shitstorm I'm flying into."

8

ALEX SANTOS'S fingers flew over the keyboard. In seconds, he was on the dark web, navigating his way to the private chat room where some of the world's most talented hackers talked to each other.

It was late and Buzz and Snip, the two old veterans who practically lived at Lancy's Bar, were serving last-call drinks. Alex had promised them free drinks if they covered for him for ten minutes. Alex had cleared the bar of bugs already that morning, had just sent a plane to refuel Grant and Valeria's helicopter, and now he wanted to check in with his fellow hackers.

The last time he had been online, they had all noticed something going on. There was online chatter about missing bombs, political upheaval, and hacking of financial institutions. Alex said as much as he could without giving anything away. But after the bombing that had hurt Tate and Birch, he was sure the board would be lit up.

And he was right. Rock Star, a hacker from London, was sending out messages to him. *Did you see it coming? I think there's more.*

火龍, or Fire Dragon, as the Chinese hacker was known, posted: *The military shot a man with a bomb outside of the Shanghai Stock Exchange. It was hushed up, though, and reported by the government media that the person died of a heart attack. They didn't bother explaining why someone having a heart attack was shot eight times.*

Alex typed: *First London Stock Exchange is attempted to be hacked and then a bomber outside Shanghai. Is this all about money? But if it's about money, why target the president? And no, I didn't see it coming.*

Dark Surfer, a hacker from Australia, joined them: *I wonder if the missing bomb from here ended up in Shanghai?*

Alex paused as he looked at the screen. There was a missing bomb from the FBI lab in Quantico as well. Where would it be used . . . Birch.

Rock Star: *There's chatter that a whole shipment of weapons from Russia is missing. A shipment that was supposed to be medical aid, but what my sources are saying was really five suitcase-sized bombs. Russia is scrambling to find them.*

Alex blew out a breath: *Five bombs from Russia, one from Australia, and one from the US are missing.*

Fire Dragon: *One dead in Shanghai and one president almost assassinated. There are still five bombs out there.*

Dark Surfer: *But what are the targets? Are they places or people or both?*

Rock Star: *I sent the intelligence to MI-6 anonymously. I didn't know what else to do.*

Alex blinked in surprise. Most hackers were completely against the governments they believed were decades behind them in technology and whom they generally didn't trust since they knew all about the spying the government did through technology. Many hackers had been taken from jail to work for the NSA or MI-6 to hack on behalf of the government, just like Alex had been. He expected Rock Star to be flamed, but instead the boards were quiet.

Dark Surfer finally responded: *It's the only thing you could do. We have to save as many people as we can. But where do we even start?*

Alex: *Mollia Domini*

Fire Dragon: *What?*

Alex: *It's the group from the shadows that I believe tried to kill the president.*

His fingers shook as he waited for a response. If any of these people worked for *Mollia Domini,* then Alex would be dead by that night. They were anonymous to most people, but even the slightest hint of a digital trail would be enough for this group to track down. But something had to be done. Some information had to be out there and if it was, these hackers would find it.

Rock Star: *I'll look into it and let you know what I find.*

Fire Dragon: *Me too.*

Dark Surfer: *If they are behind it all, then be extra careful. I'll also see what I can find out. Cover your tracks and cover them well. Good luck.*

The chat room went quiet and Alex trembled as he closed his laptop. Either he'd just helped his group or he'd signed their death warrants. He looked at his watch. He had time to close up the bar, clean up, and head to DC.

GRANT WAITED PATIENTLY as he flew through the night. After hanging up with Lizzy, he thought Valeria would launch into an explanation. But she didn't. She was quiet instead. She thought she was hard to read, but she wasn't. The worry was as clear as the confusion. She was trying to work it all out in her head, so Grant left her to it.

The radio crackled and Valeria jerked out of her trancelike state. "What's that?"

"Easy, it's just the refueling plane."

Grant wasn't sure, but he thought he saw Valeria swipe away a tear. Instead of asking what was wrong, he concentrated on hooking up to the refueling plane. Soon enough, they would be alone again, and he could ask her what was going on.

Until then, he enjoyed seeing a side of her he doubted Valeria showed many people. She may be turned away from him and quiet, but he sensed the concern and compassion she had for her team. So, he'd do what he does best—sit back and let the woman come to him.

HUMPHREY SAT on the chair next to the president's bed and watched through the glass as the nurses and doctors read over the president's reports and generally got in the way.

"When will they let you leave?" Humphrey asked, wondering if any of them were spies for *Mollia Domini*.

"Three days is what they said last. I'll have two doctors at the White House at all times for another two weeks. It's just the two of us in this wing, so they are constantly around to check on us. You better tell me what news you have and fast," Birch told him.

Humphrey felt bad asking when Birch could leave while he was still pale and bruised. Tate didn't look any better with her arm in a sling from a bullet wound and her leg in a cast from major surgery. However, war was coming and they had to be ready.

"Valeria has been found."

Tate gasped and sat up too fast. She winced but didn't sit back down. "Where is she? Is she safe?"

"She's safe. Lizzy called. She and Dalton are on their way back. Valeria called them for extraction from Mexico. Since they couldn't make it, they sent Grant Macay to rescue her."

"Grant Macay? Who's that?" Tate asked, cutting off Birch.

"He was the pilot from Dalton's PJ team. He helped out with the South China Sea incident. They are in flight now to Laughlin and will be in DC by morning. Lizzy has ordered Val to read him in."

Birch nodded. "Does Valeria know about Brock?" Humphrey shook his head. "I want to tell her. He died saving our lives."

"Valeria says she can bring *Mollia Domini* down. She found the information when she was in Mexico. We need to find a way to get them in here to see you," Humphrey said, looking over his shoulder at a nurse coming toward them.

She opened the door and smiled. "Here's your medicine, Mr. President." The nurse seemed to take forever as she gave Birch his medicine, gave Tate hers, took their blood pressure, and recorded their vitals. Finally she left, leaving the sliding glass door open a couple inches. Humphrey got up without saying a word and closed it.

"I don't think we can," Birch said as he eyed the doctor coming toward them yet again.

"Video call," Tate said quickly. "Get a secure video link, and we can put in headphones and take the call from here. I'll wobble to put a broomstick against the door if I have to."

Humphrey nodded. "I'll have Alex get me a secure, untraceable laptop."

The door opened and the doctor walked in. "And how are we feeling tonight?"

Humphrey rolled his eyes as he went to work sending what he needed to Alex. He'd meet him a short distance from the hospital and bring the laptop back to the hospital that night.

He waited for the doctor to leave and rose to shut the door yet again. "Now, onto the rest of the matters affecting the country."

VALERIA LOOKED out across the Mexican landscape. Another hour and they would be back in the US. Grant hadn't asked to be filled in yet. Instead he'd been quiet, allowing her time to think. And that was what she needed to do. She still hadn't revealed the thumb drive located in her belt buckle, and she hadn't informed him of *Mollia Domini* and what they were up against. The idea that Tate and Birch were hurt because she couldn't get the intel to them had hit her fast and hard. Harder than she thought it would.

Valeria wasn't the type of person to get close to others. The one time she did, the man turned on her and had her fired from the DEA. But Little Miss Sunshine, Tate Carlisle, had snuck up on her.

"So, you were with Dalton when the helo went down in Syria?" Valeria asked, finally coming out of her thoughts.

"Aye."

Valeria rolled her eyes at the one-word answer. "Why did you go with him?"

"It was the right thing to do. We don't leave anyone behind."

"Even if it gets you discharged?"

Grant nodded. "Even if it got us thrown in a cell for a month."

"Are you ready to do something that will land you in a grave if you're caught?"

"I picked you up, didn't I?" Grant winked at her, and Valeria felt a small smile tug at her lips. His confident attitude was something she could relate to, and by his actions tonight, he had the skills to back that attitude up.

"There's a group called *Mollia Domini* that wants to control the world from the shadows. Assassinations, media manipulation, and political interference. Some of the biggest names in the world are part of it," Valeria told him, expecting a reaction but only received a grunt instead.

"What were you doing in Mexico without backup?"

That wasn't the question Valeria was expecting or wanting. "I had a lead."

"So you go it alone instead of filling in your team?" It sounded like a reprimand, and it probably was, but this guy didn't have the right to comment on a group he only was now learning about.

"I don't think you—"

"Don't work yourself into a lather. If I'm joining this team, I need to know the strengths and weaknesses. To be a strong team, you have to acknowledge those strengths and weaknesses. Don't try to tell me shooting off to Mexico half-cocked on some lead and leaving your team behind is a strength."

Valeria felt the familiar urge to defend herself, but the knowledge that she could have possibly prevented the bombing of Tate and Birch stopped her. "I thought at the time I was protecting my team."

Grant flashed her a smile. "See, that wasn't so hard."

Valeria narrowed her eyes. "Then what's your weakness?"

"Stubborn women. It's the Scot in me," he said, sending

her a wink. Valeria blinked as she realized he wasn't disparaging her. In fact, he admired it. "But I do have a tendency to disobey orders I don't think are right. Now, are you going to tell me what you found in Mexico?"

"There's a lot more to tell before we get to that point." Valeria looked out over the controls and began laying everything out.

HE LOOKED at the map and smiled. Soon, very soon. He would bring the world to its knees and then they would turn to him to save them. Countries, presidents, monarchies, and working people alike would hail him as their savior as they handed over everything he wanted. So what that Shanghai didn't go according to plan. That's what test runs were for. He had many other more important locations ready and waiting. However, the president was another matter. One that he needed to take care of immediately.

9

Lizzy unlocked the door to her townhouse and walked inside. Soon she'd have to make a decision whether or not to keep the place or if she would move to Quantico full time. However, since finding out her father had been murdered and getting tangled in the web of lies she found herself trying to unravel, the future didn't seem so futuristic. It seemed more like an hour at a time.

"Valeria and Grant are on a plane to Andrews. They'll be here in three hours. Alex is meeting us here, and we'll video call with Tate, Birch, and Humphrey," Lizzy called out as she set down her keys and turned on the kitchen light. A thin layer of dust covered the kitchen table and all her plants were turning brown.

"Jason will meet us here as well," Dalton told her as he put his phone on the kitchen table and looked around. "Seems strange that Dave isn't here."

Lizzy smiled at the thought of her rescued Bichon Frise being doggy-sat by Snip back in Quantico. "I'm looking forward to seeing that furball again." Lizzy poured a glass of water into one of her plants but figured it was a lost cause.

Her therapist had told her to care for the plants to help her recovery. Then she'd rescued Dave. Dave had helped more than the plants. But what really helped was finding out she hadn't messed up and caused the death of her ex . . . well, until she killed him in the South China Sea. She didn't feel too badly about that since she found out Dan was with *Mollia Domini*.

Lizzy felt Dalton's arms wrap around her from behind as his lips nuzzled her neck. "We have three hours, and you told me you loved me." Dalton's hand slid up under her shirt and cupped her breast. "I can think of a way to mark this milestone in our relationship."

"Sandra—" Lizzy started to say until Dalton pulled her head back and kissed her.

"Can wait three hours. We need a plan on how to handle her anyway, and right now my plan is to make you forget everything except me," Dalton said roughly as he spun her around to face him. "In three hours you'll no longer be mine. You'll be at the will of the president. Right now you're mine."

Dalton lips were on hers, coaxing her mouth open as his hands worked her body. He knew where to touch and how to touch her in ways that left her breathless. Never one to surrender, Lizzy snapped the button of Dalton's jeans and reached inside. His erection was ready for her as she stroked him, earning a carnal growl for her attention.

Dalton dropped his sensual torture of her breasts long enough to shove down his pants, slip on a condom, lift her onto the counter, and delve into her. Lizzy's head dropped back in pleasure as his head lowered to pull one taut nipple into his mouth as his thrusts assaulted her senses. Lizzy arched her back, her mouth falling open on a silent cry as

Dalton sent her over the edge. When she looked up, his jaw was clenched, his face looking as if he was battling for control. Lizzy clenched her legs tight around him, and his control snapped as he came. They only had hours to be Dalton and Lizzy. And she'd be damned if they spent it sleeping.

VALERIA WOKE up feeling warm and safe. She blinked her eyes and realized she was looking at a very close-up view of Grant's neck. The warmth was coming from his large arm wrapped around her, holding her against him. Her face rested on his rugged chest. The man was a heater, and Valeria wanted to curl up closer to him, but the plane jerking to a stop told her they were home.

"Ah, you're up," Grant whispered. Three words . . . yet because of how kindly they were spoken, Valeria felt calmed. After what she had endured for the last week, and then to know two people she cared about had nearly been killed, she welcomed Grant's gentle tone. It was like a balm to her battered heart. But it simultaneously worried her. She liked banter and arguing, and how it kept people at a distance. Kindness, trust, and respect were things that brought people together. She didn't need to be on that level with a man again while she was a part of this team. Not when her life depended on it. She'd already made that mistake once, and Valeria wasn't going to repeat it.

"Sorry. I guess I fell asleep," Valeria said, sitting up and looking at the sculpted face of Grant Macay.

Grant chuckled easily. "You did more than that. You passed out. It's okay, though. I also have a weakness for women who fit perfectly in my arms."

Grant stood, stepped out of the seat, and began walking down the aisle, leaving Valeria once again sputtering.

"Major Washington?" a soldier asked as if it were common for two people to come off a plane at four in the morning.

"Yes," Grant said to the fake name, with all the command of an officer.

"Here are the keys to your car. It's sitting over there." The officer pointed outside the gates surrounding the airfield.

"Thank you."

Grant walked off leaving Valeria, his assistant, to follow. She let out a deep breath of annoyance and followed. "I'll drive."

"No, I will," Grant countered as he opened the driver's door.

"You don't know where we're going. I do."

"Then you can tell me. Now get in. We're being watched, and you're injured."

Valeria looked over her shoulder and saw the soldier watching them as he made his way to one of the nearby buildings. "Fine," she grumbled.

Grant winked at her again, and she flipped him off. At least she'd be back with her team. The thought surprised her. She was never a team player, but she found herself wanting that camaraderie. She shoved it aside. With what she was going to show them, they didn't have time for warm fuzzies and bonding.

AT THIS TIME OF MORNING, the drive went quickly. Val hated to admit it, but Grant drove like he flew—with utter confidence and competence, and she found herself relaxing into the seat as they talked about their Scottish histories.

"I'm so jealous you competed in the Highland games. I always wanted to see them, but our trips to Scotland were rare, and I never got to see one," Val told Grant.

"I'd spend every break from school there with my grandparents. I'll show you around if you're ever up for going."

Val was about to say her automatic no, but taking in Grant's profile and sincerity, she said instead, "This is the place." Val pointed to Lizzy's townhouse.

"We'll park a block away and cut through the back," Grant said before she could suggest the same thing. "Has anyone ever told you that you are cute when you make that pissed-off face?" Then Grant touched the wrinkled bridge of her nose and smiled. "Cute as a button."

Valeria growled. If she had a gun on her, she'd have shot him right then. No one had ever called her cute before.

Grant parked and looked around as he got out of the car. "You can jump that, right?" he asked, pointing to the privacy fence. Valeria responded by pulling herself over despite the recent wounds and flashing him a victorious smile before dropping to the ground on the other side.

"There's my lass," she heard Grant chuckle as he easily bounded over it. For being such a large man, both height and muscle wise, Grant certainly had moves.

"Val!" Lizzy cried as she pulled open the sliding door and raced out into the backyard. Valeria stood stiff as Lizzy wrapped her in a hug. "I am so glad to see you. I was so worried about you."

Val brought her arms up and patted Lizzy awkwardly. "I should have told you where I was going. I'm sorry."

Lizzy pulled back, her blue eyes flashed with annoyance. "I won't lie and say it didn't piss me off. But I figured you thought you were doing what was best. But now that attacks have been made on the group, I think it's time to be all in. If you can't be part of the team, it would be best if you left."

"But there's so much to do," Val blurted out, realizing she let her tough demeanor slip.

"Then no more lone-wolfing it. Are you ready to be part of the team or not?" Lizzy stepped back, crossed her arms over her chest, and stared her down.

"After I show you what I have, you'll need all the help you can get. You'd have to kill me to get me to quit."

"Good. Then before you do anything, run it past me." Lizzy held up her hand as Val opened her mouth to complain. "In or out?"

Val closed her mouth and took a deep breath. Lizzy wasn't her ex-boyfriend, Anthony. Lizzy was maybe the only person who truly knew Valeria's pain after being scapegoated and dumped from her life's calling. Valeria had to take a step of faith and trust again. "In."

"Good. We're all inside."

Grant was already at the door pounding Dalton on the back before his grin grew. "Jason! You old pain in the arse. I'm damn sorry to hear about Michelle. She was one hell of a woman."

The light quickly dimmed in Jason's eyes at the mention of his wife. Val knew that look all too well. It was a look of not caring about life any further. She'd had it before Humphrey had broken into her house to recruit her. There was never an option to simply block out the pain. But she had learned to move forward when she became a part of this team. Maybe the team would give Jason something to live for as well.

Val walked into the small kitchen and headed for the living room as she said hello to Jason and got a hug from Dalton. Alex sat on the couch with his head bent and his hair falling in his eyes as he worked on the computer. He looked up at her and frowned. "Hey, dude."

Val stopped dead in her tracks as the normally hyper Alex went back to work. Apparently he wasn't ready to forgive her for leaving yet. "Hi, Alex. What are you working on?" Val asked, taking a seat by him.

"Calling the prez." Suddenly Alex sat up and looked at her. "That wasn't cool, dude. You shouldn't ditch your team. Lame. Real lame. Do you know how worried we were? How much time I took trying to find you, hoping you weren't dead? Not cool, dude. Not cool." Alex shook his floppy-haired head and went back to work.

Somehow his words hurt even more than Lizzy's. Maybe because Alex wasn't like her or Lizzy. He was somehow innocent, even though he'd served time in prison for hacking. Valeria imagined this was how a mother felt when a child was disappointed in them.

"I'm sorry, Alex. It won't happen again," Valeria said softly. She went to move when two string-bean arms were flung around her. Alex's mop of a head was pressed against her as he hugged her.

"Good," he sniffled as he hid his face from view. She felt him take a deep breath and sit back up. "Are you ready?"

The group nodded, and Alex connected with the laptop in the hospital. He moved it to sit on top of the TV stand as everyone sat on the couch or the floor in front of the coffee table so they could all see the computer.

The secure connection linked up, and Tate was the first person Valeria saw. She sucked in a breath at her friend's bruised and battered body. "Jesus, Tate."

The perky press secretary just smiled wide. "Val! Oh, I am so happy to see you. Are you okay?"

"Am I okay? Are *you* okay?"

Tate nodded and reached across to grab Birch's hand. "We both are. I channeled my inner Valeria."

Fuck. She would not cry. Valeria looked at the ceiling and tried to take a breath without anyone noticing she was choked up. But when she looked back she saw Grant had noticed everything. "I'm proud of you, Tate. You bought me enough time to get the evidence we need to blow the whole thing wide open when you talked to Manuel's man."

"Not only that, but she took down the entire media arm of *Mollia Domini*," Birch said proudly.

Tate shook her head. "No, *we* did. We all did it together."

Val cocked her head. "I don't know what's been going on. I haven't been near a television or radio in over a week."

"I guess this is where we come in," Dalton said, drawing everyone's attention. "Thanks to Tate, we knew that Claudia Hughes was following a script of talking points that were setting Birch up to fail and to shake the people's faith in the country. The talking points revolved around wars that were going to be fought and an economy on the verge of collapse, which wasn't true."

"So," Lizzy picked up, "thanks to Alex running the fingerprints Humphrey helped us get, we found out Secretary of State Sandra Cummings was the person placing the orders for Phylicia to carry out. Sandra fled the country, and Alex tracked her down. And this is where it gets interesting. When you called us, we were in Romania, trying to find Sandra. What we found instead were the dead bodies of George and Helena Stanworth."

"And at two in the morning, police were called to the Stanworth mansion. Apparently his much younger wife, Christine, hung herself," Dalton added. "I guess she was the one who found the bodies of Fitz and Hugo that Jason left for George."

Dalton nodded to Lizzy who picked the story. "We found the house where George and Helena were killed. Alex is working on tracing ownership, but we believe it was a meeting of the inner circle of *Mollia Domini*. George and Helena's time of death lines up with a phone call from Christine, most likely when she found the bodies. Our guess is the head of *Mollia Domini* took them out since they were made. And probably killed Christine as well since she found the bodies. Alex?"

"Yeah, so I found out the house is under an estate, but I'm having a real hard time finding who the relatives are. I'm still working on it," Alex said, running his hand through his hair, making it stick up more. "Also, there's something else I need to tell you all before we turn it over to Valeria. Um, so you know I'm like a hacker, right?"

Everyone rolled their eyes.

"Yes, I think we know that," Birch said dryly.

"Well, I kinda sorta told some hackers about *Mollia Domini*."

Lizzy reached out and smacked the back of his head. "Why the fuck would you do that?"

Alex winced. "There was a reason! Dudes, really. It's big. There's a small chat room with some of the best hackers from all over the world in it. I have a couple friends in there, and there was already chatter about something big going on. Well, they told me some interesting things. First, there was a bomb stolen from Australia. And second, there were five Russian bombs stolen as well. Third, the Chinese police killed a man outside of the Shanghai Stock Exchange with a bomb in a large duffle bag."

Everyone was quiet as they looked at each other. They all knew what it meant.

"So, there are five more bombs out there," Birch said, shaking his head. "This is very bad."

"I think this is where I come in." Valeria stood up and pulled off her belt.

"Dude," Alex whispered with wide eyes.

Valeria rolled hers at him. "I'm not getting undressed, I'm getting you a thumb drive. Can you make it so everyone can see it?"

"Dude," Alex said in such a way it was obvious Val was underestimating his skills. Who knew one word could mean so many things?

Valeria pulled out her knife and wedged the point into a small pinhole as she pulled hard. The belt buckle popped open, revealing a small plastic baggie with a thumb drive no bigger than half an inch. She tore into the plastic and handed the small drive to Alex.

Valeria looked around as Alex walked toward the computer. "Hey, where's Brock?"

10

VALERIA KNEW the moment she asked the question that something was wrong. Everyone in the room froze and stared at her. Where was he? What weren't they telling her?

"Who's Brock?" Grant asked as Dalton shook his head to indicate he should shut up.

"Brock Loyde," Valeria said, slowly looking around at each person in the room. "He is a Secret Service agent who was supposed to help guard Birch. Did he decline?"

"Alex, move," Birch said sternly. Alex stepped out of the way of the camera and she saw Birch's face more serious than normal. "Come here, Valeria, so I can see you better."

Valeria felt numb as she approached the laptop. The computer at the hospital was moved to Birch's lap so only he could be seen.

"Where's Brock?"

"Val, I'm sorry to tell you that—" Birch started to say, but Valeria was already shaking her head back and forth.

"No. No. Don't tell me," Val ordered, her voice strangled by unshed tears.

"He died saving my life during the bombing. He was a

hero and will be buried as such. I thought you would want to handle the funeral. I'm so sorry, Valeria," Birch finished, telling her even though she didn't want to hear it.

"Val," Tate said, her voice heavy with sympathy. Sympathy was something Valeria didn't want to hear right now. She spun away and pushed past Lizzy. She needed an escape from it all. She needed to control herself.

Valeria darted into the first room with a door and closed it. It was a small half bathroom with a white pedestal sink, sea foam walls, and not much else. Valeria turned on the sink and let the sound of running water cover the sound of her tears.

"Who's Brock?" Grant asked into the silence.

"Valeria's boyfriend," Tate answered. "He was in the Secret Service and was with us at the bombing."

Grant gave a nod of understanding. The woman just lost her love, and he'd been hitting on her. Now he felt like an arse.

"You can still leave if you want to," the president said with a sigh.

Grant looked back at the closed door and then at Dalton. He'd never left a soldier behind, and he wouldn't do it now. "No. I'll stay."

Alex moved in and began to work on the computer as Grant headed over to stand next to Dalton. They had worked together so long words weren't needed to communicate what they felt at this moment. Grant knew going into this it was a small group, but now he and Dalton felt just as they did flying out to rescue the downed Syrian—this operation was FUBAR.

"Duuuuuuude," Alex said, all wide-eyed and open-mouthed. He looked up from the computer. "Dude, dude, dude!" His voice raised an octave with every dude he said.

"What is it?" The president's voice came through the computer even though Grant couldn't see him since Alex was working.

"She followed the money."

"I'll go get her," Lizzy told them, but Grant reached his hand out and wrapped his fingers around her wrist, stopping her.

"I'll do it."

GRANT KNOCKED ON THE DOOR. Nothing but the sound of running water greeted him. He twisted the knob and the door opened. He found Valeria sitting on the toilet lid, her head buried in her hands, and her shoulders shaking as she silently cried.

Grant wedged himself into the small bathroom and closed the door. Valeria turned away from him and wiped at her face as he crouched down in front of her. "Ah, lass. I'm so sorry about your boyfriend."

His heart broke as he said the words. He enjoyed their playful banter and the challenge Valeria presented. But if he'd known about Brock, she would have been off limits from the beginning. Instead he'd hit on her while her boyfriend was dying for the president.

"I'm fine," Valeria mumbled as she finally looked at him. Grant saw the bloodshot eyes and the stiff upper lip. She was hurting but refused to admit it.

"It's okay to mourn. You lost someone you love. He must have been very special."

Valeria nodded and then looked away again. "He was. And it's my fault he's dead. He didn't ask for this. He was happy in France, and I dragged him into this just like I'm dragging you. You rescued me, now let me rescue you. Leave now. Go back to your base and forget we exist."

Grant reached out and clasped her hands in his. "You're not dragging me into anything I don't want to be in." He paused. He didn't want to push her, but they needed a game plan. "When you're ready, Alex has all the information up that you got in Mexico."

Valeria took a deep breath, her eyes hardening. "Let's finish this." She stood up at the same time Grant did. He stepped back against the sink as they came chest to chest. His arms automatically wrapped around her to catch her as she stumbled. Shit. He'd had women in his arms before. Many, if he was honest. But Valeria? The beautiful, fiery force of nature felt like she was made to be in his arms. *He wanted her.* And damn the luck that her heart belonged to someone else.

Grant looked into her blue eyes streaked with electricity and rimmed with dark clouds. Her eyes were as wild as she was. Some men would want to tame that wildness, but not him. He longed to set her free. To do that, he had to let her go. Grant dropped his arms, opened the door, and watched the woman he desperately wanted in his life walk away from him.

LIZZY WATCHED the closed bathroom door open and a red-rimmed Valeria step out. Her back straight and stiff, her eyes for a second showed confusion as she glanced back at Grant, but then hardened. That was the Valeria Lizzy knew. The one who would look death in the eye and give it the finger.

"That's interesting," Dalton whispered next to her.

"It's distracting."

Dalton's eyebrows rose in response. "Am I a distraction? Sometimes love is a motivation, a reason to keep going, not a distraction, Lizzy."

Lizzy looked at the resignation and longing etched in Grant's face. He'd shaved since she had seen him last. His big thick beard was now what she'd consider a day's overgrowth of scruff. It was dark auburn and only highlighted the sharp angles and muscles of his face. His matching dark auburn hair was slightly wild in an I-just-had-sex kind of way. And then those green eyes—they were like looking at the Highland mountains. This literal mountain man looked as if his heart ached for Valeria, but he was too tough to ever admit it. And it broke Lizzy's own heart.

Lizzy leaned close to Dalton. "You're right. Love isn't a distraction. Love saved Birch. If Tate didn't love him with all her heart, she wouldn't have risked her life to protect him."

"And love brought me to the South China Sea. I wanted to protect you. I wanted to soothe the hurt and deception Dan caused. And it's what's keeping me by your side through everything that may come."

Dalton placed a kiss right below her ear as Valeria turned from talking to Alex. Grant stood next to Dalton, and everyone stopped talking and gave Valeria their full attention.

"Manuel Hernandez is the head of the *Hermanos de Sangre* cartel. He owns the local bank that I traced all the payments to Phylicia to, along with a $5,000,000 withdrawal made by Sandra Cummings that corresponds to the briefcase full of cash Branson Ames was supposed to deliver to the terrorists in Syria." Valeria pointed to the records she'd pulled off Manuel's computer.

"It's imperative we pick up Sandra immediately," Birch ordered.

"I've secured Thurmond in a former CIA black site here in DC. It hasn't been used for five years but is still useable. I can pick her up and take her there," Jason offered.

"Do it," Birch ordered.

"And speaking of Sandra," Humphrey's little nasally voice said, "Alex has Thurmond's computer and the dossier he put together at her request on natural disasters. We'll discuss that next."

"Actually," Val said, "I bet that has to do with what else I found on Manuel's computer. See, I followed the money not only to Sandra, but payouts to Dan, Hugo, Fitz, Phylicia, and about twenty other names."

Val went to the next image and Lizzy gasped. "Stanworth."

"Wait. Does that say SA Tech?" Birch's voice sounded hollow at seeing his friend's company listed.

"Yes. Sebastian is somehow tangled up in this. He told me he had to pay Manuel a fee in order to not have his business harassed in Mexico. However, it seems as if they do quite a bit of business." Valeria didn't seem too surprised or saddened by this fact. Lizzy, on the other hand, knew the feeling of betrayal Birch must be feeling.

"Here," Val said, pointing to the screen, "is a $5,000,000 deposit by Sebastian just two days before Sandra's withdrawal. It's sloppy and obvious. Either they needed the money fast or he is being set up. I can't tell which," Val answered.

"Lizzy," Birch said, his voice empty of emotion, "you're to accompany Sebastian to the White House. I'm tired of being stuck in this hospital. You bring him to me as soon as I'm back home. I'll be the one to question him. Go on, Valeria."

"Well, you can see there are also payments to and from Bertie Geofferies, the Kamerons, and Governor Orson Benning. It reads like a who's who of international players. Geofferies is Sebastian's biggest competitor, the Kamerons make their money selling various products made in Mexico, and New York Governor Benning's family owns a small but very luxurious resort on the Mexican coast. The trouble is figuring out who paid to do business and who paid to launder money. There are so many payments being made back and forth, it's pretty much impossible to tell. However, we now have a list of names. Plus we have this."

Val opened the next file. It was filled with communication and orders from Roland Westwood.

"Roland Westwood. I should have known," Birch said.

"Who's he?" Alex asked.

"Roland Westwood is the spoiled grandson and heir to Davenport Bank," Tate told everyone. "His grandmother spoils him even as his not-so-loving father tries to keep him on the straight and narrow. For his twenty-fifth birthday, his grandmother handed the Davenport Bank in South Africa over to him after Roland told her he enjoys the surfing there. I did a story on the corruption coming out of those banks."

"And Davenport Bank is one of the most prestigious banks in the world. Everyone who is anyone banks there. It would be nothing to have all those people on that list as clients," Humphrey pointed out.

Valeria nodded. "It's how they launder the money. Manuel put $5,000,000 into his bank, then invested it into a stock market account. Then someone at the Davenport Bank in South Africa liquated that account and wired it through private banking to Davenport London, who would then send it to Davenport Bank in DC or anywhere else in the world. When it's pulled out, it's clean."

"This is good, and we can now stop the free-flowing money that is funding *Mollia Domini*, but what does this have to do with the bombs?" Jason asked.

"This." Valeria went to the next file. "It's a list of the world's most influential stock markets, power grids, and water plants."

"It's the dossier Thurmond prepared," Humphrey said, stunned.

"They're going to blow up some or all of these targets. We know they have five more bombs, thanks to Alex's hacker friends. But we don't know if they have more than that," Dalton said with a seriousness they all felt.

"We do know where and who the money is coming from, though. We need to cut off the money and cripple *Mollia Domini*. And let's make sure we find Roland Westwood. Maybe then we can find out where these bombs are. We can't wait any longer. We need to move now. Westwood could be the head of *Mollia Domini,* and without him we may never find all the bombs," Lizzy ordered.

"Sandra doesn't know we're onto her, though." Humphrey said, his bald head coming into view as Alex took down the documents from the shared screen. "She could lead us to Roland or even others who are in the inner circle."

"I can get that information from her," Jason said coolly. "She's responsible for Phylicia."

That said it all. Jason blamed *Mollia Domini* for his wife's death. But he blamed Sandra most as Phylicia's handler. Lizzy looked at Dalton, and she looked at Birch. They understood what was happening. If she gave Jason permission, she was signing Sandra's death warrant. Of course, Sandra never had much of a chance at living anyway. Not when she'd committed treason.

"Do it," Lizzy ordered.

"Wait," Birch called out. "I'll call her to the hospital. Meet me here at eight. I'll have the floor cleared. Alex can get you past any security. I'm taking a risk, but I need this as much as you do. Then you can take her to the black site."

Jason looked out into some unknown before acknowledging the president. "I'll keep myself in check. I'll see you in a couple hours."

"Valeria, you're with me," Lizzy said as she took control. "We need to find Roland Westwood."

"You've got it."

"Dalton and Grant, you'll provide support if we need it. Alex, you do your thing to shut down the money. If you have to, bring in only those hackers you can trust. No more public boards and screen names, though. I need details on them so I can vet them before I clear you to bring them in. And even then, they only need to know the bare minimum. Okay?"

"Yup," Alex nodded, already getting to work on his computer. "I'm posting their details on our secure site."

"Tate, are you able to work?" Lizzy asked.

"I can type with one hand," Tate smiled.

"Then start working on press releases for the disappearance of Thurmond and Sandra. We need something to account for their absence or someone will come looking for them. I want it to be specific enough that *Mollia Domini* knows we have them and are coming for them."

"I can do that. I'll have something tomorrow for you to look over."

"Good. We have our assignments. Good luck, everyone."

11

ALEX HEADED BACK to the bar, Jason disappeared into the night, probably to the black site, and Valeria found herself and Lizzy sitting at the kitchen table researching Roland Westwood until darkness turned into light. Valeria leaned back in her chair and ran a hand over her face.

Grant was asleep on the couch and Dalton had disappeared into the bedroom a couple of hours before. Valeria was beyond exhausted, but she had a job to do. "It would be easier to get to Roland with Sebastian's help."

Lizzy shook her head. "You know as well as I do that we don't know if Sebastian is involved with *Mollia Domini*. The bank records, the spyware, I don't know if we can trust him."

"At the worst, he's one of the inner circle or even the leader. Sebastian has the power, money, and influence to pull it off. He could be funding us just to keep an eye on us," Valeria pointed out.

"And at the best he's someone who doesn't mind crossing lines to get things done."

"Isn't that what we do?"

Lizzy thought about that. Valeria had a point. "Yes, but

our goal isn't self-serving. With Sebastian, I think everything he does is meant for the betterment of his situation. That's why I worry about turning to him now. There're times I would swear he helps us, but I'm learning nothing is free with him. *If* he's not with *Mollia Domini*, then he will still expect payment in terms of us doing something questionable for SA Tech. And I don't know if we can risk turning to him."

"Well, unless you can think of a way to get into Kerra Ruby's summer bash, I'm afraid we won't have a choice. And trust me, and this is hard for me to say because I agree with everything you've said about Sebastian, but I don't know of any other way."

"We could break into his home," Lizzy suggested.

"Which one?" Valeria asked, pointing out the difficulty of hunting Roland down. "We know exactly where he'll be tonight. There're so many people at these things, it makes it easier to get in and out. As long as we have an invite, we can move freely once inside."

Lizzy groaned. "I'll call Sebastian to find out when he will be back in town so we can meet. I find it's better to try to read him before asking for anything. In the meantime, let's get some sleep."

Valeria looked around and settled on a chair in the living room as Lizzy picked up the phone to call Sebastian. He was going to love this early wakeup call. Grant sat up, stretched, and patted the couch for Valeria to lie down. Lizzy watched out of the corner of her eye as Valeria lay down, resting her head on Grant's tree trunk-sized muscled leg. In seconds, she was asleep with Grant's protective hand on her hip.

"Hello?" Sebastian didn't sound sleepy at all even though it was five in the morning.

"It's Elizabeth. Where are you?"

"I'm in my gym. Where are you?" Sebastian asked, his voice dripping with a mix of seductiveness and demand.

Lizzy wanted to roll her eyes. Sebastian didn't like giving anything away. "Which city are you in?"

"DC. I got here as quickly as I could after hearing what happened to Birch. The country would be a worse place if Birch weren't in it. I was waiting to call him to see how he is doing until later this morning."

"He's alive, which ruined someone's plan." Lizzy tried to be casual, but she was sure Sebastian knew she was acting. "I know he'll want to see you. I need to see him as well. How about two SA Tech employees visit him this morning? Meet at the hospital at nine?"

Sebastian was quiet for a moment. "I can do that."

"Good. See you then."

Lizzy hung up without waiting for Sebastian to say goodbye. She had just enough time to rest for a couple hours before seeing which side Sebastian truly fell on. She sent a secure message to the team informing them of the plan. As Lizzy left the kitchen, Valeria had a hand resting on Grant's upper thigh. He rested one hand on the top her head and the other on the indent of her waist.

"Come to bed." Lizzy looked up to see Dalton standing shirtless at the bedroom door. In seconds, his body wrapped around hers as he held her. The warmth and the utter feeling of complete safety had Lizzy instantly falling into a heavy and dreamless sleep.

IT TOOK Birch screaming at the doctors to get them to leave. His Secret Service had to stand guard on the other side of the thick doors leading to his closed wing. His doctors were great and all, but one, Birch didn't know if any of them were reporting to *Mollia Domini*. And two, they enjoyed eavesdropping way more than Birch was okay with.

He had two hours to see both Sandra and Sebastian without anyone coming in. Jason was allowed in with a credential saying he was with the chief of staff's office. Humphrey joined him as they walked in together wheeling a large suitcase filled with papers to be signed and cards from well-wishers. The suitcase would be checked by his agents before they would be allowed onto his floor.

Humphrey and Jason arrived just as the floor was being locked down. "Did you see that Sebastian is coming in an hour?" Humphrey asked, tossing all the "important presidential papers" in the trash as Jason set the piles and piles of get-well cards on Birch's table next to his bed and then dragged a chair over toward the door to sit.

"Yes. I hate that I have to do it here. I feel weak in the hospital, but at least I'm getting it over with. I don't know what I'll do if Sebastian—" Birch couldn't finish.

Tate reached over and grabbed his hand. She knew how important Sebastian was to him. He was more than a friend; he was like a brother to him. But brothers could be betrayed as easily as friends.

"Do I need to stay?" Jason asked.

"No. Lizzy will be here." Jason just raised an eyebrow and continued with his cold stare. "She can handle herself, trust me. I've seen video of her in action."

"No offense, but if push comes to shove, I don't think she'll shove as hard as she should."

"She put a bullet between her ex's eyes. I think she'll be fine."

Jason shrugged. "You're the boss."

The door down the hall opened and Sandra stepped in.

She looked around as Humphrey hurried from the room. "Ah, Sandra. We're down here. Sorry, we had to clear the hall so we could discuss any national security issues that come up."

Sandra walked in with worry written all over her face. Worry for herself or fake worry for him, Birch didn't know, although he did know she was one hell of an actress. Sandra glanced at Jason questioningly and Jason smiled. For a split second he looked like a kind, caring man. "I'll be just outside, Mr. Orville."

"Oh, yes. We'll head back to the office shortly." Humphrey smiled as Jason headed to a chair on the other side of the door. He would still be able to hear them, but Sandra didn't know that. "One of my aides. We had a ton of get-well cards to bring the president."

"Mr. President, Tate," Sandra said, shaking her head. "I can't believe this. How are you feeling?"

Tate smiled kindly. "Thank you for your concern, Sandra. We're getting there."

Birch frowned. "Although two very good men of mine and fifteen civilians were killed. But, you know that, don't you?"

Sandra blinked and then looked sympathetically at them. "Yes, I read that. Are you sure you should be running the nation at a time when you should be focused on getting better? I'm sure the vice president can take of things while you heal."

"I'm quite all right to run the country. After all, that's why I asked you here. To get down to business."

"Right. We need to address the executive order for contracting private security that President Mitchell proposed. Some key embassies have received terror threats recently, and we don't have enough soldiers to increase security and go after the terrorists. So the State Department has already called in some National Guardsmen to help, but now the states are lacking in security. New York City, Chicago, and Los Angeles have all asked for funds to hire private security to help replace the National Guard."

"Good point. What else do we need to address?" Birch asked, keeping his suspicions hidden. Like hell he would authorize that much power to private security.

"I think we need to address the rumors of our collapsing stock market. I have foreign leaders contacting me about pulling out of their investment in American companies," Sandra said as she took out her notebook and scribbled some notes.

"Yes, yes. That's no good at all," Humphrey bumbled. It seemed to put Sandra at ease.

"Great. Since Tate is here, I'll put out a press release through her assistant. How is the investigation going on the explosion?" Sandra asked with such concern Birch would almost think she cared. But he knew better.

"Thank you for asking. We've made big strides in the investigation." Birch watched Sandra's reaction. She seemed surprised but covered it quickly.

"I have heard the Chinese are angry about our ships keeping the peace in the South China Sea. Is it them?"

"No. It's not the Chinese. In fact, it's a new group I've never heard of before that has been responsible for a number of bombings and assassinations around the world. I'm just their next target."

Sandra looked shocked. "A new group? Who are they? Syrian?"

Birch shook his head. "No." Birch looked thoughtful for a second. "We know who they are, but we don't know how they knew about my plans for that night. They were rather spur-of-the-moment."

Humphrey bobbed his bald head up and down in agreement.

Sandra looked confused and then horrified. "This group has a mole in the White House?" Her eyes shot around the room. "Who is it?"

"We don't know yet," Birch told her sternly. "But we will find out soon enough."

"How?" Sandra asked.

Birch blinked his eyes at her. "Why, you're going to tell us who it is."

"Me?" Sandra asked puzzled. "Oh no. You don't think it's Thurmond, do you?"

Humphrey stopped bobbing his head. "Thurmond? Why do you think it's Thurmond?"

Sandra leaned forward and lowered her voice. "Well, he's a great assistant, but he is very power hungry. Everyone knows that. I was waiting until the end of the term to replace him. He knows so many people; I have to admit I was lax in letting him go. But I've caught him in my office a couple times. I'm suspicious enough that I started locking my office and desk, but I had no real proof."

"Interesting that you say that because we've already talked to Thurmond," Birch told her, never taking his eyes off hers. Sandra swallowed and closed her notebook.

"You have? Is he the one?"

Birch nodded. "He told us everything." Sandra went white. He could see her moving her feet to better leap up. She was going to make a run for it. "But here's the thing. We didn't need him to tell us anything. We already knew."

"You knew he was the mole?"

"No. That you were in the inner ring of *Mollia Domini*."

Sandra made her move. She threw her notebook at Humphrey as she leapt from her chair. Humphrey let her go. She yanked the sliding door open only to be met with a punch to the face by Jason. Sandra's head snapped back as her body followed. Gone was the nice, polite Jason. In his place was someone so empty and lost that Birch had had second thoughts about including him in the group. Sandra shrieked as she looked around like a caged animal. Blood trickled from her split lip as she crab-crawled away from Jason.

"Shut up, Sandra," Birch yelled over her. Sandra leapt up and grabbed at him. Birch grunted with pain as she tried to pull him from the bed. In one long stride, Jason had his hand around her throat and was dragging her off Birch.

"You killed my wife," he said so softly between clenched teeth that Birch barely heard him. But Sandra did. She stopped struggling and began shaking her head.

"No. You have the wrong person. I didn't kill anyone."

Jason squeezed tighter, and Sandra opened her mouth in a feeble attempt to get air into her lungs. "Don't lie. Phylicia Claymore got orders from you. You are responsible for what happened."

"Okay, Jason." Birch didn't yell the command, but the steel in his voice had Jason loosening his grip on Sandra's throat instantly. She gasped for air, filling her lungs as Birch watched her mind working.

"You have the wrong person. I don't even know who Phylicia is," Sandra cried as tears ran down her wrinkled face.

"You left a print on the message that went into the rock," Birch said as if he were tired of hearing her excuses. "We know about your meeting on the beach of the Black Sea in

Bulgaria. We know about George's and Helena's deaths as well. Why don't you just tell us your side of it?"

"No. You can't know." Sandra was breaking quickly. Her body was trembling, her face bloodless. "He'll kill me."

"I'll kill you first if you don't start talking," Jason growled at her.

"Why don't you start with the missing bombs?"

"How?" Sandra stared at him. "How do you know this?"

Birch didn't answer. Instead he just smiled.

"The bombs, Sandra," Humphrey said quietly.

Instead of answering, Sandra opened her mouth and screamed for all she was worth. Birch nodded his chin for approval, Jason slid the needle into Sandra's neck. She collapsed instantly.

"Dammit. She gave us nothing." Tate stared at Sandra's body as Jason dragged in the suitcase and folded her into it.

"I'll get something from her. I know women like her. They think they're tough. They prepare for the attack, but when all she's met with is silence, she'll break. It might take a couple days, but I'll break her," Jason swore. "How far can I go?"

"As far as it takes," Birch decided. He may be violating the very laws he swore to uphold, but if he didn't . . . Birch took a deep breath. Five more bombs were out there, and he'd do what it took to get them.

Jason zipped the suitcase. "Are you sure you don't need me to stay and help with Sebastian? What I gave her will have her out for three hours or so. That's plenty of time."

"No. Lizzy can handle it. I want you to be with Sandra the second she wakes." Birch took a deep breath as he looked at the people in the room with him. "Humphrey, can you take Tate for a stroll in her wheelchair? I need a moment alone with Jason."

"Sure." Humphrey pushed the wheelchair next to the bed and held out his hand. "Your ride, madam."

Humphrey angled Tate out of bed and the two of them chatted happily as he wheeled her out.

"Jason, sit down. It's time we talked as only two men who have lost their wives can."

12

LIZZY WALKED into the hospital two steps behind Sebastian. Sebastian exuded power and control as he walked in his form-fitting black suit and dark gray tie—a dark gray tie that matched his eyes perfectly. Humphrey was waiting at the door to the hospital room for them. He greeted them in his typical bumbling way, but Lizzy knew he was more than the snoring, drooling, blundering man he projected himself to be. Just as she knew the man they'd passed in the parking garage wasn't some assistant delivering letters, but Jason taking Sandra away.

"Tate and I are heading out to pilfer the ice cream while the nurses are off the floor. Do you want anything?" Humphrey asked as he pulled Tate's wheelchair out of the room.

"No, thank you," Lizzy said, smiling at them both as Sebastian just shook his head. His eyes were locked on Birch's as he took in the wires, the IV, and the bruises. Lizzy closed the door. Humphrey would be right outside as a last resort if she needed help.

"Shit, Birch," Sebastian whispered with more emotion

than Lizzy had ever heard from him. Sebastian stood rooted to the floor as Lizzy took a seat at Birch's bedside. She sat unobtrusively between them, preventing Sebastian from touching Birch unless he allowed it.

"Yeah, it's hard to fight someone trying to kill you when you don't know who it is. In war, we know who they are. With this, they are all around and you would never know." Birch kept his eyes locked with Sebastian's as well.

"What can I do?"

"You can cut the bullshit, Seb."

Sebastian didn't react. It was an art, really. Only the tiniest flare of Sebastian's nostrils showed he was affected by Birch's words.

"How so?"

"Stop being Sebastian Abel, tech genius, business mogul, billionaire. Be the man I grew up with. Be my friend."

"I'm always your friend, Birch."

"See, I don't know if you are. You're so caught up in this God complex, thinking you should be running the world, that I'm not quite so sure you are my friend anymore."

Sebastian blinked. Birch's words hit harder than Lizzy thought they would.

"How can you say that? I'm funding this whole secret mission you have going on and don't know a thing about it. I hand over my planes, my connections, my money . . . all because you're my best friend. Shit, you're my only friend."

Birch sat up and stared at his friend. "Then why are you using my agents to spy against your rival, Bertie Geofferies? And why are *your* name and *your* money showing up in the records of the largest drug dealer in the world, a drug dealer who just so happens to be funding *Mollia Domini*? Now, I can forgive the fact that Roland Westwood is your private banker. After all, he's known for making his clients a lot of money. However, he's also known for being ruthless and power-hungry, just like you have become. And he also is a member of *Mollia Domini,* the same group that tried to blow up your supposed best friend. And you had to know that. I know you better than anyone, and you never go into anything blind."

Lizzy sat in silence as both powerful men were motionless. They looked at each other as if trying to read into the other's every move and motive. Sebastian's lips thinned as he pressed them together so hard that they turned white.

"You knew, didn't you?" Birch asked quietly as he let out a long sigh. "Seb, just be honest with me."

It was as if all the air was let out of Sebastian. "Yes, I knew. Or at least I suspected. I knew about Manuel. That was why I was trying to get that other woman to let me go with her to Mexico. I guessed that was where she was going when she hopped on my plane with me and compared me to him. I'm guessing she's dead now."

"No, she's not," Lizzy said with her jaw clenched. She stood up and poked Sebastian in the chest. "You should have told me!"

"I assumed you knew where she was going and why."

"But you shouldn't assume that I knew," Birch said, stopping Lizzy from poking Sebastian again. "Tell me what you know."

"Well, know and *know* are two different things. Manuel is the go-to man for business in Mexico. All those manufacturing plants, resorts, anything . . . they all make payments to Manuel. But last time I was down there checking in on my resort, Roland was there. It was two months ago now. He couldn't stop bragging about how big he was and that he was in a new investment. I gathered it had to do with Manuel. Then when you told me about *Mollia Domini,* I figured that's what he was talking about."

"Why didn't you tell me?" Birch asked with disbelief.

"I had no evidence. It was just a feeling."

"What else do you know or think you might know?" Lizzy asked as she clenched her fist. They could have been miles ahead in this operation if she'd known about Roland.

"That's about it. I know I've been approached by numerous people about a particular secret investment, but those people have mysteriously disappeared recently."

"Is Roland the head of the investment group he talked about?" Birch asked.

"I don't know. I'm sorry—"

Birch shook his head, cutting Sebastian off. "Don't say something you don't mean. I don't even know who you are anymore, Sebastian. You would sit back and let me be killed instead of coming to me? How do I know you're telling me the truth now? How do I know you're not the head of *Mollia Domini,* and you're just stringing me along so you can know what's going on?"

"I am not a part of that. I would never hurt you, Birch."

"How can I know that? Look at your actions. You're playing both sides, waiting to see who the winner is so you can take advantage, aren't you? Well, Sebastian, your time is up. Choose right now. Whose side are you on?"

Lizzy moved to the edge of her seat, ready to stop Sebastian if he decided to either run or attack. By the way Sebastian's jaw was moving as he ground his teeth, Birch had hit the nail on the head. Sebastian was playing both sides.

"What can I do to prove to you that I'm on your side?"

"Well, since you're so good at laundering money, you're

going to transfer $20,000,000 and one jet into an account we'll set up. That way we'll be completely autonomous from you from now on," Birch told him, knowing it was just a drop in the bucket for Sebastian.

"Done."

"And I want you to get me two invites for Kerra Ruby's birthday party in Los Angeles," Lizzy told him.

"Done."

"Any strings?" Lizzy asked, knowing every time she'd asked for a favor there had been strings attached.

"No."

Birch looked at his childhood friend and shook his head. "It's not easy, you know. This hurt more than the fact someone tried to kill me. Who have you turned into, Sebastian?"

"Someone who will never be beat up again," Sebastian said softly. Lizzy saw the pained look in Birch's eyes.

"We've come a long way from the two boys who would get into trouble on the base. We had a rough start, but would you change it? I wouldn't."

"No, I wouldn't. We were innocent then." Sebastian looked at the floor and took a breath. "I'll have everything done in a couple of hours."

Lizzy stood to leave with Sebastian, but he held out his hand. "Not now, Miss James."

Sebastian walked out of the room and down the hall, never looking back.

"Shit, Lizzy. What have I done? He's my best friend, but you saw it, didn't you?"

Lizzy's heart broke for Birch. And even for Sebastian. Friendships should never be taken for granted. Sometimes they were as dear to you as family—even more so since you chose your friends. But even family and friends sometimes lose their way and no one sees it until it's too late.

"Yes. He's still withholding information."

Humphrey wheeled Tate back into the room. "How did it go?"

Birch just shook his head. He was lost in the past and the future while trying to figure out where his best friend fit into all of that. "Lizzy, you better go. They're opening the wing back up soon. We get to go home tomorrow, or I guess the day after tomorrow technically since it won't be until the middle of the night. We're hoping I'll have a chance to get home without the press knowing to give me time to settle in."

"Is there anything I can do to help?" Lizzy asked.

"No. Gene Rankin, the butler, is taking care of my arrival at the White House."

"Lizzy," Tate said, drawing her attention from Birch. "Be careful tonight."

"Thanks." Lizzy looked at her group and walked out the door. She only hoped she'd make it back to them.

ALEX SLUGGED BACK another energy drink. He hadn't slept in . . . well, long enough that he needed at least two more drinks to make it through the work he had to get done. His eyes were dry and bloodshot and his fingers were cramped, but he couldn't stop now. He had turned the IRS and DEA onto Davenport Bank. He'd sent all the information they'd need to make their case. But he's also sent it to the heads of every intelligence agency and multiple DEA offices all over the US to make sure no one would drop the ball.

Then he'd hacked Manuel's bank and locked them out.

They couldn't wire any money in or out without a password, a password they'd never get. If Manuel was good, and he was, he'd have his own hacker on it, but it would take time. That would allow the IRS and DEA time to move in and shut down his US contacts. The money for *Mollia Domini* was drying up.

The chat screen on the private secure group with his hacker friends popped up.

Dark Surfer: *Roland Westwood has his hand in everything and everyone. And I mean that both figuratively and literally. His clients read as the top 100 richest people in the world. Or, I should say, his grandmother's bank. Roland has been investigated numerous times for insider trading, but walks away each time. It seems with each cleared investigation he gets more and more whales as clients. It's hard to tell who is legit and who isn't. Personally, Roland has been linked to actresses, models, and most recently to heiress Blythe Sterling, the granddaughter of George Stanworth. They are going to be at some birthday party for Kerra Ruby tonight.*

Rock Star: *I found plenty linking Roland to Manuel. The trouble is, like Dark Surfer, I have found too many ties with powerful people to know what to make of it. I'm slowly hacking into as many accounts as I can. I can't get into Sebastian Abel's or Bertie Geofferies's accounts yet. They must hire even better hackers than us at their tech companies. I already lost one computer to a virus SA Tech's firewall installed as I was trying to hack them. I did get into Trip Kameron's accounts and social media. It's clear Trip and Manuel are close. But what was interesting was the money that Vivian Geofferies was paying to Trip who was then sending part of it to Manuel. What I also found out from Vivian and Trip's private messages to each other —Manuel will be in LA tonight for that same birthday party. He'll be on US soil.*

Alex read the message three times, thinking his eyes were deceiving him. Valeria, Lizzy, Grant, and Dalton were already en route to that very party. Dalton and Grant weren't invited, they were going to be keeping an eye on the perimeter, but Valeria and Lizzy had invitations. Manuel would recognize Valeria instantly.

Alex dove for his phone. In his sleep-deprived, artificially hyped state, he hit the phone and sent it crashing to the floor behind his table. Falling to the floor, Alex crawled on shaky arms and legs under the table to the phone. He sat down hard and slowly reached for the phone. He took a deep breath and called Lizzy.

"Dude."

13

"I DON'T LIKE THIS," Dalton said, crossing his arms as Lizzy and Valeria stepped from the private jet.

"I don't either," Grant said, similarly crossing his arms over his chest and glaring at Valeria.

Valeria looked down at her mini dress. It was the most expensive dress she'd ever worn and surprisingly loved it. "It's designer."

"If there's a slight breeze, your arse will on display."

"I think that's the point." Valeria smiled happily. She looked at Dalton pulling Lizzy's top up to cover her breasts. They had boarded the jet and found two packages waiting for them from Sebastian. There was a handwritten note saying they needed to dress appropriately for the party. Valeria's dress was silver and draped in a halter top down her front, leaving her back exposed, and then down to a very short skirt. Lizzy's was the same, but in black. The headlights of a limousine broke the bickering. Valeria reached up her skirt and pulled out her gun.

"Where did that come from?" Grant asked as his voice

changed from demanding to seductive. Apparently he wasn't concerned about a nearing car.

Valeria wanted to roll her eyes, but they were glued to Grant's as they trailed down her body and stopped between her legs. Her body flushed as she read his wanting look, but then, in an instant, he stepped back and was all business.

Valeria watched the limo pull to a stop next to them, the back window rolled down. "Get in."

"Sebastian?" Lizzy sputtered with anger as she replaced her gun in the depths of her cleavage. "What the fuck are you doing here?"

"I'm your way into the party."

Dalton and Grant felt the tension and stepped forward, shielding the women. Lizzy rolled her eyes at Valeria and the two pushed past them. "You said no strings."

"There aren't any strings. I was invited to the party. The only way I could get you invitations was if you were with me. You're my dates."

Grant went stiff. "Sorry, laddie, I don't think so."

Sebastian turned to stone. His eyes bore into Grant. "I'm perfectly capable of protecting two women."

Grant smirked. "It wasn't the women I was worried about."

Sebastian flung the door open, and Valeria leapt forward as the men came toe to toe. "That's enough, unless you want to whip your dicks out for Lizzy and me to measure. That could be entertaining, compared to this macho bullshit."

"Sebastian," Lizzy said without raising her voice but with enough steel to it that had Sebastian looking away from Grant. "Thank you for the invitations and the clothes. But we have a problem."

"I'm not going to hurt you. I'm not part of *Mollia Domini*!" Instead of raising his voice, it only got lower.

"Then prove it. We have a problem. Manuel Hernandez is also attending the party tonight."

"So . . . oh," he said, looking to Valeria. "I'm guessing he knows what you look like."

Valeria nodded.

"No problem. Get in. Your men can follow." Sebastian turned and got into the limo, leaving the door open for them to follow.

"Lizzy," Dalton warned.

"Val and I will be fine. Everything goes on as planned. Put in your coms and we'll see you on the other side." Lizzy leaned over and kissed Dalton as Val and Grant put in earpieces so small that they wouldn't be visible at a glance.

"Valeria," Grant said quietly as Lizzy got in the limo and Dalton went to get their car parked nearby. "Be careful and watch your arse."

He winked and Val smiled. Grant was courageous, loyal, skillful, and so freaking sexy that she struggled to simply smile at him. As she had watched Dalton kiss Lizzy, she knew what longing felt like. She wished it were Grant by her side instead of Sebastian, but wishes didn't have a place in her life anymore. She knew her strengths, her capabilities, and part of her wanted to prove to Grant she was a team player. *With this team.* But all that had to be put aside, especially when she didn't know if she'd make it out of this party alive.

THEY WERE quiet in the limo ride to a small but beautiful home in the Hollywood Hills. Like many of the houses not in gated communities, it sat right off the road behind a thick columned hedge. The walkway to the pale blue house was flanked by tall Italian cypress trees that also ran the length of each side of the small property.

"Where are we?" Lizzy asked as Sebastian got out of the limo.

"A friend's house. She'll have a solution for Valeria's problem." Sebastian walked away, leaving them sitting in the limo to follow.

Val looked at Lizzy who just shrugged as they watched the front door open. A woman with pink hair and more tattoos than Valeria could count smiled up at Sebastian before giving him a hug. They watched as she listened to Sebastian and then looked toward the limo and nodded. She smiled and waved at them before going inside the house.

"Come on," Sebastian said, somehow without really raising his voice.

"Let's do it." Valeria slid out, followed by Lizzy. They saw Dalton and Grant park their van across the street, but they didn't stop to talk to them.

Lizzy took the lead as they went into the bungalow that looked the complete opposite from its owner. It was neat, elegant, and filled with old Hollywood antiques and fixtures. However, what sat in the front room was anything but traditional. There were shelves full of wigs, counters full of makeup, mustaches, beards, beauty marks, and thick paste.

"Imogene is a makeup artist for one of the studios. I told her how you wanted to change your look for the party tonight, and she said she'd be happy to help." Sebastian took a seat on a gold silk couch and the little pink-haired, tatted-up twenty-something smiled up at Val.

"This is so exciting. The dress you have is killer, so I think we need to go with a killer look."

Oh, she had no idea.

"Ice blonde. A beauty mark. And can you wear contacts? I'm thinking silver eyes to go with the ice blonde. You're so tan I want to make the contrast very sharp."

Sounded good to Val. Colored contacts would be particularly useful since her blue eyes tended to get noticed. "This is so exciting. Thanks, Bashy," Valeria said in her best Southern California voice as she blew a kiss to Sebastian.

An hour later Valeria didn't even recognize herself in the mirror. The wig was a short, sharp-edged chin-length bob. Her eyes seemed glacial under the silver contacts. The deep blood-red lipstick made her lips pop and the one little beauty mark on her cheek, "for glam," as Imogene said, made her a mix of Marilyn Monroe and an assassin. It was kinda perfect.

"This was fun, thank you." Valeria hugged the woman even though it went against her nature.

"You're welcome. You want me to do you next?"

Lizzy shook her head. "I wish we had time, but the party already started."

Imogene laughed. "Oh, honey, no one who is anyone shows up on time. The more important you are, the later you arrive. And as Sebastian's escorts, you all have oodles of time."

"In that case—" Lizzy took a seat and Val watched as Imogene applied makeup, a matching beauty mark, and a black wig in the exact cut as hers. They were polar opposites except for the beauty mark. Where Val was white hair and dark makeup, Lizzy was dark hair, bright makeup. On each side of Sebastian they looked like an angel and devil whispering in his ear.

"What the fuck is taking so long," she heard Dalton ask

as they got ready to leave. The door opened and they walked out, each holding onto one of Sebastian's arms. "Holy shit. I wouldn't know that was you, and I sleep with you."

They got into the limousine as Lizzy blew Dalton a kiss. It was late now, well after midnight as they made their way through the gates of Laughlin Park. They wound their way through the old neighborhood and stopped in front of the wooded drive leading to Kerra Ruby's house.

"We'll get out here," Sebastian told his driver. "Ladies."

Sebastian got out of the car and held out both arms. Valeria and Lizzy didn't think twice as they hooked their hands into the crook of his arms. Sebastian, no matter his faults, was someone who drew attention. Tall, handsome, wealthy, and powerful—a lethal combination to the women at the party tonight.

"We are on the street closest to the back of the property," Dalton's voice said over the coms as they walked to the guarded entrance.

Three security guards stood at the entrance with clipboards, walkies, and stun guns. "Name," the tall man with no neck and bulging muscles demanded.

"Abel." Sebastian said calmly as he handed over his invitation.

The guard looked at Lizzy and Valeria and back at the clipboard. "Okay, you and your guests are good to go. Enjoy your evening, Mr. Abel."

The house came into view after a short walk along the heavily wooded driveway. It was a tan stucco Spanish colonial with red clay shingles and iron light fixtures. The sound of music grew louder as they walked around the fountain in the middle of the circular drive, which showed off Kerra's expensive cars all lined up.

People stood talking in groups out front, inside the

entrance to the mansion, and packed in the hallways and living room leading out to the pool area. Valeria saw actors, directors, models, singers . . . basically the whole list of people Tate had discovered were the influencers for *Mollia Domini*. And tonight *Mollia Domini* was on everyone's lips. Even if they didn't say it by name. They used the Stanworth name instead. Everyone was discussing what would happen now that Stanworth and Helena were dead. The morning news had reported they'd been identified by George's son, Auden.

"Blythe is, like, so brave." Valeria heard a group talking as they strolled by.

"Totes. And I even hear she's going to go to battle with her uncle over control of the company."

"OMG! So brave. Like, all that money could be hers."

"Then maybe I could get a lead in one of the movies. Blythe and I are like besties."

No one seemed sad that George and his daughter, Helena, had died. They were more concerned about profiting from their deaths. Of course, Valeria was thinking the same way.

"I see Roland. He's talking to Manuel and Trip Kameron," Sebastian said as he lowered his lips to her ear. "Giggle."

Valeria giggled. Then Sebastian whispered to Lizzy and she giggled. Somehow the sounds of them giggling seemed all wrong. They weren't the giggling type.

Sebastian strutted forward and stopped. They were only a couple yards away from them when he used his arms to pull them toward him, forming a triangle as he lowered his head. Lizzy and Val did the same so they could hear him.

"What are we doing?" Lizzy whispered with a smile on her face even though she was just as confused as Val.

"You always let what you want most come to you first. Now, ladies, it's time to play your cover." Valeria saw Lizzy's eyes momentarily flash as Sebastian's hand dropped to her ass. Before she knew it, Sebastian had pulled Val to him and his lips were on hers as his hand grabbed her ass and squeezed. She thought about kneeing him in the balls, but the sound of Trip Kameron's laughing yell of, "Sebastian, you're my fucking hero," stopped her.

Sebastian raised his head slowly as if he were mad at Trip for interrupting. Lizzy had moved her hand to Sebastian's chest as she looked up longingly at him. Valeria looked back as Sebastian took a handkerchief and wiped the lipstick from his lips. Sebastian had made Trip look, resulting in Manuel and Roland also looking. They recognized Sebastian and waved him over.

Sebastian dropped his arms to their waists and maneuvered them the ten feet or so to the small group of men. Manuel dismissed Val and Lizzy after one appreciative glance.

"Apparently, we are *hermanos*," Manuel said, welcoming Sebastian into the group.

"You get that, too?" Sebastian said, sounding slightly annoyed.

"*Sí.*"

Sebastian didn't react. He also didn't bother introducing Val or Lizzy, which was probably a good thing since it was Valeria who had told both men they looked alike.

"Sebastian, good to see you," the man Val recognized as Roland Westwood said, holding out his hand for Sebastian to shake. Roland was exactly what a rich heir to a banking empire would look like. His body was money-bought. Rich clothes, rich haircut, the whitest teeth anyone had ever seen, and a body made by a private chef and a personal trainer. And underneath all that, he was a cocky bastard.

"Roland. How's my money doing?"

Roland laughed and tossed back a whiskey. "You're still rich. Richer than me, at any rate."

Valeria knew how much each man was worth, as best as she could tell. But there were always ways to hide money, and she was sure they all did. It was still a shock to think about how much Sebastian had made on his own. She might even be impressed if he weren't such an asshole. It was more than Roland had inherited, and it was more than Bertie Geofferies, who had once been the richest man in the world, obtained.

"Actually, that's something I'd like to talk about with you and Roland," Manuel said easily.

"Me being rich?" Sebastian asked, taking a drink Trip offered him.

"In a way. Trip, take the ladies to the bar and get them a drink," Manuel ordered as if telling his lap dog to get down.

"My pleasure," Trip sneered. "I always love sharing with Sebastian. He has the best taste."

"If the laddie touches you, you rip his *doaber* off," Grant's Scottish accent became stronger with anger in their ear coms.

Lizzy leaned over so that her lips were by Val's ear. Trip, probably thinking they were going to make out, stopped and stared. "I wish you had some of the drugs I gave him last time."

Val's lips twitch up at the thought.

"Can you hear them?" Lizzy asked as she trailed her hand down Val's arm.

"Barely. I need to get a foot or two closer."

"Aw, come on, girls. No one likes a tease," Trip whined.

"I want to dance," Lizzy pouted as she wrapped both arms around Val's neck and began to sway. Valeria took the lead as they slithered their way closer to Roland, Manuel, and Sebastian.

"Oh, yeah. Can't leave the Trip out of this. After all, three is always better than two." Trip pushed his way between the women, making a Trip sandwich. Valeria rolled her eyes as Trip rubbed his hands over her body.

"I can kill him," Lizzy mouthed from behind Trip. She moved her hands up toward Trip's neck. Valeria laughed, which drew Trip's eyes to her bouncing breasts. Whatever kept his attention away from them drawing closer to Sebastian and his group.

Valeria swayed closer to the men in order to hear better. She only heard bits and pieces and thought about pulling her top down to shut Trip up. She tuned out his blathering about his large dick and prowess in bed as she closed her eyes and focused.

"*Puto* DEA," Manuel swore. Valeria pushed Trip's head toward her breasts as he decided to start talking dirty in her ear. Although, it really wasn't very well done. Telling a woman how she'll please him when she does all the work isn't really a turn-on.

"Tell that *tolla-thon* to go fuck himself," Grant practically growled over the coms as his accent deepened in anger.

"Shut up," Valeria cursed, even if Trip was an asshole she was trying to hear what Manuel was saying about the DEA.

"Oh, you're no talk, all action. Trip likey."

"Suck my finger, it turns me on," Valeria said, not even looking at Trip as she shoved her finger in his mouth to shut him up.

Lizzy had to turn away from the group as she tried not to

laugh. But Valeria closed her eyes again and focused on the deep voices floating on the thumping music.

"They cut your money off?" Sebastian asked seriously.

"I still have it, I just can't send it anywhere," she heard Manuel explain. "I'm meeting a DEA contact tonight to see if we can fix this."

"We need your help," Val heard Roland say a couple seconds later. "It's an exclusive group of the most powerful people in the world. We help each other out."

"And you want me to help by funding whatever it is until Manuel pays off the right people and gets his accounts unfrozen?" Sebastian asked as if funding a secret group was no big deal.

"Yes, but it's more than that. We'd also help you," Roland said, his voice fading as he tried to seduce Sebastian to join *Mollia Domini*.

"This is so hot," Trip mouthed around her finger.

"Then take two." Val jammed another finger into his mouth as she saw Lizzy tense. She heard Sebastian's voice over the music, but just barely.

"Is there a leader? I have a problem being the richest person and not being in charge."

"Well, sure there's a leader," Roland said, suddenly sounding nervous. "But you must first prove yourself before you can climb the ranks."

"Let's fuck," Trip bumbled around Val's fingers.

"Okay," Lizzy whispered. "We like to play games. Why don't you find a room, get naked, and we'll come find you."

"Oh man, so hot."

Trip took off, and Lizzy threw her hands around Val's neck as they swayed to the music. "What did Sebastian say?"

"I don't know. That little shit made me miss some of it."

Lizzy turned her head. "They're walking away."

Val turned and watched. There was no way they could follow without being noticed as the three men walked into a distant shadowed part of the yard. Val looked around to find any way of getting closer when she felt as if the air had been punched from her lungs.

"What is it?" Lizzy asked in a whisper.

"Anthony." Valeria said, barely moving a muscle.

"Who?" Lizzy asked at the same time Dalton and Grant did.

"My ex-boyfriend with the DEA."

"The one who set you up and got you fired?" Lizzy asked.

"The very one."

Lizzy spun them around so that Valeria's back was toward him. "Which one? Oh, never mind. He looks like a wanna-be biker?"

"Yeah."

"Sticks out like a sore thumb. No wonder he took a bribe. He'd be outed as an undercover agent in a heartbeat. Doesn't he know bikers don't wear designer clothes?"

Val sighed. "He knew enough to have me blackballed at every government agency."

"He must be Manuel's contact. He's seen Manuel and is heading in that direction."

Lizzy kept turning Valeria so her back was toward him. "He stopped by the pool. Manuel sees him. Manuel's looking around. His eyes are on us," Lizzy laughed as she looked at Valeria. "We need to leave."

"Why?" Valeria felt her stomach knot. It was the same feeling she had when an operation went wrong.

"Because Anthony is walking this way. Manuel pointed to us."

14

"GET OUT," Dalton's calm words came over the coms.

"Like hell. I can take Anthony with my eyes closed." Valeria was ready. It was time for payback.

"He's stopped," Lizzy giggled, spinning and sending her skirt flying up. "He's staring at us."

"Fuck," Dalton cursed. "This party is busted. Get out, now."

"Sebas—" Valeria started to ask.

"Leave him. He has identification, neither of you do." It was remarkable how calm Dalton and Grant were under stress. Grant calmly told them how to leave the party as the first sounds of "DEA!" were being shouted at the front of the house.

Lizzy and Valeria moved quickly, shoving their way through the crowd. Some of the crowd panicked, some laughed and snapped selfies while others kept drinking and dancing.

"Left through the mimosa trees," came Grant's steady voice.

"The white or pink ones?" Lizzy asked as she led the way.

"Pink."

"Go first," Lizzy ordered Val.

"You go. You're already there," Valeria called from where Lizzy was already halfway up the tree looking over the eight-foot stucco privacy fence.

Lizzy nodded and climbed from the tree to the top of the fence and then disappeared from sight. Valeria reached up and grabbed the branches of the tropical tree with the fuzzy flowers. She hiked her foot and pulled herself up.

But suddenly she was being pulled back down. Instinctively she tightened her grip on the branches and tried to free herself. "It's been a long time, baby."

Anthony's voice slithered over her.

"I'm not your baby."

"Did you think a wig and some makeup would fool me? Your back gave you away. How many times did I trace those freckles that make up a crescent on your shoulder blade?"

"Do you need assistance?" Grant's granite-hard voice said over coms, but before she could scream, the DEA and police flooded the backyard.

"Freeze!" someone yelled right behind them.

"Calm down, I'm with you. DEA Agent Anthony Gomez. I'm taking a suspect into custody."

"I'm not a suspect!" Valeria said, fighting against the cuffs Anthony was putting on her.

"Hold on, lass. I'm coming," she heard Grant's voice say over the coms as Anthony flashed his badge and began to drag her across the yard and away from her team.

Valeria fought. She darted out in front of Anthony and spun to face him. "*Hijo de puta!*" she cursed as she slammed her forehead into the bridge of his nose. She smiled as she heard the crunch of his bone. His grasp loosened enough for her to jerk away, but then she felt it. The pinch of taser prongs and everything went black.

GRANT SHOVED the side door to the van open and went to leap out. Dalton's iron-tight grip on his arm stopped him. Adrenaline surged through him harder and faster than when he was taking on enemy fire.

"Let go!" Grant growled as he tried to shake him off.

"We have to think about this. If you go charging in there, you're no help to her at all. Listen, she's not talking. It's that Anthony guy talking."

"Thanks for your assistance, officer. I'll take her from here," Grant heard Anthony say, followed by the sound of car door closing.

"Steal a car and follow them. We need to find Sebastian, Manuel, and Roland," Lizzy ordered as she neared the van. Dalton let go of him. Lizzy reached into a duffle bag and tossed Grant a gun and a burner phone.

"What's this?" he asked as he turned on the phone. A little dot was moving along the private road heading out of the neighborhood.

"I learned my lesson the last time and put a small GPS dot sticker on the inside of her dress. Follow her and get her back."

Lizzy climbed into the driver's seat of the van and tossed a second phone to Dalton. "I also tagged Sebastian."

"They're moving deeper into the neighborhood," Dalton said as he watched the dot move. "Go!" he yelled at Grant, who didn't wait to jump out of the van.

Grant slid the gun into his waistband at the small of his back and took off down the street. Contrary to belief, it would be easier to steal a car from behind a gated driveway than not. People felt safe behind gates and tended to not lock up like they should.

Grant hopped the first gated driveway he found. A plum purple Bentley Continental convertible was parked in the round driveway near the front door. Even better, he didn't need to break glass.

Grant leapt over the door and slid into the front seat. He let out a silent whoop when he saw the key fob in the cup holder. He pressed the brake and pushed the start button, and the Bentley's V8 roared to life. As he waited for the gate to slide open, he looked at the map. Anthony was speeding east, about to get onto Interstate 5. The gate opened and Grant peeled out the driveway. Unlike Anthony, he didn't have a way to get past the blockade. Grant smashed his hand against the steering wheel when he was stopped in a long line of cars by police and DEA as they looked for Manuel Hernandez.

Time slowed to a crawl as one car was finally cleared and allowed through. Grant thought his heart would explode as he tried to keep his cool. He grabbed the fake military identification and the car registration.

He put his cell phone on his lap and dialed Alex.

"What's up, dude?"

"I've just stolen a car and have to get through a checkpoint."

"Duuuude."

"Can you help?" Grant asked, agitated.

"Duh. What's the car owner's name and registration number?"

"Stein, Cecilia," Grant said, spitting out all the information Alex would need to find her.

Another car cleared the checkpoint. Grant had three more cars and then he'd be on the spot. As Alex did his thing, Grant stared at the dot on the phone. Anthony had gotten on Interstate 5 and was already turning onto Interstate 10 heading east toward San Bernardino. At this time of night and with sirens, Anthony was able to put miles in between them with every minute Grant was stuck waiting to get through the checkpoints. As the minutes ticked by, Valeria was slipping farther and farther from his grasp.

"You're set. You're married to Cecilia now. Just got married last Saturday. Nice, she's the daughter of a producer. Of course, she's nineteen so you kinda look like a cradle-robber. But whatever, dude."

"Thanks, Alex." Grant hung up and took a deep breath as the next car went through. It about killed him, but twenty minutes later he finally pulled up to have his car checked.

The officer looked at his ID and the registration. "These don't match up," he said suspiciously, shining the mag light into Grant's eyes.

"It's my wife's car. We were just married last week. What's going on? I was at my in-laws' house." Grant motioned back the way he'd come. "And can't get home now."

The officer looked at him again, not believing the story. "I'll be right back. Search the car," he ordered the officer on the other side of the car.

"Pop the trunk please," the officer ordered as the one with his fake ID and car registration walked to the police barricade. Grant opened the trunk and prayed Cecilia didn't have any drugs or weapons in her car.

The officer checked the trunk, opened the glove box,

and used a mirror to check under the car. With every second that ticked by, Grant battled for control. He had to get to Valeria. The second that dot stopped moving, he knew she would be dead.

After ten minutes the officer walked back with his ID and registration. "Here you go. Just had to confirm the marriage since you aren't listed on the registration. Congratulations, now move along."

Grant gave the man a smile and a nod and slowly drove through the barricade. The second he was out of sight he pressed the gas and took off. Anthony had over a thirty-minute head start on Grant and he was flying.

"Dammit!" Lizzy cursed and slammed her hand against a beautiful wood patio table. Lizzy and Dalton had driven halfway through the neighborhood trying to follow Sebastian, Manuel, and Roland, then right before the checkpoint for that end of the neighborhood became visible, they had turned into a driveway.

Lizzy had followed, but a gate had been in the way. She'd left the van in the drive, and she and Dalton vaulted over the gate only to watch a helicopter lifting off from the backyard with Sebastian in it. They'd sprinted around the back, but the helicopter was already flying away.

"The fucker betrayed us! He helped Roland and Manuel escape. Ahhh!" Lizzy screamed as she balled her hands together. "So help me, I will kill him myself."

"So let's follow him. He doesn't know he's being tracked. Get me to a helicopter, and we're good to go," Dalton said calmly. After all, being a PJ was synonymous with calmness under pressure.

"First we have to get out of here."

"I'd advise driving straight out the back."

"What?" Lizzy asked, looking around the backyard. There was a pool, a privacy fence, and a basketball court, which is where the helicopter had landed. "There's nowhere to drive."

"Right through that fence," Dalton told her, holding up his phone. "We go through the fence, onto the neighbor's driveway, and we're on Hobart Boulevard. No checkpoint."

Lizzy looked around. It would be a tight fit between the trees, but it was doable. "Can you get the gate open?"

Dalton just smiled. "Help me tip over this statue."

Lizzy looked at the large nude stone woman lining the drive. There were five of them on the side of the drive farthest from the house near the gate, all sculpted in different poses. "Why?"

"See this slight indent in the driveway's concrete? It's the trigger line for the gate. It'll open when a certain amount of weight is put on it," Dalton explained.

Lizzy looked at the small indent running in a straight line across the width of the drive and up at the statue. If they pushed her over, she'd land on the indent, open the gate, then she could walk out and drive the van through.

"Okay, let's do this." Lizzy said as she and Dalton moved behind the statue.

"Just put your hands right on her feet." Dalton instructed. Lizzy looked up at the stone feet at chest level. She put both her hands on one foot and Dalton put both of his on the other. "One. Two. Three."

They pushed with everything they had and the statue slowly slid off its base. They strained, bending their knees to put more force behind the push until the nude woman teetered on the edge of her pedestal and fell.

The statue slammed into the ground, breaking an arm and sending it rolling away from her. Lizzy looked at the statue and then at the gate as it slowly began to open. She didn't wait to marvel that it actually worked. Instead, she took off up the drive and jumped into the van. In seconds, she was driving through the gate and into the yard in order to get around the fallen statue.

Dalton got into the passenger seat and put on his seat belt. "There's a sightseeing helicopter tour company a couple miles from here. Turn right out of the neighbor's yard to get there."

Lizzy angled the car into the backyard and around the pool. "Ready?"

Dalton nodded and held on. Lizzy floored the gas as the old van shot forward. They hit the privacy fence and Lizzy's foot was momentarily knocked off the gas pedal as she was flung forward. The seat belt caught and sent her slamming back into her seat.

"Pool," Dalton said easily as she cranked the van to the left, knocking the side mirror off on a tree to avoid the water. The van bounced over the decorative cement patio and plowed through a wooden privacy gate. They came to a stop on the driveway as lights were turned on in the house and yelling could be heard.

Lizzy took a breath and looked at a neighborhood street. "Okay, here we go." She turned right and headed toward the tourist helicopter tours. "How's Grant doing?"

"I don't know. I'm not going to ask, though. He's focused on saving Valeria and that's where his focus needs to be. Turn left, and it's five blocks up on your right."

Lizzy made the turn and saw the big bright sign promising to show you the stars from the sky. "Where's Sebastian?"

"Heading south."

"Will we be able to catch them?"

"Doubtful, but we'll be able to hunt them."

Lizzy stopped in the parking lot of the helicopter tours. "Then let's go hunting."

15

VALERIA CURSED as the cuffs bit into her skin. Somewhere along the way she'd been zapped again and tossed into the trunk. Probably after she tried to bite Anthony's carotid artery open. Normally this would be a good thing. There were lots of ways to escape being in a trunk. However, this time her mouth was taped shut, her arms were cuffed behind her, and her feet taped together.

It was hot, dark, and muggy in the trunk. She was on her left side, facing away from the taillights. Valeria was also lying on top of the spare tire and a couple of bulletproof vests. It wasn't the most comfortable way to travel. She wondered how long she'd been with Anthony and where they were going. Her bet was back to his jurisdiction or into Mexico to be handed over to Manuel. Either way, it wasn't good.

The car sped up and then slowed down. Valeria rolled uncomfortably from the back part of her left shoulder she was lying on to the front part of her shoulder, causing her nose to bump into the vest. What was going on? Then suddenly there was a loud bang and then there was the scraping sound of metal against metal. The tires of the car spun and suddenly she was flying as the car flipped.

GRANT HAD DRIVEN close to one hundred thirty miles per hour since he'd gotten out of the city. He'd rejoiced when Anthony turned off the interstate and onto State Route 79. He'd sped through the mountains and along the small two-lane road on the desert side of the mountains as fast as he could. It had taken about an hour and a half to catch up to Anthony some one hundred fifty miles away on the deserted San Felipe Road. There was nothing around at night except dirt, tumbleweed, and foothills. The closest landmark they were approaching was Scissors Crossing, which was nothing more than part of the Pacific Crest Hiking Trial.

When they'd come to a straightaway and his headlights appeared in Anthony's mirrors for the first time, Anthony didn't do anything. Grant kept his emotions in check as he looked at the GPS dot on the phone. Valeria, or at least her dress, was still with Anthony. Grant sped up slightly to get a good look through the rear window. He only saw what he guessed was Anthony's outline in the driver's seat. As Grant pulled closer, Anthony sped up, but then slowed down as if allowing Grant to pass. Grant pulled into the opposite lane and slowly pushed the Bentley's gas pedal so he could pull even with the car.

In the glow of the dash, Grant saw the sharp outline of a nose and thin face. The man looked to be in his mid-thirties and his tie had pulled loose while his sports coat rested on the passenger seat. The empty passenger seat. Grant looked into the backseat and saw nothing. Where? Grant slowed and looked at the trunk.

When Grant looked back at Anthony, a gun was

pointing out the window. Grant swerved hard to the left, but the bullet ripped into his tire. There was only one way to stop Anthony now. He just hoped Valeria could hang on as he jerked the steering wheel to the right and drove the Bentley right into the side of Anthony's car.

Grant held onto the steering wheel as metal crashed against metal. He pushed his car harder, sending the other car fishtailing off the road as Grant struggled to keep control despite having burst a tire or two. With a final ram of the crumpled Bentley into Anthony's car, Grant held onto the wheel as smoke poured from under the hood before flames began to creep out. Through the smoke and flames, he saw Anthony's back tire catch in the dirt and rock, sending the car flipping into the air. It all felt like slow motion. The back tire hit a low-profile rock, sending the tires closest to Grant swinging up into the air. Grant was out of his car running toward the wreck as the car settled with the tires pointed toward the sky.

Grant had his gun drawn and raced toward Anthony's car as the front door was kicked open and a man crawled out. His face was burned from the airbag and his lip and nose were bleeding, but he was standing and he was armed.

"You picked the wrong guy to fuck with tonight, you asshole," Anthony yelled until he saw the gun Grant had pointed at him.

"No, you picked the wrong woman to take."

Grant watched as Anthony Gomez's dark brown eyes processed what he was saying. He gave a small half laugh of amusement. "This is over Valeria? The bitch is dead and soon you will be too."

The sound of grunting drew both men's attention as a tussled Valeria wobbled to stand. The trunk had been thrown open during the crash and Valeria had rolled out as if the back trunk's hood were a slide. Grant would have laughed if his heart weren't so relieved to see her alive. Her wig was falling off, her breast was hanging out of her skewed top, and she was giving Anthony a death stare.

"Aye, she does look like death, but she's mine nevertheless."

Grant kept his eyes trained on Anthony as Valeria began a hunched bunny jump toward him. When she stopped next to him, he reached out without looking at her and ripped off the tape from across her mouth.

"*Follar una carbra! Pinche pendejo*," Valeria spat in Spanish.

"Give me the handcuff keys, and I won't let the lassie kill you," Grant called out over Valeria's constant stream of cussing. She was working her way through Spanish and heading straight into Gaelic.

"Who are you?" Anthony asked, not bothering to move to hand over the keys.

"Doesn't matter who I am. It matters that you're helping Manuel Hernandez, and you had Valeria fired from the DEA."

"I don't have time for this. I'm just going to shoo—"

Bang!

Anthony let out a scream as he fell to the ground. "Don't talk about shooting someone, just shoot them," Grant said, finally shutting up Valeria's rant. He stepped forward, and as Anthony raised his gun to fire, Grant shot again. He may be trained to save lives, but Grant was trained to take them as well. He was an elite soldier trained to enter hostile fire and fight his way to the target.

However, a shot to the knee and a shot to the hand wouldn't kill Anthony. Grant bent down and picked up Anthony's dropped gun, then reached into the man's pocket.

He pulled out the key ring and walked back to where Valeria stood, shooting daggers at him.

"I wanted to shoot him." If her arms weren't cuffed behind her back, he figured they'd be crossed over her chest as she glared at him.

"I can't let you have all the fun, now can I?" Grant was so relieved to see her safe. The agonizing drive, the fear she'd be dead when the car flipped . . . it was all too much. He lifted his hand to her face and cupped her cheek. Instead of pulling away, she leaned into it. "I'm glad you're all right, lassie."

"Thank you for coming after me."

"I'll always come for you. Now, let me get your hands free." Grant stepped behind her and unlocked the cuffs. Valeria shoved up her skirt and Grant got a nice view of her ass.

Bang!

When Grant looked up, Anthony was leaning back against the car with a bullet to the head. A second gun was in the dirt on the ground next to his hand.

"Well, now it's my turn to thank you. Are you hurt?" Grant asked as he bent and cut the tape from her ankles, trying not to ogle her exposed cheek. When he ripped the tape from her skin, she grunted with a mixture of pain and anger.

"Just stiff and pissed. I should have found a way out of this situation before it got to this point."

"Sometimes you can't do everything on your own. I thought we talked about this," Grant said with a little smirk to let her know he was teasing.

"He was there with Manuel. Did you get him?" Valeria asked as she slowly stretched her neck and then her arms.

"I don't know. I came after you. Lizzy and Dalton went

after Manuel, Roland, and Sebastian. What is going on with them?" Grant asked as he pulled out his phone.

"I think Sebastian just joined *Mollia Domini*. They were asking him for money."

Grant nodded. "They need someone to fund the operations since Alex shut down Manuel's money outside of Mexico. We better duck."

"What?" Valeria asked as Grant shoved her to the ground just as the Bentley exploded. Grant shielded her body with his as debris rained down near them. His body fit snuggly against her as the curve of her ass cradled his quickly growing erection—one he'd fought since the lass wasn't his to have. She was in mourning, and he was a real arse for thinking of what he wanted to do with her naked body in this position.

"Well," Grant said, sitting up and putting some space between them, "we need to start walking. My phone blew up in the car and the nearest town is seven or so miles away. We don't want to be found here by anyone and have to explain why there's a dead body."

Valeria's brow creased as she stared at him over her shoulder. She gave her head a little shake. "Then we better get going."

Grant stood up and held out his hand for her. She placed her hand in his, and he pulled her up. She tucked herself back into the dress and looked at her spiked heels. "Here," Grant said, holding out his hand for the shoes. "I can help with that."

Valeria gripped his shoulder for balance as she took off each shoe. Grant attracted women who wanted to be rescued. Women with the girl-next-door looks and shy voices. Women who felt safe with him and women he felt safe with since they never asked for anything from him.

Certainly never a woman who would shoot someone between the eyes. A woman who would demand everything from him because, while Valeria would deny it, she wanted love. He knew that because it was what he wanted deep down, too.

"Here you go," Valeria said, handing him the shoes. No batting eye lashes, no simpering, so fawning over being rescued. That wasn't Valeria's style. For the first time, Grant felt as though he'd found his equal in every way.

Grant reached for the knife on his belt and set the shoe on a rock. He bent over and with a strong swing he chopped off the heel to one shoe, then the second. "Not the most comfortable but better than trying to walk on stilts."

Valeria slipped them on and tried them out. "Thanks, Grant."

Grant felt as if he'd been handed the world. He had a feeling she didn't say that word often. "You're welcome. Now, let's go."

~

"WHERE ARE THEY?" Lizzy asked as she scanned the sky from their stolen helicopter.

"They're flying southwest toward Mexico. They're south of the small town of Ocotillo," Dalton replied as they flew across the western base of the Peninsular Range near Palm Grove.

"I see it," Lizzy said, scanning the map of the area and looking closely at the GPS coordinates from the tracker on Sebastian. "They're about twenty-five miles ahead of us. They're over someplace called Jacumba Wilderness Area near the border."

"If they get over the border, we'll never be able to get to them. Manuel has protection everywhere."

"Wait," Lizzy said, keeping her eyes on the GPS signal. "They've stopped."

"Where?"

"I don't know," Lizzy said, pulling up an image of the area. "It's nothing. It's a small mountain range about a mile from the border. Okay, he's on the move. They're moving into the mountains. They're going slowly, so they must be on foot."

"They're trying to sneak across the border. We might be able to catch them."

Agonizing minutes passed as Dalton flew closer to the targets. They ate up the miles as Lizzy readied a parachute. If they were in the middle of the hills, the helicopter may not be able to land and there was no way she would let that stop her.

"Lizzy!" Dalton yelled into the headset. "Where'd they go?"

Lizzy looked at the map on the phone. They were gone. There wasn't even a blip of a signal anywhere on the map. "They were just there," Lizzy said, pointing at their last location. "They can't be gone."

"Do you think they found the tracker?"

"They could have. Let's find out."

Dalton nodded his head as he headed for the last location.

16

BIRCH GRIMACED as he was moved to the wheelchair. It was the first time he'd been allowed out of the hospital bed, and he couldn't wait to get back to the White House. The hospital was quiet this late at night—or this early in the morning, depending on how you wanted to think of it.

The cleaning crew had just left, leaving the halls smelling of antiseptic. The white floors and walls glowed under the artificial light as the staff lined up to say goodbye. The staff was minimal with only two nurses and a couple doctors that had been treating him. However, the army of Secret Service agents ruined the calm of the moment. Six agents flanked him as Dr. Wilson, his personal White House physician, pushed his wheelchair to each person. Birch held out his hand and shook the doctors' hands and then the nurses'. "Thank you for such excellent care." Birch wasn't given long to say goodbye as his agents kept him moving.

Ahead of them, Humphrey pushed Tate, but Birch couldn't see them through the wall of agents there to take them home. He knew Humphrey was there because of his constant history lessons on different presidents being admitted to the base hospital.

What a pair he and Tate made. Both banged up and in wheelchairs, although Tate would be moved to crutches soon since her shoulder injury was healing faster than expected. They would have to talk to the media soon. Her undersecretary had been handling all the press since the bombing, but the people would need to see the president to know he was capable of governing the country. While work had been handled, he was isolated at the hospital. Meetings were delayed and instead of a steady flow of people coming and going, it was just he and Humphrey getting things done. He'd need to meet with members of Congress, his cabinet, and the world leaders he'd had to reschedule. This was the last calm before the storm.

The sterile white was broken up by silver doors of the elevators at the end of the hall and the few posters of smiling soldiers and doctors that hung on the walls. The elevators were on lockdown, but two of the four were open for him by the time they reached them. Tate went into one, while he and his wall of agents went into the other.

It was strange to ride down the elevator in complete deafening silence. He'd grown accustomed to Humphrey's lectures. Birch found them soothing, especially when the situation was as tense as it was now—moving a president someone had attempted to assassinate. But now it was all business. The agents had hands on their guns as two kept an eye on the ceiling and the others formed a barricade between him and the door. Birch didn't think anyone breathed as they rode down to the garage.

It seemed like an eternity of listening to blood pounding in his ears before the door opened and the agents exited with guns drawn and cleared the area. "We're all clear, sir," the lead agent told him, holstering his gun, and Dr. Wilson moved to push him out of the elevator and over to the presidential limo nicknamed The Beast.

The garage was musty and humid, even with the cooler night air. It felt strange to Birch to feel non-air conditioned air and to smell something other than medical cleaner and sterilized air. He couldn't wait to get into the car and back home. He was tired of being watched as if he was about to die, and he was ready to get back to work.

His doctor stopped the chair as two agents helped Birch stand. His legs ached, but the energy coursing through them as they were finally used again made him want to run around the garage. Instead, he shuffled his way to the car and slowly lowered himself to the leather seat. His legs may have wanted to run, but his ribs did not.

"How are you feeling?" Tate asked from her seat next to him when the agents shut the door.

"Good. I'll be up and moving soon. My legs want to, so I think I'll try the bike later today. How are you doing?"

Tate smiled. Even without a speck of makeup on, she was stunning. Her light pink lips tightened with annoyance, though. "I can't wait to get the pins out of my leg. They're irritating. I can see and feel them under my skin."

"It feels strange going back to the White House, doesn't it?" Birch asked as he looked out the window. He reached and took Tate's hand in his and squeezed. They were alive, and they were ready to fight.

"It seems as if it's been months when it's only been days," Tate said, summing up exactly what he felt as they pulled into the White House entrance.

The parade of agents began again as they were moved to

the residence where his butler, Gene, looked both relieved and worried. "Sir," the older man in his tux said, stepping forward as some of the agents broke away to search the entire residence even though police dogs had probably just left, "it is so good to have you home. We've all been so worried."

"Thank you, Gene. It's good to be back. You didn't have to stay up for us, though. Go get some sleep. In a couple hours we'll be all ready to go for the day."

Gene shook his graying head and cleared his throat. "Absolutely not. When they called to prepare us for your arriva,l I insisted on being here. I wouldn't dream of leaving you right now, sir. And you too, ma'am." He looked at Tate and smiled warmly. "There's a piece of chocolate cake in your old room and a hot bath with something special in it to help with your aches."

Tate practically started drooling. "You're the best, Gene. I hope we tell you that enough."

"Thank you, ma'am," he said, bowing his head briefly. "There is also a bath waiting for you, sir. I know it must feel good to get out of the hospital. Is there anything you'd like, sir?"

"Not right now, but I want a real breakfast and not that stuff they forced on me at the hospital."

"It's all clear, sir," an agent said, stopping in front of them. "We'll move to our regular posts. Call if you need anything." Birch thanked the agents and breathed a sigh of relief when they were finally gone.

"Gene," Dr. Wilson said, "could you take Tate to her room while I get the president in bed, and then, Tate, I'll be down to help you get in the bath."

"Of course," Gene said, taking Tate's chair from Humphrey.

"See you soon, Tate. Goodnight, Gene. I'm heading out." Humphrey smiled as he pecked a kiss to Tate's cheek.

Dr. Wilson pushed Birch into his bedroom and helped him get ready for the couple hours he was going to sleep. A bath sounded good, but so did sleep. "How about a shower, Doc?"

FIVE MINUTES LATER, Dr. Wilson, who was in his late fifties with a full head of light brown hair and the body of a huggable grandparent, led Birch back into the bedroom. "Oh, let me help!" Humphrey jumped up from his seat and took Birch's other arm.

"Thanks, Humphrey. What are you doing here? I thought you left."

"I figured I'd just sleep in my office tonight, but I got a call I thought I should talk to you about." Humphrey sat on the chair on the other side of the room as Dr. Wilson made sure Birch was reclining comfortably.

"I'll leave you to it. I'm going to help Tate and then head to bed myself. Call if you need anything. You can get up and around now, just slowly and carefully. Rest, move, rest, move. And ice. I'll have Gene bring some to you. Good night."

"Night, Doc. Thanks," Birch called as his doctor left, closing the door behind him. Humphrey was across the room, so Birch had to turn his head slightly to the left to look at Humphrey. "So, what call did you get?"

"A very worried Alex. Some hacker named Rock Star, whom I think Alex likes, found a wire transfer from Sebastian to Roland Westwood that went through an hour ago. A wire of $1,000,000. She's trying to follow it, but it's being transferred and broken up all over the world by Roland."

It hurt more than the physical pain he was in. His best friend had betrayed him. "Tell Alex to notify the group to apprehend Sebastian immediately and hand him over to Jason for questioning."

Humphrey grimaced. "Are you sure you want to do that?"

"I'm sure. I can't show him mercy, and right now Jason is the only one who isn't going to show mercy to my best friend. They may not mean to, but they would subconsciously do it out of fear of upsetting me. And check in with Jason. Let's see if Sandra is talking yet."

"Will do." Humphrey went to stand, but Birch stopped him. He felt the smile tug on his lips.

"So, you think Alex likes this hacker?" He felt as if he and Humphrey were parents talking about their teenage son. The whole group felt that way about Alex.

"Oh yes. His voice changed when talking about her. I asked him and he replied with an embarrassed and shy 'dude.'" Humphrey smiled.

The door opened, partially shielding Humphrey from view as Gene came in with ice packs and a plate of food. "Dr. Wilson said you needed these." Gene walked into the room, not seeing Humphrey, and handed the packs to Birch. He set the plate on the nightstand. Large chunks of apple filled the plate. Birch's stomach rumbled.

"I guess you did want a snack." Gene held up the plate and Birch took a slice and popped it into his mouth. Gene set the plate down and picked up a pillow Birch had thrown on the floor.

"Don't worry about that," Birch said between chews as he reached for another piece of apple. He went to swallow and everything went black as the pillow Gene held was smothered over his face with such force that he couldn't breathe. His ribs burned with pain as he struggled. He clawed at the pillow suffocating him, but then the pressure was gone.

Birch ripped the pillow from his face, spit out the apples, and dragged in big gulps of air. His vision had been blurry, but it refocused onto Humphrey holding Gene tight in a chokehold. Gene was kicking and fighting, but Humphrey had his face set and a solid hold. His left arm was behind Gene's head and anchored to his right bicep as he dragged Gene backward. Gene lost his footing and ended up on his ass where Humphrey used his now-heightened advantage to leverage his arm and send Gene into unconsciousness.

"What the hell?" Birch gasped as he stared at Humphrey who wasn't even breathing hard.

Humphrey dropped his hold and straightened his pink and green striped bowtie. "I think we found our White House mole."

"Gene was here when I planned our date night. Why? Why would he do this?" Birch had thought of Gene as a friend. Sandra, no. She'd always been hostile toward him. But Gene had always been someone to talk to after a long day. Someone who cared how he was. Birch knew all about his family . . . well, at least he thought he did. Had Gene been lying this whole time?

"Thank you, Humphrey," Birch said, slowly moving to stand. "You saved my life."

"I'm glad I was here. In your weakened state . . . Do you want me to call the agents?"

Birch shook his head as he slowly walked toward his closet. "No. Call Jason." Birch grabbed a handful of ties and belts, and when he made it back into the bedroom, Humphrey was already on the phone with Jason.

"The tunnels. See you then." Humphrey hung up and grabbed the belts. Gene was already stirring as Humphrey trussed him up and used a tie as a gag as Gene lay on the floor.

Gene groaned as his eyes finally blinked open. Birch watched as realization that he was trapped set in. The man freaked out. He was screaming behind the gag, tears streaming down his face as he fought the ties at his hands and knees.

"Why?" was all Birch asked. Gene looked up at him, his eyes pleading with him. "Go ahead, Humphrey."

Humphrey helped Gene to sit up and then pushed down the gag far enough for him to talk. "They made me. It was my debt to pay. They would kill my family. And because I failed, my girls—oh God, my girls are dead!"

Humphrey and Birch shared a look over Gene's head. "Who made you do it?" Birch asked as he held onto one of the bed posters.

"I don't know!" he cried. "I . . . I . . . I have a weakness. I'm addicted to drugs. I can't stop. I was arrested right after you were sworn in, and this man shows up at the jail. I knew I would be fired. Decades of working in the White House gone, just like that. And this man, he tells me he can get me out of jail and make the arrest files disappear as if they never existed because they wouldn't exist if I agreed to his proposal."

"And you didn't ask who he was?" Birch asked in disbelief.

"Of course I did. He said he was representing an interested party. He was clean-cut. Maybe forty-five years old. Five feet ten inches. Dark brown hair, stylish glasses, expensive suit. And he was there with cash in his briefcase. He claimed he was my lawyer. I asked what I had to do and he said I just had to keep my ears open and call this number to report what was going on at the White House every day. If something out of the ordinary was happening, like your date or Tate moving in, then I was to call immediately. I would call, leave a message, and that was it. I put two and two together after the bombing."

Gene began to cry again. His nose turned as red as his bloodshot eyes. "It's all my fault those people are dead."

"Yes, Gene, it is," Birch said quietly. "Then what?"

"They must know I couldn't handle it. As soon as reports came in that you were alive, I received a phone call. They were with my daughters. Rebecca is twenty-two and Stephanie is twenty. They're in Mexico for a vacation together. Sisters' trip, they called it. I got a picture of them lying on the beach. They told me they would kill them if I didn't kill you."

"Where are they now?" Birch asked.

"They're still in Mexico. They leave day after tomorrow. If I hadn't killed you by then, they die. When I heard you were coming back tonight . . . I don't care if you kill me, just save my girls. Please!"

"Gene, I'll get your girls. And you'll live, for now. Where's this phone you use to talk to them?"

"We're not allowed to have personal phones on us, so it's hidden in the locked cabinet in the staff room. I'm the only one with the key." Humphrey moved and felt his pockets until he found the keys.

"I'll give this to someone to look it over after I deliver Gene." Birch nodded and knew he was talking about Alex.

"I won't be safe. They'll kill me as soon as my name pops up on the jail register," Gene sighed, but sounded resigned.

"You're not going to jail. You're going to disappear. No one will know where you are or what happened to you until I want them to. Gene, a bit of advice. Tell the man you meet everything you know." With a nod of his chin toward Humphrey, he put the gag back on Gene and tied a blindfold over his face before dragging him from the room.

17

DALTON SET the helicopter down near the last location of Sebastian's GPS. The half moon lit up the desert, but not nearly enough to see if someone was waiting to kill them. He looked around and saw nothing. No lights. No movement. Nothing.

"I don't see anything," Lizzy said as she scanned the area.

"Me either. Let's get out and have a look around." Something wasn't adding up, but Dalton couldn't figure it out. A helicopter full of people didn't just disappear like that.

He and Lizzy fanned out, sweeping the area with his phone light and a small flashlight they found in the helicopter.

"Over here!" Lizzy called out. Dalton gave the small mountain one last glance before heading her direction. When he rounded an outcropping, he saw what she found. The helicopter. It was hidden under camouflage material and would blend perfectly into the desert landscape for any drone or helicopter patrolling the border.

Dalton looked over the helicopter. "This is the same one. But I don't see the GPS tracker anywhere."

"I couldn't find it either," Lizzy said as she slowly scanned the dirt ground around them. Her flashlight moved over the ground and then stopped as it went toward the small mountain. "Dalton, I think I know where they went."

"Where?"

"Down." Lizzy's light had found a metal door in the base of the mountain painted to look like the desert surroundings. It looked identical to the mountain it sat in, except for the heavy-duty keypad lock on it.

"Do you know how to get through that lock?" Dalton asked. His skill with lock picking was minimal. Blowing stuff up, sure. But he didn't have anything with him to be able to do that.

"I can try, but I don't have my tools with me."

"Now we know where they went, at least. We're practically on the border. I bet it's a tunnel into and out of one of Manuel's warehouses in Mexico. Let's look around more and see what we can find."

Dalton took off in the night, slowly scanning the mountain and surrounding area. By the time he had covered a half-mile grid search, he'd found three cars, the helicopter, and close to twenty large drums of gas. However, what worried him was that there was an empty space that a fourth car normally occupied. The tarp that would have been covering the car was staked to the ground. Under the tarp was a small oil stain darkening the dirt and sand. Somewhere, there was someone from Manuel's cartel out in the United States and who knows what they had planned.

∾

"I'M GOING TO STEAL IT," Valeria whispered as they watched an old man set his cell phone down on his outdoor table as he sipped his morning coffee.

"Just be patient, lass. Wait and watch. Or do what I thought we should do and let me walk up and ask to borrow it," Grant calmly replied.

Valeria almost snarled. She didn't like sitting back and waiting. Of course, that's what got her in trouble the last time. They'd walked side by side through the night, not stopping once. They seemed to feed off of each other naturally. If she started to slow, he would smile at her and say, "You're not getting tired, are you?" He knew it would spur her on because if there was one thing Val wasn't, it was a quitter.

So they'd kept going. Grant never seemed to tire as they talked and walked through the night. It was strange to think the man standing next to her knew her better than Anthony ever did, and she'd dated him for years. Grant had asked about Brock, and so in the darkness, she found herself telling Grant about her best friend. Valeria shook her head and dislodged the feeling—a feeling that appeared to be more than lust when she looked at Grant. A feeling she shoved aside. He might have a physical reaction to her, but no matter how she flirted, he had kept his distance since Brock died.

She knew one way to kill two birds with one stone. She could satisfy her curiosity and get her way with the phone with one little kiss. She'd distract Grant as she distracted Sebastian, then she'd be able to see if there was anything between them. And she'd be able to get halfway across the yard to steal that phone before Grant could stop her.

Grant looked around the shed again and then turned to face her. He lowered his head to whisper something to her, and that's when she made her move. Valeria grabbed fistfuls of his shirt and pulled his lips toward her. The days' growth of his thick scruff rubbed against her face, tickling her as his lips greeted hers. Valeria arched into him as his large hands moved up her ribcage to cup her breasts. Being with Grant was wild, heart-racing passion, and he was—gone. Valeria blinked open her eyes. Where the hell was he? "Son of a bitch," she cursed with a smile still on her face. Grant was halfway across the yard, calling out a greeting to the old man.

DALTON PULLED out the ringing phone as they made their way back to the helicopter. Lizzy hadn't been able to break the lock so it was time to get some tools and come back. He didn't know the number, so when he answered he didn't say anything, opting to listen instead.

"I can hear you breathing."

"Grant! Where are you? Do you have Valeria?"

"I have her," Grant said, rattling off the coordinates for his location.

"That's not far from where we are." Dalton could tell Lizzy was trying not to yank the phone away from him as he gave her the thumbs-up to let her know everything was okay.

"I'm borrowing a phone from a nice man. Could you pick us up a mile west of town? There're wide open spaces there," Grant told him.

"You bet. Be there soon."

Dalton hung up and turned to tell Lizzy about the call when his phone rang again. This time it was Humphrey. "Why isn't anyone answering their phones?"

"I'm answering my phone."

Dalton didn't think Humphrey found it amusing. "Gene tried to kill Birch."

"So, finally, the butler did it." It spewed from Dalton before he could stop himself. Humphrey was deadly silent on the other end. Dalton cleared his throat. "Since you said 'tried,' I'm assuming he's okay?"

"Yes. I was able to take Gene down, and now he's with Jason. Gene has a drug problem and was arrested a while back. A very expensive lawyer with no name came in and had all records of the arrest erased so Gene wouldn't be fired. In return, he was to spy on Birch."

"Shit, he was the mole who informed on the location of Birch's date with Tate. I am also assuming he's with *Mollia Domini*."

"We think the lawyer was. Alex is working on the phone Gene used," Humphrey explained. "I tried calling everyone, but you're the only person who answered."

Dalton filled him in on the night as he pulled the hose from one of the gas drums out of the helicopter. "We'll be back this afternoon."

"Not so fast," Humphrey said. "One of you needs to make a little detour to Mexico first."

GRANT WHISTLED as he walked across the backyard of the man's house. He could practically see smoke wafting up from behind the shed as he walked around it only to be grabbed by Valeria. She tried to shove him, but Grant held his ground.

"What the hell?" She growled as she poked him in the

chest with her finger. Only this time he knew what was under all that bravado.

"Oh, I'm sorry. Did you think you could kiss me into getting your way? You're free to try again, lass." Grant's smile widened at the outraged look on her face. "But first, I think we need to clarify something. You don't have to kiss me to get your way. Especially right after losing your boyfriend. No matter how much I enjoyed it, don't mistreat his memory like that."

Valeria blinked in confusion. "How am I mistreating Brock's memory by kissing you?"

"I'm sure you kissed him before he died. That should be your last memory of him."

Valeria shook her head. "No, I didn't."

Now it was Grant's turn to blink in confusion. "Then what did you do with your boyfriend if it wasn't kissing?"

"Brock and I broke up after college. Years ago. My last boyfriend was Anthony, the creep that kidnapped me. Did you think Brock and I were still together? Is that why you haven't—?" Valeria trailed off, suddenly looking shy.

"Fuck," Grant cursed as he realized what she was saying. He'd gotten the order of her boyfriends mixed up. She'd been waiting on him to make a move, and now he couldn't make one because they had a helicopter to catch. And by the look she was giving, she was expecting him to make that move now. "We have to move. Lizzy and Dalton are picking us up."

Grant grabbed her hand and practically dragged her out into the open area behind the town. The town disappeared until only the sound of their angry footsteps hitting the hard ground was heard. He'd been so freaking stupid. What was it about this woman that caused his brain to shut off?

"For fuck's sake," Valeria finally muttered before yanking on his arm, bringing him to a halt.

When Grant turned around, he saw she had worked herself into a real lather. Her eyes were narrowed and her mouth was set in a tight line. "You don't go storming off after something like that. Shouldn't we"—Valeria looked wildly around as she gestured with her hands—"I don't know, talk about it?" she asked as if she'd just taken a bite of spoiled food. Her face held such dread at the idea of talking about their feelings that Grant laughed.

"Ah, lassie, I have a better idea." Grant stepped up close to her, and she didn't step back. He knew she wouldn't. She'd never back down from anyone or anything. He'd seen Valeria take on groups of armed men. He'd seen her kill the man who betrayed her. And yet, this was the first time he'd actually seen her nervous. But what he loved was she didn't run from those nerves. She faced them head on, like she faced everything else thrown her way.

Grant slid his large, rough hands over her cheek to cup the back of her head as he pulled her lips toward his. "You have no idea how badly I want you," he whispered against her lips before taking them in his. The kiss started with a graze of the lips, but didn't stay that way. Grant used one hand to control the kiss and the other to pull Valeria's hips against his. They moved together as if they were naked. The kiss went from soft to hard in a heartbeat. The kiss was as wild as Valeria was. It was no gentle caress of tongues; it was a battle of passion, each giving way completely to their desires as they ravaged each other.

His heart beat hard, and he let her take control of the kiss. He dropped his hand from her head and shoved aside the draped material of her dress, baring her breasts to him. Valeria arched forward, telling him exactly what she wanted. Perfect handfuls of firm breasts filled his hands as he rolled her nipples between his fingers, capturing her moans with his kiss.

It took everything he had to not take her completely in the open desert, not caring for anything except making her come. But that was not in the cards as the sound of a helicopter had him breaking the kiss and dropping his hands from her breasts. Placing his hands on the curve of her hips, he kissed her quickly one last time. "We'll continue our talk very soon."

Valeria smiled up at him, keeping her hands flat against his chest. "I like the way you communicate, Macay."

They shielded their eyes as the helicopter landed and then jogged toward the open door. Lizzy was already opening the door by the time they reached it. She held out her hand for Valeria and helped her up. She was hugging Val as Grant got in.

"So, how do you two feel about a trip to Mexico?" Dalton asked as soon as they were strapped in and taking off.

"Do I get to kill Manuel?" Valeria asked in return.

"No, you need to rescue two college girls," Dalton told her, filling them in on what had happened at the White House along with what they'd found out about the tunnels and Sebastian's GPS disappearing.

"Then it could pop back up when they make their way through the tunnels," Grant said.

"If Manuel doesn't have his compounds carefully scrubbed that is," Lizzy pointed out. "But if he has jammers and such, we're not getting anything until Sebastian is heading back home."

"So, where are we going?" Valeria asked. He could understand her anxiety about heading back into *Hermanos de Sangre* land.

"A fancy resort outside Tijuana owned by one Sebastian Abel," Lizzy told them. "You don't even need to make contact with the girls. You just need to take out those watching them and make sure they get on the plane day after tomorrow. Alex got you a reservation in the penthouse. We will be there in a bit and drop you on their helicopter pad and then take off so no one gets a good look at us. Then take the plane with the girls back to DC. Alex has that all taken care of as well."

"I don't have any identification," Valeria told her.

"Alex said it will be waiting for you at the hotel along with a credit card."

"What will you and Dalton be doing?" Grant asked.

"We'll head to San Diego, ditch the helicopter, fly back to DC, and wait for Sebastian to show up," Lizzy answered.

Dalton turned around to shoot a quick smile at Grant. "I was thinking of joining Jason for a little chat with Sandra."

"Good idea." Grant put his arm around Valeria and let her rest her head against his shoulder. Her eyes closed almost immediately. They had a full day ahead of them, and they both knew it was necessary to catch a couple hours of sleep whenever they could find it. In seconds, Grant drifted off.

18

"WHAT DO YOU THINK?" Tate asked as she watched Birch read over the speech for later today.

"When are Elizabeth and Dalton getting back?" Birch asked instead of answering.

"Five tonight, why?" Tate asked, suddenly worried her speech was too much. She hadn't held anything back. She was ready to go after *Mollia Domini*.

Birch closed the laptop and looked up from his desk in the oval office. Tate was sitting on the couch, and Humphrey sat across from her. Her wheelchair was parked next to her. Two more days and she'd be on crutches.

"And Grant and Valeria?" Birch asked Humphrey instead of answering her.

"They are at the resort already. They are catching the red-eye back to DC and will be here with the girls the day after tomorrow around noon if all goes well."

"What are we going to do with them?" Birch asked to no one in particular as Tate began to fume.

"Why don't we send them on another trip? They don't have to be back until school starts. Tell them they won something and ship them to Saint Thomas or something," Tate said agitated.

"That's a great idea. Humphrey, make it happen."

"Birch," Tate said with warning in her voice. "The speech you're supposed to give tonight?"

Birch shook his head. "It's too good. I can't do it tonight."

Tate felt her mouth fall open. "What do you mean?"

"I mean, your speech is perfect, but we need all our ducks in a row before I give it. Tonight you release a generic press statement saying we're back at the White House and settling back in. Tell them I'll give a live primetime talk on all the networks soon. More information will be forthcoming." Birch paused and held her eyes. "Once I read this, there's no going back. *Mollia Domini* will know we're talking about them and the threat level will increase."

"I know. I thought about that, but it's time to challenge them head on."

"I agree, but it's still a matter of timing."

Tate let out a breath. "You're right. I'll make it happen." Tate stood up on one foot as Humphrey hurried to her side and helped her into her chair. Birch stood up and slowly made his way around the desk. His left hand never left the desktop as he used it for balance and support.

"Get an advanced copy to Flint. Tell him he can publish it as soon as the speech is over. I'm sure he'll have something to write about by then," Birch said about the blogger who had been brought into their fold.

"Should I tell him about Sandra?" Tate asked.

"Yes," Birch agreed. "But wait until we talk to Jason. I'll have Dalton check on him. The man is walking on a precipice, and I don't want him to fall. I thought giving him a mission to focus on, but—"

Tate knew exactly what Birch was worried about. Jason

was blank. He had no emotion left but anger. It would be beneficial when it came to interrogation, but deadly for Jason if he decided there was nothing else to live for.

"Good idea. I'll send everything to Flint as soon as I hear. I'll see you at dinner. Don't push yourself too much," Tate chided as Humphrey pushed her out the door and handed her off to Jessica, Birch's private secretary.

BIRCH SLOWLY SHUFFLED BACK to the desk. The pain in his side started once again, and he just wanted to sit down. Humphrey didn't say anything as he came up and offered his arm for support.

Birch slowly lowered himself back in his chair, closed his eyes, and took some deep breaths. The pain began to fade, and he opened his eyes again. Humphrey was standing by the desk, looking at his phone.

"Sebastian is back," Humphrey said with dread. Having your best friend involved in trying to kill you and take out the government wasn't a subject he liked to talk about. "Alex said his GPS came on at a private airfield in Mexico. FAA records show his private plane just landed and has filed a flight plan to DC. He'll arrive at five-thirty."

"Pick him up at the airport. Take a couple agents with you if you think you can't handle it. Although, after seeing you in action, I believe you could."

"We all have our secrets, don't we?" Humphrey joked, although it was true. "Mine just happens to be I enjoyed working out with the cadets I taught."

"And I'm glad you did. Bring Sebastian to me, and let's put an end to whatever game he's playing."

Humphrey nodded his bald little head and shoved his

round wire-rimmed glasses up his nose with his finger. "You've got it."

Birch watched him leave the room and closed his eyes. He didn't know if they had time to wait or not. This mission with Gene's kids had blown his timeline, but he couldn't let them die. By saving them, he was defeating *Mollia Domini*. He didn't know if this small battle was important to the war cause or only a distraction.

VALERIA SCANNED the group on the beach from behind her dark, oversized sunglasses. It was the first time they had a moment to scan the guests. The second they had arrived, they'd been presented with the fake IDs in a sealed envelope that Alex had said one of his hacker friends had delivered, and immediately headed to the boutique to buy clothes. From there, they went to their room. Valeria had almost gasped as their concierge had shown them around the massive suite. There was a kitchen, a full bar, a living room, and a balcony that ran the entire length of the floor-to-ceiling windows in the living area. That was before they went back to the king-sized bedroom with electronic blackout shades and a separate balcony.

Their new purchases had been put away for them as Grant flipped on the television, and she'd made them lunch with the food that had been stocked in the kitchen. When all the attendants finally left, Grant flipped off the television and they ate before putting on their suits. Sadly, Grant had shaved, although he'd left enough scruff to show his wild Highland side.

He lay next to her in a couple's cabana with his arms under his head. A tattoo of a Celtic trinity knot, with its horizontal and vertical lines combining in the intricate design, stood out on his left shoulder. Women were noticing, to say the least, considering his shoulders and chest looked to be sculpted from granite.

"Two o'clock," Grant's deep voice drew her attention from a twenty-something in a thong bikini who just dropped her sunglasses right in front of them. Val looked over at Grant and wanted to laugh. He wasn't even looking at the woman. Instead, he was focused on a man on a lounge chair in the row behind Gene's daughters.

"I see him."

"Keep watching. Every couple minutes he looks to his left," Grant said, putting his arm around her and pulling her against his side. The thong-clad woman huffed and sashayed away. Valeria watched the target as Grant's hand dropped from her shoulder to fondle the top of her blue triangle bikini top. He turned his head and placed a kiss on her neck as his hand dipped into the thin material of her top.

"Grant," Valeria squeaked on a gasp when he pinched her nipple into a taut peak.

"Shhh, I'm keeping our cover," he said, kissing his way down her neck.

Valeria chuckled as she heard a group of women sitting nearby sigh. They'd been talking about Grant for the past thirty minutes. "You're drawing attention."

"Good. I want the men to know you're off limits. Plus, it's fun." He pulled his hand from her top and placed it on the indentation of her hip. "Did you see it?"

Valeria nodded as she rested her head on his chest. "The guy that's getting up, right?"

"Right."

Valeria watched the man walking off the beach and onto

the private path leading to the villas. The path was obstructed from view by various palm trees and flowering bushes.

"I'll be right back," Valeria said, placing a quick kiss on his cheek. She climbed off the queen-sized padded lounger and adjusted her bikini bottoms as she casually strolled after the man in the short-sleeved, salmon-colored button-up shirt that was opened to his belly button. The outline of a gun was clearly seen under his shirt and against the waist of his dark blue swim trunks.

Valeria grabbed a fruity drink left abandoned beside one of the lounge chairs and went to cut him off. She hurried to an entrance farther down the beach and began to jog toward her target once in the privacy of the path.

"No, the girls are oblivious," she heard the man say in Spanish. Valeria stopped and pressed herself into the leaves. The man was around a bend, and she couldn't tell if he was walking toward her or just standing there talking. "Tonight? Do you want it to be an accident?"

Valeria crept forward when she noticed he wasn't moving. She peered through the thick foliage and saw the man standing in the middle of the path and slowly circling to make sure he was alone.

"I'll put something in their drinks. It'll look like alcohol poisoning. I'll call you when it's done."

Valeria stepped back as the man started walking in her direction. "Oops!" she giggled as she weaved toward him, stumbled, and sent the drink flying down his shirt.

"Stupid drunk," he muttered in Spanish as he picked a pineapple wedge from where it got stuck in in shirt.

Valeria bit her lip and looked confused. "I am so sorry. I don't speak Spanish, but let me help you." She started brushing the drink from his chest. "Oh, dear. I have club soda in my room," she gestured behind her and then frowned before laughing. "But you don't speak English so you probably have no idea what I'm saying."

"I speak *Inglés*."

"Oh good!" Valeria tittered and felt stupid for doing so. She sent a slow look from his head to his crotch and then looked back up in embarrassment. "I'm here with my girlfriends this week, and they're all down at the beach."

It didn't take long for the man to realize what she was insinuating, just like it didn't take long for Valeria to notice the tattoo above his heart showing him to be a member of *Hermanos de Sangre.*

"You have something to clean it, yes?" he asked, his voice dipping lower.

Valeria bit her lip and nodded. "Right this way." She reached out and took his hand in hers. He didn't even question it when she led him behind the villas and into the overgrown lushness surrounding the resort. Not when she reached behind her as she walked and unlaced her string bikini top. And not when she turned and jabbed her fingers into his Adam's apple. Not even when she spun behind him as he bent over gasping and slipped her string bikini around his neck and pulled.

He struggled, but she put her foot on his back and pulled until he fell lifelessly to the ground. Letting out a deep breath, Valeria tied her bathing suit back on, picked up his gun, and dug around his pockets for his key and cell phone. She dragged him off the path and tossed the gun into the dumpster behind the villas before making her way back to Grant.

"Shall we go for a swim?" he asked when she stopped in front of the cabana and tossed him the phone and key.

"I've been dying to."

"Then let's go." Grant took her hand in his as they walked down toward the water. The girls were swimming and the man was nearby watching. He kept looking back at the path, then out to where the girls were.

"Everything go okay?" Grant asked.

"It's been taken care of," Valeria told him as she submerged herself under the water.

Grant dove under and came up behind her. He wrapped his arm around her waist and pulled her to sit on his leg. Valeria leaned back, and they floated there for a moment in complete silence, watching the two sisters splash in the water.

"Do you ever remember being that innocent?" Valeria asked quietly from behind her shades.

"*Aye*. I grew up like that. It wasn't until I was active duty that I saw the evil of the world. I knew evil existed, but I had never seen it in person. I threw up after my first bad mission. Dalton was with me. It changed my life forever. That was years ago now. Now I'm no longer surprised by evil. I only hope to rid the world of as much of it as possible before my time is up."

"I've thought about walking away. It used to bother me to kill someone. It doesn't anymore. What if I'm becoming just as evil as those I kill?" Valeria asked, tears welling in her eyes as she admitted her biggest fear.

Grant tightened his hold on her, pulling her against his chest. "There's a difference between doing bad things for a bad reason and doing bad things for a good reason. Stopping *Mollia Domini*, stopping *Hermanos de Sangre*, those are good reasons."

Valeria nodded as she broke apart in the middle of the ocean. Silent tears rolled down her cheeks and plinked into the water. While killing didn't bother her like it used to, what Grant said resonated. She wanted to do good. She wanted to make the world a better and safer place. And she would see this to the end, knowing she was doing what was necessary to keep good people safe.

GRANT KEPT Valeria in his arms as they continued to watch the young women smiling and laughing while they swam in the ocean. However, when the man watching the women got up and headed for the path to the villas, Grant had to make his move.

"Why don't you sun for a while? Rest, order us some drinks, and I'll be right back." Grant placed a long kiss to her temple before letting her feet touch the soft sand beneath them.

"I can do it," Valeria said stubbornly, and Grant knew she wasn't talking about ordering drinks.

"I never thought you couldn't." Grant winked and waded out of the ocean. He didn't look back. He didn't want Valeria taking that as a sign that she could kill the last target. It wasn't that Grant wanted to either. But feeling Valeria cry silently almost broke him. And while she said it didn't bother her, she was wrong. Otherwise she wouldn't be crying into the Pacific.

Grant grabbed the key to the men's room and the towel with the gun wrapped inside the folds. What they did wasn't easy. It wasn't supposed to be. But they were here because they could do what wasn't easy. Lizzy, Dalton, Valeria, all of them. They were involved because of a deep drive to protect innocence. To protect vulnerability. To protect those who didn't know they needed it.

As he put the key into the door, kicked it open, and fired, he knew no one would know he saved two young women that day. No one would know these wicked men would never kill anyone ever again. They wouldn't be able to sell drugs to children or the weak and desperate. They wouldn't hurt anyone ever again. And he was fine with that because two women could now live out their lives free from danger. They may go on to save others' lives, invent the cure for cancer, teach children, or simply raise families of more good people.

VALERIA WAS WAITING for him in their suite. Her tears were dried, but the look she sent him said she understood. When you lived in the shadows, when you saw evil, you needed light. And she was his light. Valeria stood, her back to the large tinted windows and held out her arms.

Grant came to her, starving. Starving to clear the memory of death, starving for life, compassion, and understanding that Valeria held. Grant might be a stubborn Scot, but he knew when he had something special in Valeria.

Their kiss was hard and hot as he pushed her against the windows. His hips pressed against hers as she ran her hands over shoulders and down his chest. She shoved his trunks to the floor, and he kicked them away as his mouth broke from her lips and traveled down her neck, across her collarbone, and to her breast. He reached behind her and with two quick tugs tossed the bikini top to the side. His tongue circled her puckered nipple before latching on and sucking until Valeria tossed her head back and cried out with pleasure.

VALERIA HELD Grant's head to her breast as he fell to his

knees before her. Heat radiated from his body as the cold glass pressed against her back. She raked her fingers through his dark auburn hair as he moved his other hand to strip her of her bikini bottoms.

Grant moved lower, kissing his way down her stomach, and circling her navel with his tongue before sliding his tongue and fingers between her legs. A wave of heat flashed through Valeria as she felt her body coil and then snap with release.

Breathing heavily, Valeria leaned against the window, now seeking its coolness. Her body was flushed with her pleasure as Grant reached for the package of condoms she'd picked up on the way back to the room. His eyes had turned dark green with anticipation, but Grant paused.

"Lass?"

Val nodded once and saw the flare in his eyes as she silently told him to take her. And he did. In one quick motion, he had her against the window with her legs wrapped around his waist. Grant lifted her, tilting her hips toward him, and slid into her. Valeria let go. She let go of the past and the future. Instead, all that remained was the present, being in Grant's arms. The sensations curled her toes and made her dig her heels into his lower back. An aching feeling fell on her as the walls crumbled from around her heart. Before she knew it, she tumbled over the edge screaming out his name.

19

DALTON KNEW it couldn't be good when Alex met them at the airport. He stood in baggy olive-green cargo shorts, shifting from side to side on his untied tennis shoes that had to be worth more than any kid had the right to spend on shoes. He shoved back his unkempt hair as he scanned the crowd.

"Dude!" he called out as soon as he saw them and frantically began to wave them over.

Dalton had slept hard and long on the plane ride home, but he was still exhausted, and Alex's puppyish exuberance only annoyed him right now. "What is it?" he asked with dread as Alex's bouncing increased.

"Sebastian is arriving in a private jet in ten minutes. Humphrey is meeting him, but—"

"But you're worried Humphrey won't be able to handle it," Dalton finished for Alex as he opened the door for Lizzy.

"Yeah. I mean, he's an old dude," Alex shrugged.

"Then let's go," Dalton sighed as he lowered himself into the sedan.

Alex hurried around the hood of the car and leapt in.

"Oh, and I need to take you to talk to Jason. I can drop you off there and take Lizzy back to her place before picking you back up. That is, as long as Humphrey can get Sebastian to go with him."

Alex tore out of the arrivals line and sped toward the private hangars. They wouldn't be able to waltz right in, but they would be able to watch to make sure Humphrey had Sebastian in hand. If not, then Dalton would go to Plan B.

They saw Humphrey's car before they saw his head. He was leaning against the side of the car with his arms crossed. Dalton and Lizzy peered out the windshield and through the chain-link fence, watching him.

"I don't see any agents with him," Lizzy said, scanning the area.

"Nope, and here comes Sebastian," Dalton replied, his eyes never leaving Sebastian's tall frame as he walked down the stairs of his jet. "He doesn't seem surprised to see Humphrey."

"Sebastian would never show if he was. That's part of his image," Lizzy answered.

Humphrey walked over to Sebastian and shook his hand. He gestured to the car. Sebastian nodded and said something. Humphrey nodded then and pulled out his phone. Lizzy's phone rang and Alex jumped. "Dude, weird."

"Hello?" Lizzy put the phone on speaker.

"It's Humphrey. I'm at the airport with Sebastian. He wants to talk to you."

Lizzy looked at Dalton, and he instantly knew what she was asking. He gave a single nod of his head. "Then turn around. We're in the sedan."

Humphrey spun as Lizzy and Dalton opened their doors. Lizzy still had the dress from the party on, but it was now covered with a black T-shirt. Sebastian was in the same suit as well. Sebastian and Humphrey got into his car and drove through the guarded gates toward them.

"What do you think he wants?" Alex wondered. Lizzy and Dalton didn't answer. They spread out to cover the car as it came to a stop next to them. Sebastian and Humphrey got out and Dalton tensed, ready for anything.

"I'm glad you're alive," Sebastian said, not sounding all too glad.

"I could say the same, but I don't know if it's true yet," Lizzy shot back in the same nonchalant voice Sebastian had used as she patted him down for a wire. "How are your new friends?"

Sebastian seemed amused, and Dalton fought against punching him. "Roland isn't the head of *Mollia Domini*."

"I guess you'd know this since you joined them. At least that's what it appears when you wire a million dollars to Roland Westwood right after you disappear with them," Alex chimed in.

Dalton blinked at Alex's statement. First, Alex was standing up to Sebastian. Second, a million dollars?

"You paid them?" Lizzy asked, her voice soft and deadly.

The moment of shock that had registered and then quickly passed over Sebastian's hard features was masked with elitist indifference once again. "A million is nothing. You know that. It was enough to learn that Roland isn't the leader. Isn't that worth a million dollars?"

"At what cost?" Lizzy asked. "The cost of you now being an enemy of the country? What did they need that money for? To try to kill your supposed best friend again?"

"Again, again," Alex mumbled.

"What?" Sebastian snapped.

Alex began to shuffle his feet again. "Someone tried to kill the president again overnight."

Sebastian didn't react. Instead he turned to Humphrey. "Let's go."

"Wait," Lizzy ordered. "What else did you learn?"

"I'm an enemy of the state, remember? If you want to know what I know, then I need a favor."

"So much for no strings," Lizzy spat. Dalton could tell she was close to letting her temper fly.

"I've put a lot on the line to get you information on Roland. Now I need something in return. It's a simple quid pro quo," Sebastian shrugged.

"What do you want?" Lizzy asked between gritted teeth.

"Nothing from you, love. I want Alex, or whoever discovered I'd wired that money so quickly, to get me all of Bertie Geofferies's financials, private emails, text messages, everything."

"Why?" Dalton asked.

"Bertie is my rival, and we all know knowledge is power. I'm helping you, you help me, and I continue to feed you information on *Mollia Domini*."

Lizzy shook her head. "No. I won't let him. You're not in control here, Sebastian."

Sebastian raised one eyebrow over his cement-gray eyes. "We'll just see what Birch has to say about it. Speaking of my friend, let's go, Humphrey." Sebastian slid into the back seat as if Humphrey were his chauffeur and closed the door.

"I'll let you know everything," Humphrey promised before getting in and driving away.

"What an arrogant ass," Dalton muttered as they all got back into their car.

"I can't tell with him. Is he on our side or not?" Lizzy asked as Alex drove out of the airport.

"He's on his own side." Dalton sighed, exhaustion rolling

over him, knowing he still had a full day before he could get some shut-eye.

"This is the second time he's asked for information on Bertie Geofferies. I think it may be time for me to find out why," Lizzy said with the decision made. "Alex, can you get that information Sebastian wants?"

"Some, but Rock Star can get more."

"Rock Star?" Dalton asked with a quirk of his lips. The way Alex said the name showed an admiration and respect, but it was the way little hearts practically leapt from his eyes that told Dalton that Rock Star was more than just a hacker buddy.

Alex cleared his throat. "Yeah, she's the hacker from London."

"I remember," Lizzy said, not bothering to hide her smile. "Our little boy is growing up." She held back the laughter.

Alex turned apple-red. "Not cool, dude. Not cool."

"But Rock Star is," Lizzy said, and she surrendered to the laughter.

"Okay, okay, we embarrassed him enough." Dalton was laughing as well. "Can you get what we need?"

"Duh. I'll get working on it immediately. I'm assuming I'll give it to you and not Sebastian."

"You've got it," Lizzy said, finally leaning back in her seat and closing her eyes. "And make sure Rock Star meets us before you take her on a date. We have to make sure she's good enough for you."

DALTON WALKED HESITANTLY into the building Jason was using as a black site. It was an abandoned building made to look like office space. He knew Jason had seen him on the cameras, and sure enough, Jason appeared at the office door.

Dalton stood in the aisle surrounded by empty cubicles and looked at his friend and mentor. Jason was empty. His eyes were blank, his lips were in a thin line, and his body that had plumped after retirement was now sagging. It was evident that Jason wasn't dieting; he wasn't eating, period.

Jason leaned a shoulder against a steel doorjamb and crossed his arms. "You come to check on the prisoners?"

"Are they still alive?"

"For now."

"Jason, you need help," Dalton told his friend, knowing it was the last thing Jason wanted to hear.

"I'm getting my help here."

"Is revenge the only thing keeping you alive?" Dalton asked, fearing he already knew the answer.

Instead of answering, Jason turned and walked down the dark stairwell, leaving Dalton to follow. The stairs led into a secret network of rooms behind a false wall in the basement of the building. Down there, no one would hear a gunshot, a scream for help, or any other noise that might occur during interrogation.

Interrogation rooms lined the hallway as they walked to the cells in the back. Each cell was a small cement block room lined with thick metal walls and exposed steel beam ceilings. Behind each steel door with the small square Plexiglas window was a cot and a toilet. The first cell contained Gene, huddled on the cot as his body shook.

"Here," Dalton said, stopping Jason. "What's wrong with him?"

Jason pulled out a set of keys. "Drug withdrawal. This one wouldn't shut up. He told me everything he knew the second I set him in the chair. Unfortunately, it's not much.

Mostly, he was a patsy. I kind of feel sorry for him. Michelle would have taken him under her wing." At the mention of his wife, he looked away from Dalton and opened the door.

Dalton walked in and knelt before the old butler who was still in his White House tuxedo. Next to him was plenty of food and water, something Dalton was betting the others didn't have.

Gene opened his eyes. "Are you going to kill me?"

"No. I'm here to tell you that your daughters are safe. There were two operatives following your girls. They've been eliminated. Your daughters will be getting on a plane tonight and coming home only to discover they've won an all-expenses paid trip out of the country for the rest of the summer. They're going to call you, and you're going to tell them you are stuck at work and are so happy for them. You're going to tell them to leave immediately and enjoy themselves. And you're going to tell them how much you love them."

Tears began to stream down Gene's face. "The president did that?"

"Yes."

Gene began to cry harder. "I didn't want to do it."

"I believe you," Dalton said sadly. Gene was another life ruined by *Mollia Domini*. How many more people would be dead or ruined before this was over?

Dalton stood, and Gene reached out and grabbed his leg. Dalton didn't jump back. There was nothing Gene could do to him. Not with Jason aiming a gun at his head. "Thank you. Thank you for saving my girls. They're all I have left after my wife passed."

Jason faltered. His gun momentarily dipped at the mention of the loss of Gene's wife. "You're welcome. Gene, are you willing to testify about what happened?"

"Only if it doesn't hurt my girls. They're all that matters to me now."

Dalton gave him a tight smile showing he understood and walked out the door. Jason shut it and locked it again. "Who is next?"

"Thurmond. But he doesn't know anything more than he's already told us. It's clear he was set up to take the fall if Sandra started to come under suspicion."

"Will he testify against Sandra?" Dalton asked.

"Maybe if it means he doesn't get the death penalty. I'm sure he'd enjoy writing a tell-all book and doing interviews from prison."

"Then let's ask him."

Dalton waited for Jason to open the cell door. Thurmond was sitting on the cot with his back against the wall, waiting for them when they entered. "Who are you?"

Jason rolled his eyes. "He's still a little shit."

"I can tell," Dalton said seriously.

"Will you testify about everything you've told him?"

"Testify to whom?" Thurmond asked as if he weren't sitting in a black site.

"The court and Congress, if need be."

"What do I get out of it?"

"How about not dying and a chance to be on every channel live as you're telling Congress what role you played along with Sandra?" Dalton casually answered.

"I want immunity," Thurmond said, crossing his arms over his chest.

"How about you die in a secret prison? You'll be that asshole they're glad disappeared," Dalton countered.

Thurmond looked ready to argue, but one look at Jason had him changing his mind. "Fine. I'll testify. But I want a lawyer."

"You'll get one. Here's the deal. If there is anything you haven't told us, and we find out, the deal will be as dead as you will be. Got it?" Dalton asked as he stared a mutinous Thurmond down. Thurmond was trying to be tough while clearly petrified of Jason at the same time.

Thurmond looked away and then back to Dalton. "Deal. I, um, know something that Sandra could tell you that I may have forgotten about until now."

"What?" Jason snapped.

"Um, a private security group that Sandra and President Mitchell wanted to contract through the State Department. They had something to do with the report I was generating. They were to be part of the response team to the financial district and the Department of Energy."

"Which private contractor was it?" Dalton asked, knowing they were onto something big here.

"CBL Services Group."

Neither Dalton nor Jason said anything. They were intimately aware of how dangerous CBL was. The head of the company was retired Col. Brandon Locke. He was now in his early fifties, but Jason had worked with him quite a bit before Locke was quietly pushed out of the military. Dalton had worked with him for a year before the rumors became too much and the military was forced to either admit what happened under their watch or quietly pension him off. They chose to pension him off and bury the evidence as much as they could.

"Anything else?" Dalton asked.

Thurmond shook his head. "Not that I can think of. So, we have a deal?"

"Yes, we do. If you think of anything, knock on the door and tell him. No matter how big or small it is. Okay?"

"Okay. When do I get my attorney?"

"If you can use half of your brain to figure out why we're asking this and connect the dots, then you'll realize how much trouble you're really in. When it's over, you will get your lawyer. Until then, you will be fed, clothed, and treated well, unless you start withholding information. You are considered an enemy of the state and you need to understand that."

Dalton turned to leave and Jason followed him out. They didn't say anything until the door was locked. They walked a couple paces away and huddled together, dropping their voices.

"Why am I not surprised Locke is involved?" Jason asked rhetorically.

"All I know are the rumors. I met him a couple of times when we were overseas for rescues. I'd never met anyone so cold-blooded. He didn't care if civilians were in harm's way and that's where the rumors came into play," Dalton remembered.

"Brandon Locke is a disgrace to the military. He ran an elite group of black op soldiers who were just as bad as he was. They had absolutely no moral code. Sometimes you need that in war. But you need someone who can control them. Locke was more interested in riling them up and letting them loose than focusing on the mission.

"I remember a rescue that I was called in on before you joined us. They went into the mountains to try to find one of the high-value targets. They were caught in a shoot-out and one of them was injured. My team was called in for a medical evac. In the meantime, the terrorists were hiding among innocent families. By the time I arrived, they were all dead, and not from the terrorists. Locke had gone in and wiped them all out. Innocent or no, he didn't care. He got his target. Children as young as two were murdered. My team found women with clothes ripped off and a single bullet in their head." Jason looked down the hall as if he were there, looking at the casualties.

"I shoved Locke against the helo, but his men were on me in a heartbeat. They threatened us all and said what we saw were the casualties of war. We took it to our commander and were told, very clearly, to drop it. I heard there was an incident with a foreign ambassador and his family that finally ended Locke. It was a rescue mission and during the blood lust that followed the rescue, the ambassador's daughter was raped by one of Locke's men. Allegedly she was a very beautiful nineteen-year-old woman and was being held alone in a separate room. When the soldiers killed her captors, they thought they deserved an extra reward for saving her. The woman caused a scene, and Locke killed the girl to keep it quiet. The ambassador went straight to Sandra Cummings, who was the head of the Senate Foreign Affairs at the time, and it was covered up the best it could be, and Locke retired," Jason said with a disgusted shake of his head.

"That's the connection we needed, though," Dalton said, pulling out his phone. No service. "Let's check on Sandra and hear what she has to say about it. Then I think it's time to renew our acquaintance with the colonel."

Dalton followed Jason down the hall. Jason stopped at the door and then rushed to get it open. "Fuck!" he yelled, flinging the door open so hard it echoed off the metal wall. Dalton saw what it was the second he got through the door. The cot was leaning partially upright against a wall as if it had been stood on its end lengthwise and then kicked over. Sandra was hanging from the exposed beam by her bra a couple feet away. She'd found a place where a bolt had fallen out and slid her bra through making a noose. She'd shoved her cot upright and climbed up, kicked the cot away and hung herself.

"When did you last see her?" Dalton called out as he raced over to try to lift her in case she wasn't dead.

"Right before you arrived. I took her pantyhose. Dammit, I didn't think of her bra." Jason moved the cot and took Dalton's place, holding Sandra's body so Dalton could climb up and cut her down.

Dalton cut the bra and Jason laid Sandra down on the ground, feeling for a pulse. "She's dead."

20

VALERIA WOKE with her body pressed against Grant's. She didn't know how, but she'd somehow fallen asleep as they watched over Gene's girls from their cabana. Grant was reclined with one arm behind his head and the other around her back and resting on her hip.

"I'm so sorry. I've never fallen asleep on a stakeout before." Valeria made a move to sit up, but Grant kept her pinned there.

"It's okay, lass. Rest. We leave in a couple hours for our red-eye anyway. They've just been swimming and sunning. We had a long night last night." He leaned down and kissed her upturned lips, reminding her of the pleasures of staying up late with a man like Grant.

She rested her head back onto his chest and watched the girls being handed strawberry daiquiris. Since her time with Anthony, Val had been a one-night kind of girl. She didn't trust. She didn't want to have to decide ever again between love and the law. Instead, Val preferred no-strings-attached dates. However, she wasn't ready to shove Grant out the door. Somewhere, over the rescue in Mexico, the rescue in

California, the night in the desert, and time together at the resort, she had begun to trust him. And trust was dangerous in her book. It gave Grant power over her and that was something she didn't know if she was ready for.

"You're thinking so hard I can hear it," Grant said softly as he began to absently stroke the curve of her hip with his thumb.

"Just trying to plan out our next step."

"Of the operation or of us?" Grant asked, knowing her better than Anthony ever did. Not since Brock had any man really known her. Valeria had never thought she'd have those feelings again. Trust, affection, love.

"Both," she said honestly.

"I know you're blown away by my animal magnetism. It's scary and intimidating, but as long as you don't look deep into my eyes, you'll be okay."

Valeria burst out laughing. Maybe it was time to take a risk with her heart along with the mission. Grant smiled at her as she leaned up and kissed him.

"Hmm," Grant said, pulling back. "Phone. It's Dalton."

Valeria sat up as Grant answered. She had enjoyed their moments together, free from the reality of their mission. But reality had a way of never really going away. The more you fought it, the harder it picked you up and slammed you back to earth.

"Fuckin' A," Grant cursed, sitting up quickly and looking at Valeria as Dalton continued to talk. "Yeah, we're still here. We leave in a couple hours. Sure, we can catch an earlier flight. Tell Alex to get the girls on the same one. I don't want to leave them here alone. I think they're safe, but I don't want to risk it until we're out of the country."

Valeria took in Grant's hand as it opened and closed as if

he were trying to remain calm. He finished his phone call and Valeria knew reality had just slammed them yet again.

"What is it?" she asked as he stared out over the open water, searching for signs of trouble.

"Have you ever met someone so evil they scared you to your core?"

Valeria thought about it. "Angered me, worried me, threatened me, sure. But scare me that deeply? No."

"You will. Retired Colonel Brandon Locke. He's the owner of CBL Services Group. Private security of the worst kind," Grant told her. The more he told her, the colder Valeria felt. It didn't matter she was in the hot summer sun. To know that kind of evil was out there chilled her,but sadly didn't surprise her.

"Dalton wants me to go with him and Jason to see Locke. They believe he's with *Mollia Domini* and will be used by them as their own private army."

"Where are their offices?"

"New York City."

"We'll all go. Lizzy and I certainly aren't ones to sit back keeping the home fires burning."

Grant shook his head. "Locke will talk even less if you're there. He finds women worthless. He'd order you taken out the second we have our backs turned because no matter how hard Dalton and I hide it, he'll see we care about you both."

It rubbed Valeria the wrong way to be considered a liability, but she understood. She threatened family members all the time to get people to talk. "We'll be invisible. We'll stay in the van or in lookout positions."

"I think we can handle that."

"Rebecca or Stephanie Rankin," a hotel staffer called out

as he walked through the sand in his white shorts and bright blue polo.

"Here!" Rebecca called out from her chair in front of Grant and Valeria.

"We have you scheduled for a shuttle to the airport this evening, however, your flight has been changed. You leave in two hours. I'm sorry for the inconvenience."

The sisters quickly gathered their things as Grant called the man over. "I just got notice our flight was also cancelled and rebooked for earlier. Can you arrange two more seats on that shuttle for us?"

"Of course, Mr. and Mrs. Browning."

Valeria watched the staffer hurry back to the resort as she gave one last look out over the ocean. It had been twelve blissful hours, but reality was a bitch.

DALTON, Lizzy, and Jason were the first to arrive at the tunnels. She hated waiting but knew it would be safer to go through the tunnels all at once. With the increased security, she didn't want to have to open and close the hidden entrance to the White House residence more than necessary.

Dalton had given her the abbreviated version of what had happened, and since then, neither he nor Jason had said much. Lizzy didn't push. She had said she would go with them and they'd both said no with such force she didn't bring it up again. She'd see what Valeria said because she had no intention of staying behind.

The secret door leading from the basement of the hotel opened and Valeria entered, followed by Grant and Alex. Grant looked around in wonder, and Lizzy wondered if she'd ever looked so awestruck. Then she remembered the first time she came through the tunnels she had a sack over her head.

Lizzy greeted them as Dalton began to lead the pack up the tunnels. Lizzy hung back and put a restraining hand on Valeria's arm for a brief second. It was more than enough as Valeria instantly slowed and moved to her side.

Lizzy leaned her head close and whispered, "Has Grant said anything about New York?"

"Yes," Valeria whispered. "I thought you'd want to talk about this. He said the guys would want to leave us behind."

"Dalton already said I couldn't go."

"Well," Valeria said, before looking up to make sure they weren't overheard. "I knew you'd feel the same way I do, which I told Grant. He said this colonel is scary evil, and I agree after hearing about him. He's worried if we go with them, neither he nor Dalton will be able to hide the fact they care about us."

"So?" Lizzy started but then stopped and smiled. "Grant cares about you?"

Valeria blushed slightly and Lizzy's grin widened. She had thought relationships would hurt the operation, but instead they made them stronger. Tate's rescue of Birch would never have succeeded if she didn't love him.

"Grant believes the colonel would purposely hurt us just to throw them off. I actually agree with him."

"There's no way I'm staying behind if he's that bad," Lizzy hissed as she tried to keep her voice down.

"I agree. I told Grant that, and he agrees that we can be outside the facility in a backup vehicle or in a sniper position. While we won't be inside with them, we'll at least be nearby if they need to make a quick exit."

Lizzy wanted to say no, but it was a good plan. "Let's do it then. I'll take sniper and you take driver. Then we'll have both positions covered. I'm sure Dalton and Jason will agree to that."

They were all quiet as they climbed the stairs. Lizzy sent a message to Humphrey and a few very long minutes later the secret door opened and Humphrey's bald head poked in.

"It's all clear. We're meeting in the Treaty Room." Was it just her or was Humphrey walking a little taller today? Saving the president's life could do that to a person.

Birch was standing when they walked in. His hand and a hip were leaning against the polished table, but he looked better than he did on the video chat a few days before. He was back in a suit and tie. His light brown hair had been freshly cut, he had shaved, yet he still looked tired. There was pain etched along the fine lines around his mouth and eyes.

Tate was sitting in a chair with her leg propped on a small ottoman. She smiled to the group. Her blonde highlighted hair was pulled back into a loose bun at the base of her neck, and while she looked worried, she remained the optimistic go-getter.

"It's so good to see you both in person," Lizzy said, shaking Birch's hand and leaning over to hug Tate. Every one else fell in line behind her making their rounds to welcome Tate and Birch back into action.

Lizzy watched as Valeria hung back. She was the last to shake Birch's hand and then she almost pulled Tate from the chair with her hug. There had been a time when Valeria thought Tate was nothing more than a talking bobble-headed reporter. Now, as they embraced, it seemed they were family. Well, they were. This crazy mix of people was family. They had her back and now she needed to have theirs.

"It's great to be together again, but I'm afraid we need to get back to work. Dalton, why don't you fill them in," Lizzy said, raising her voice slightly over the greetings.

"Sandra Cummings is dead."

"What?" Birch asked, shocked. "How?"

"She hung herself with her bra," Dalton told him along with what they had found out from Gene and Thurmond.

"Brandon Locke? Shit." Birch shot up from where he was sitting and grimaced in pain. "When they mentioned private security, I thought it would be someone reputable. But Brandon Locke? He'd kill someone out walking their dog . . . and then kill the dog."

"We want to go talk to him," Jason said quietly from the corner of the room.

"Why would you do that?" Birch asked.

"I want to ask him to his face what's going on," Jason said, standing now. "I'm tired of hiding."

Birch was quiet for a moment. "Alex," Birch called out, turning to Alex instead of answering Jason, "what have you found out?"

Alex was bouncing even as he sat. His right leg bounced so hard the table was moving. "I'm telling you, dude. Mr. Dude? Sorry, President? Sir? Birch?"

"Birch. Go on," Birch said with a faint smile.

"There's chatter everywhere. London, Switzerland, Japan, all over the world, dude. I mean, Birch."

"What kind of chatter?" Lizzy asked.

"The kind about terrorist attacks. And not the kind for the most human casualties, but the kind that can cripple a country. It's lining up with the report Thurmond made on financial and energy targets. Furthermore, I traced Gene's phone, and the lawyer who came to him is big-time bad news. The phone was a burner, so I hacked into the jail and found the security footage of the attorney's visit. Dude kept his face away from the camera the entire time. Never got a shot of his face. So I traced the burner phone to a small DC electronics store. They don't have any footage, but there is a traffic camera nearby, and I got an image. Stan Detrick."

"Stan Detrick, himself?" Lizzy asked as everyone was quiet.

"Yup. I matched the custom watch he wears. It's identical to the man who went into the electronics store and the man who met with Gene."

"Who's Stan Detrick?" Grant asked.

"He was the attorney general under President Pollock. Everyone knew he was corrupt. He used the power of the AG's office to build his client list and then left the administration before he was caught doing anything illegal. His client list consisted of huge drug dealers like Manuel, corrupt CEOs, dirty politicians, hedge fund managers who were trading inside information—you name any defendant with $500 million or more to his or her name and Stan Detrick was their attorney," Birch explained.

"And this is bad?" Grant asked, trying to understand.

"It's bad in the sense Stan Detrick won't talk. He's been threatened with everything short of torture. He's managed to wiggle out of it because he knows more people than I do. Cartels owe him, the mob owes him, politicians owe him— the list goes on and on," Birch explained.

"So, torture him," Valeria shrugged.

"I would have Sebastian talk to him, but I can't trust him anymore," Birch sighed as he sat back down.

"I, uh, have information on that as well," Alex stuttered as his bouncing knee smacked into the table above it.

"Rock Star found it." Alex turned pink. "She's better at hacking private companies than I am."

"I'm thinking we should invite her to the US. You two would make a great team," Birch said kindly.

"What did she find?" Lizzy asked instead of letting Dalton get a teasing word in.

"That Bertie and Sebastian are in a technology race. A game-changing technology race," Alex told them.

"What kind of technology?" Birch asked as everyone seemed to lean closer.

"Artificial intelligence software that can analyze every corner of every market and tell you what is likely to happen to every stock. Theoretically, it would be able to predict the stock market with amazing accuracy. Do you have any idea how much that would be worth?" Alex's eyes had grown wide as he spoke.

"Billions." Birch looked worriedly around the room. "Do you know what could happen with such autonomous software? It's constantly learning, constantly evolving. If parameters aren't put in place to keep it solely analyzing and predicting, then it could learn to manipulate variables to create its own desired outcome."

"Not just that," Valeria said, standing. "It could be sold to terrorists and turned into a market hacking tool that would do more damage than the aftermath of 9/11."

"Who's winning the race?" Humphrey asked as the room quieted down.

"Bertie Geofferies. According to the internal emails Rock Star was able to get to, they've completed the software and are ready to test it," Alex answered.

"What are they waiting for? Why isn't it being tested immediately?" Dalton leaned forward in his chair and rested his elbows on his knees. His brow creased in thought and Lizzy was pretty sure it was the same thought she had. He was waiting for something to happen.

"She couldn't find the answer. Sebastian is close to testing as well, but he's probably a week behind. That could be giving Geofferies time to test at the most optimal time or maybe Sebastian has thrown a wrench in it somehow," Alex suggested.

"When would be the optimal time?" Tate looked to Birch to answer.

"A great time to launch software like that is after a crash. The software could maximize its returns if an outside force caused an extreme drop."

"Did Sebastian tell you he wanted Alex to give him this information on Bertie?" Lizzy asked, directing the conversation to Birch and Sebastian's previous meeting.

"Yes." Birch let out a frustrated breath. "I hate to admit this, but I don't know what to do. I believed him when he said Roland wasn't the head of *Mollia Domini* and that he joined only to feed us information. But then he wanted that information in return. Not just that information, but illegally obtained corporate spying. I don't know. He's my best friend, or at least I thought he was."

"Are you going to hand the information over?" Tate pressed. Lizzy could see she was uncomfortable with this, too.

"Not yet. You want to go to New York to see Locke? Well, Lizzy, you and Valeria can pay a visit to Bertie Geofferies. We're going to get to the bottom of this now. If it's Sebastian playing me, I'll have you bring him in. And if it's Locke trying to pull a power play, deal with him. But first we learn and then we move," Birch ordered.

"We can leave tonight," Lizzy told him as the others nodded.

"And Alex, invite your crush to join us. I wonder what she's like. She must be special if you like her," Birch grinned as Alex flushed from his chin to the tip of his ears. "Oh, and before you all leave, why don't you pick up Stan Detrick and toss him in a cell for a couple days. It may make whoever is paying him a little nervous for him to suddenly disappear."

"I've got that," Jason grunted as he walked out the room.

"Jason," Birch called, stopping the man. His face, his body, and his stance spoke of a grieving, hardened man. "You're not alone." Birch looked around the room at the vagabond team, willing Jason to see that his loss was felt by all. "Be safe."

Jason barely registered the backing before he turned and left the room.

"I'll watch out for him," Dalton said softly before chasing after Jason.

"Good luck. I wish I could go with you two," Tate smiled sadly at her and Valeria.

"You keep the team together here on the home front. Give us something positive to fight for, and we'll all come back." Valeria leaned down and hugged Tate before winking at Lizzy. "Come on, Lizzy. Let's see if all billionaires are assholes."

21

"Duuuude," Alex said slowly from the backseat of the large SUV as they headed back to Quantico to pack for New York. "Oh my, I mean, dude!"

Grant turned around and looked at him. "Words, dude. Like, use them."

"She's coming. Rock Star is coming. She said she can catch the first flight out of Heathrow and meet us in New York tomorrow."

"You. She can meet you. We'll be a little busy," Valeria said, shaking her head but then smiling at Grant as he smirked.

"Remember, this isn't a hookup. This is work," Dalton called back from the driver's seat.

Grant had never seen a person turn such a bright shade of red before. "I'm not—she's not—it's not—oh no," Alex groaned as he looked at his phone.

"What?" Grant asked as he and Valeria turned to look at Alex crammed into the third row of the SUV. His knees were practically to his chest as he looked like a whipped puppy.

"This," he said, turning the phone, "this is Rock Star."

Grant blinked and Valeria let out low whistle. "Good job, dude. She's hot."

"Exactly. She's way above me. There's no way now." Alex buried his head in his hands as Valeria grabbed his phone and passed it up to Lizzy.

"Wow," she said, looking at the brunette beauty. She wore dark eyeliner, had long lashes, brown eyes, and a smile that would turn Alex into a bumbling idiot. Well, maybe then he wouldn't say *dude* all the time.

"You have to send a picture back," Valeria grinned as she took the phone from Lizzy and turned on the camera. "Smile!" Alex practically leapt into her seat to grab the phone.

"Can't we send a picture of Dalton or Grant?" Alex asked as he cradled the phone.

"Don't be a scared wee lad. Women like confidence."

Lizzy and Valeria nodded in agreement.

"I'll send a picture when I get back to the bar. Maybe do a few pushups beforehand."

Valeria shook her head. "She already likes you. She's coming all the way from London to meet you and work with you."

"You think?" Alex asked hopefully.

"Duh," Lizzy laughed from the front. "But now that we have your hacker love team set up, we need to plan our trip to New York. We need identities in case we get caught or pulled over."

"Got it," Alex said, pulling up his laptop. His fingers began to fly across the small keyboard perched on his cramped knees. "What else?"

"Everything on CBL Services Group and Brandon Locke, including his relationship with Sandra Cummings and the layout of his building," Lizzy instructed.

"Dalton, we need to talk when we get to your place," Grant said, leaning forward. "I need some gear, and we need a plan for walking into Locke's home."

"I wonder if it wouldn't be better to meet him outside rather than in," Valeria asked. "That way we can keep an eye on you guys and Locke will have to watch himself, too, since there will be people walking all around. There'd be a smaller chance of him taking you out or tossing you in a cell never to be seen again. Then Lizzy and I would have to rescue you and you'd feel insecure about being rescued by a girl."

"I think it'd be hot," Grant winked.

"Yeah," Dalton smiled. "I might get myself captured to see Lizzy storm the fortress for me."

"Yup, totally hot," Alex muttered, never taking his eyes from his screen.

Valeria and Lizzy rolled their eyes. "Hot or not, it's a good idea to try to meet him outside."

"There are cameras at the front door. Will he know you if he sees you?" Alex asked.

"He'll know Jason for sure. I don't know if he'll remember Grant or me," Dalton answered. "How do you suppose we get him out? Won't security buzz us in?"

Alex finally looked up. "It's so simple, and I thought of it. Maybe I am a badass. Rock Star will totally think I'm hot then."

Valeria opened her mouth to say something but stopped. "Is that Crew?"

Dalton pulled to a stop outside the bar as Crew pushed himself off the brick wall and sauntered to them. Valeria hopped out and hugged him. She wasn't the only one surprised by her action. So was Crew, who stood still with his arms by his side for a moment before hugging her in return. "Thank you for saving Tate."

"I know of a way you can thank me," he grinned as his hand began to slide lower.

"Ready to lose that hand? Pilots kinda need two," Grant's voice, thick with his Scottish accent, rumbled as he unfolded himself from the SUV. Grant stood a couple inches taller than Crew and a good fifty pounds more of muscle.

"Who the hell are you?" Crew spat, pulling Valeria to his side in full male posturing.

"I'm the only man whose hand gets to touch her arse. Grant Macay, Air Force Pararescue pilot and new member of this band of rebels."

"We don't need another pilot. Not when the best is already part of the group," Crew smirked.

Valeria pulled away from Crew's side. "We need to get to New York, not challenge each other to a pissing contest."

Crew took a deep breath and plastered on a fake smile. "That's why I'm here. I'm flying you all to New York. I already have a civilian helicopter and a flight plan to land at the hotel across the street from Locke's office building. We're staying in the penthouse for an engagement party. The penthouse has three bedrooms, a fold-out couch, and a cot is being brought in for our little brother."

"Where will Rock Star sleep?" Alex asked, flushing red again.

"Who?" Crew's brow wrinkled as he looked at Alex.

"Our wee laddie's lady friend from London," Grant smirked.

"Alex has a girl coming from London to see him? Way to go, bro!" Crew slapped Alex on the back, sending him stumbling forward.

"We'll get her another room in the hotel," Lizzy said, saving Alex from more ribbing. "We're not going to fill her in completely until we're sure of her. Now, let's get ready to leave first thing in the morning. And Alex, please make a reservation and ID for Rock Star."

"I'm not calling her Rock Star," Valeria said, crossing her arms over her chest.

"Roxie. Her name's Roxie," Alex sighed and every one snickered.

"Do you even know what to do with a woman?" Crew asked. "Thank goodness I'm here. Come, learn from the master." Crew slung his arm around Alex and headed to the back of the bar.

Grant slung his arm around Dalton. "Why don't you let the master see the guns you have? I bet I'll find one cute and show you how to make her fire."

"I'll text Jason and let him know we're leaving in two hours," Lizzy called out as she and Valeria dropped into line behind the guys, shaking their heads at their antics. They walked a short distance on Main Street and turned left toward their houses. The town of Quantico was empty at this time of night. It was all tucked in as they quietly talked and planned. Dalton, technically, still lived across the street, so Lizzy wasn't surprised when he and Grant walked past her house. Valeria lived farther up the street in a small rental. They silently peeled off into the shadows of the night. They knew what needed to be done. Gear would be packed, equipment loaded, and all streamlined into no more than one or two bags. It was their way of life. Be ready to go on a moment's notice. And tonight they were acutely aware they might not be back.

Lizzy opened the door to her house and Dave, her white

fluff-ball Bichon, yapped happily as he ran out of the living room.

"What, huh? Shut up, you furry rat," came the grumbling old voice from the living room.

"Buzz, is that you?" Lizzy called out.

"There's our girl. We were worried about you," Snip's tired voice said at the same time two men groaned. Lizzy hurried into the living room to find Buzz trying to get off the couch and Snip sitting in the recliner.

"You waited for me to get home." Lizzy was struck with the acute reminder that her father was gone, but she had two adopted grandfathers looking after her. She had a larger family than ever, even while all alone.

"Of course we did. When you didn't come right back, we thought something might be wrong, so we were staking out your place to see if anyone came by," Buzz began to explain.

"But sitting in the car that long really hurt our backs, and we were afraid of falling asleep so we just moved our little operation in here," Snip finished explaining.

"I'm glad you did. I have a favor to ask, again."

"We're ready to go," Buzz said, pulling out a gun from WWII from under the couch.

"Can you continue the stakeout a little longer? We have to go somewhere to check something out."

Snip snorted. Buzz chuckled.

"Okay, that was a little vague, but it needs to be. I really appreciate you both so very much, and I'm sorry I'm putting you into this position."

"Sorry? This is the most fun we've had in ages," Buzz told her as he stood up, his back cracking as he stood upright with his massive antique gun.

"Yeah, it's good to feel useful again. We'll stay right here and take care of the bar and the rat for you."

Lizzy scooped up her dog and hugged him to her chest. "He's not a rat!"

Buzz and Snip shared a look that told her they thought otherwise.

"Now, you go do what you need to do. Stay safe and take care of my grandson who is suddenly back on duty when he should be off." Buzz wiggled his bushy eyebrows, and Lizzy thought she might have underestimated their observations of the group.

Lizzy went and hugged each man. "Thank you." Lizzy kissed each of their wrinkled cheeks and hurried upstairs with Dave still clenched in her arms. She'd be gone again soon. But right now, right this minute, wasn't too soon to tell those you love that they matter to you and that you appreciate them. Especially since she had a bad feeling about this mission.

22

GRANT STOOD on the steps of the hotel, talking with Dalton. Or at least that's what it would look like to anyone else. Instead, he was keeping an eye on the front door to the building that housed CBL Services Group. They'd been watching for fifteen minutes as they talked.

Grant scanned the area and made note of where Jason sat eating his morning bagel. The morning had been all about surveillance. They'd done what they could from their hotel room. Valeria had driven the area, and Lizzy had scoped out the line of sight from the roof. Now they were on their way to attempt a meeting with Bertie Geofferies. Today was going to be an exercise in patience and restraint.

"How's Jason?"

Grant looked at Dalton whose back was toward Jason's location. "Seems calm. He's not staring, bouncing a nervous knee, or anything to draw attention. He's eating a bagel and just picked up a paper."

"I'm worried he'll make stupid and dangerous decisions if this goes south."

Grant nodded in agreement. He didn't know Jason as well as Dalton, but even he could see the man was hurting. "We'll take care of him."

"Let's walk the block to the coffee shop."

Grant and Dalton walked off as they caught sight of Jason sipping his coffee. That morning each team member was doing his or her part of the puzzle, then they'd meet again to put those pieces together. Patience. It required a ton of patience.

ALEX STOOD NERVOUSLY outside baggage claim. He tried to lean against the hood of the car and look cool like he'd seen Dalton do, but he just slid off instead. So now he was standing like an idiot, looking anxiously around for Rock Star—Roxie. He should call her that. It was a pretty name for a beautiful woman.

He'd done his own background check on her but had never pulled up a picture. He'd been afraid to look. In his mind, she was the girl next door who would instantly fall for a guy like him. Instead, he'd been blown away by her beauty. Roxie would never be interested in a geek like him.

Alex rolled up the sleeves to his dress shirt and wondered again if he should tuck the shirt into his jeans. Tate had sent him the outfit. It had been waiting at the front desk when they'd checked in. The jeans were relaxed fit, but still felt strange since he was used to them being baggier. He had to admit he did feel more confident in the outfit. And then there was his hair. Crew had taken clippers to it before they'd left. Gone was the long hair that fell wherever it dried. Now he looked clean-cut with hair still longer than Dalton's, but much more mature looking—like, twenty-five.

The sliding doors opened and there she was. He could tell she would come up to his shoulders as he watched her look around. Her brunette hair fell in long waves around her shoulders and over the tops of her full breasts. Her jeans were tight, her sneakers pink, and her black T-shirt had a picture of a power button with "Have you tried turning me on?" written in white underneath it.

She shoved a pair of black plastic-rimmed glasses up onto the top of her head, pushed her hair back from her face, and showed multiple piercings up her ear. Her long lashes batted as she turned big brown eyes in his direction.

"Dude," Alex whispered under his breath as she made eye contact with him and smiled. He hadn't realized he was standing there like a dork with his hand raised in a very exuberant wave.

Roxie's smile had all the advice Crew had given him flying out his ear as nothing but blank space filled his mind. She pushed her computer bag onto the back of her hip and wrapped her arms around him.

"Alex! I can't believe it's really you." Her soft English accent caused him to sway as all the blood rushed from his head. He wrapped his arms around her and was afraid she'd feel his attraction for her pressing against her stomach.

"I never thought we'd be able to meet," Alex said, his voice only partially cracking with nerves. He cleared his throat and stepped back to open the car door. "I'm in awe. To be with a talent like yourself is a real honor."

Roxie's grin widened. "That is so sweet!" She launched herself at him again and placed a kiss on his cheek before sliding into the front seat. Alex wanted to pump his fist into the air. Dalton had given him that line and it had worked! Holy shit. What was he going to say now?

Roxie had her computer open by the time he got into the car. "Is something going on?"

"I think so," she said, not taking her eyes from the screen. "I wish we could spend more time getting to know each other, but I'm finding references to 1400 hours. I just can't tell what time zone. Something big, that's what has me worried. When searching the dark web for that Locke guy you told me about, I came across a private chat room. Well, it would have been private to anyone else, but you know how I get intrigued by locked doors." Roxie winked at him and Alex almost drove off the road except she was onto something much bigger than his hormones.

"What are they talking about happening at 1400 hours?" Alex asked as he headed for the hotel.

"That's the thing, I don't know. I just know that there are five people who have given the all clear to proceed at 1400 hours. Your Locke guy is in this room and confirmed two hours ago he was all set."

Alex looked at the clock. It was nine o'clock in the morning. Fourteen hundred would be two o'clock Eastern time. But US Eastern time wasn't the only time zone. There were three other time zones in the US alone, not counting globally. That wasn't what was bothering him, though. It was something about the number of people in the room. Five . . .

LIZZY LEANED FORWARD and stared at the receptionist, her face only inches from the picture-perfect model these billionaires seemed to hire at their companies, like Coco at Sebastian's office. Coco was at least nice and peppy as she guarded that lobby. The same could not be said for Petal.

"No one gets past me without being on the list," she sneered. Her platinum hair was highlighted with pink, and she wore a mini-dress that looked like she belonged at a dance club, not a workplace.

"Tell Mr. Geofferies I have information he wants, and the only way he'll get it is either when I release it to the press or see him in person. His choice. Since it's about his secret project and Sebastian Abel, I think he'll want it in person."

Petal didn't look convinced.

"Pick up the phone or I'll rip your extensions off and strangle you with them," Valeria said, bored with the wait.

"I'm calling security," Petal gasped.

Valeria just stared, and Lizzy wished she had that talent. She could give a mean glare, but Valeria was glacial and deadly all at once. Petal froze and then nodded.

Petal picked up the phone and repeated what Lizzy told her to Geofferies's secretary. Then she sat quietly waiting on the phone as she tried not so subtly to signal security.

"Yes, sir. One moment." Petal handed Lizzy the phone. "He wants to talk to you."

Lizzie took the phone and looked up into the nearest security camera. "No one threatens me, you bitch."

"Artificial intelligence and market manipulation." Lizzy smiled up at the camera.

"Give me back to the girl."

Lizzy handed the phone to Petal. "Here you go."

Petal took the phone, nodded, and frowned. "Yes, sir." She hung up and handed visitor passes to Lizzy and Valeria with a pinched face. "Top floor."

"Thank you," Lizzy smiled as Valeria snatched the passes.

"Petal? Seriously? If I have a daughter, I'm gonna name her Glock," Valeria whispered as they went to the private elevator much like Sebastian's.

"Isn't that more of a boy's name?"

"Fine. Beretta then." The elevator opened, and they stepped through the doors. "What are you planning on saying?"

Lizzy shrugged her shoulder. "I don't know. I guess I'll have to wait and see how I read him."

"As much as I don't like Sebastian, I don't know how I feel about throwing him under the bus. If Sebastian is anything like Bertie Geofferies, it's a no-win situation."

The doors opened before Lizzy could respond, and Valeria didn't say anything more as another early-twenty-something model showed them the way to two enormous engraved doors: one with a script *B* on it and the other with a G.

The inside of the office was masculine. It smelled of fresh-dried tobacco and leather. The leather chairs were old and worn but gleaming. Three walls were covered in dark wood with pictures of hunting dogs on them. The other wall ran the length of the room with floor-to-ceiling windows. Standing at the window was Bertie Geofferies. He was short, around Lizzy's height, and in his seventies, but still very much in shape. His hair was turning white, but the rest of him was kept in prime condition by a well-paid staff consisting of a personal chef, a personal trainer, and probably a twenty-something masseuse.

Lounging in all his arrogance was Rue Geofferies, Bertie's son and a vice president of the company. He was in his forties with a full head of light brown hair, blue eyes, and a smirk that let Lizzy know he was the type to smack his secretary on the ass and tell himself she liked it.

"Haven't I seen you at the Blonde Beaver strip club?" Rue asked with a laugh that combined into a snort.

"No, but isn't that where you met your wife?" Valeria shot back, not looking the slightest bit offended. Rue slammed his mouth shut. His wife was one of the most stuck-up, elitist heiresses known to man. "Oh wait. That's your mistress. How do they get along? I bet they share cake recipes and talk about how you like your dick sucked."

Lizzy grinned and went to ignoring the little shit on the couch. Bertie had been observing them the entire time. "Mr. Geofferies. I'm—"

"Elizabeth James, employee of Sebastian Abel. And this woman is Valeria McGregor, an employee at the bar you also run in Quantico. Quaint little place, Quantico. Although I'm curious as to why disgraced DEA and FBI agents are here. I read your father died. That must be hard."

Lizzy wasn't surprised he knew who they were. He wouldn't have let them up otherwise. After all, Bertie made his money in tech when Sebastian was still a twitch in his father's pants. This was a man who was ahead of Sebastian in the race for artificial intelligence, and he'd easily know everything about her by the time she had hung up the phone in the lobby.

"Yes, it's always hard to lose a parent. I wanted to talk to you about your artificial intelligence software." Lizzy walked to the desk and took a seat that hadn't been offered to her.

"What artificial intelligence software?" Bertie followed and took the seat at his desk as they effectively shut Rue out of the conversation.

"You should know in a tech age like this, there is no such thing as privacy. Everything is controlled and manipulated.

The question is, what will you give me to tell Sebastian you're behind him?"

Bertie narrowed his eyes at her and examined her closely. Lizzy didn't flinch. She could do the bored look as well as anyone. Valeria was currently checking out her fingernails and sighing impatiently.

"How do I know you're not a corporate spy?" Bertie asked slowly as he leaned back into his chair and steepled his fingers.

Lizzy smiled slowly. "Of course I'm a corporate spy. How do you think I know so much already? Now, what is it worth for me to tell Sebastian whatever it is you want me to tell him?" Lizzy shrugged. "Or I can tell him about how you're ready to launch the software."

"No wonder he employed an FBI agent. But what's she here for?" Bertie asked, finally looking to Valeria.

"She's here in case you get any ideas about keeping me here," Lizzy answered as Valeria returned Bertie's examination.

"You think you two could stop us if we wanted to keep you here?" Bertie sounded incredulous. Lizzy sat back and waited. She didn't have to wait long. One of the knives that Valeria had on her was thrown. Rue screamed and shoved himself backward as the blade impaled itself in the couch, inches from his balls.

Valeria winked at Bertie who unexpectedly smiled. "What is Sebastian paying you?"

"A lot," Lizzy answered.

"I'll pay you double whatever he's paying you to join my team. All off the books, of course. You can still take your money from Sebastian and stay in DC; just report back to me with everything he's doing."

Lizzy let herself smile. "Aren't you glad you took my meeting?"

"Very. Tell me about Sebastian and where he is on his artificial intelligence software. Has he tested it yet?"

"Within a week."

Bertie nodded. "Good."

"How is that good? You haven't tested yours yet either."

"I'm not worried. My test will be done very soon. I'll bury Sebastian like the cockroach he is." He looked at Rue, who was still white as he wrenched the knife from the couch.

"Why do you two hate each other? I would think you two would actually want to partner up since you're so similar." Lizzy had weighed the pros and cons of disclosing information to Bertie and had decided the motivation behind their feud to be more important than rumors of Sebastian's software.

"There's only room for one at the top, Miss James. I didn't work my whole life to come in second. I'm sure Sebastian feels the same way. I can admire him, which I do, while doing everything in my power to make him fall at the same time. Now, what else can you tell me about Sebastian?"

23

ALEX HAD NEVER WORKED with someone before, and certainly not someone more talented than he was. He knew enough to know someone like Crew wouldn't like it. It would be a blow to his ego. However, Alex found it so sexy when Roxie bit down on her lip as she did the seemingly impossible with ease.

She would ask him his ideas, and together they found a way through CBL's firewall and into their network from where they sat parked in front of the hotel. Even though the signal was weak, they were able to hop onto CBL's Wi-Fi and into their network.

"That's fab," Roxie gasped as she followed Alex's idea on how to gain access to Locke's computer once isolating it on the network. "I'm in." Roxie's fingers flew and her eyes didn't move from the screen as she read. Alex waved off the valet once again and waited to hear what she'd found. He was going to take her upstairs to meet the rest of the team, but Roxie was onto something. Once she was onto something, she didn't stop until she'd found it.

Alex pushed his chair back and pulled out his own laptop. "How'd you get into that chat room?"

"Here," Roxie said, grabbing his laptop and showing him. "All done." She handed it back and went back to work.

Alex dug for the old posts. There hadn't been five people, there had been seven in the group. Two were no longer active. "Who are you?"

"What?" Roxie asked.

"Sorry, I talk to myself when I work. I found two other people in the group who have been inactive for the past week. I'm following up on them."

"Good. I didn't have time to find the identities of everyone. I'm into Locke's personal files. He's not a good person, Alex. In fact, he's very dangerous."

"I figured . . ." Alex trailed off as his eyes narrowed. A few more threads and then he was in the rabbit hole. And when he finally came to the end, he just stared. "Oh crap."

DALTON STEPPED BACK from the window of their penthouse overlooking CBL. There had been no sign of Locke. While there was a back entrance, they'd confirmed with the local food truck that Locke's car service dropped him off at the front door most days. He looked at his watch. "Dude, it's nine-forty. I thought Lizzy and Valeria would be back by now." Grant punched Dalton hard in the shoulder. "What the fuck?"

"You just said dude. You've been around Alex too long. I thought to break you of the habit because I can't be part of the group if two of you are duding it up. Speaking of Alex, I thought he should be back by now as well."

Dalton heard the electric lock slide open on the front

door. He and Grant turned to see who was back when the door was flung open and the sexiest little woman stumbled in with Alex practically falling over her. The two held open laptops and white faces.

"What is it?" Dalton asked as the familiar sense of dread hit him hard.

"We found the bombs," Alex said quickly. "There were seven, now there are five. One bomb was confiscated in a soft run at the Shanghai Stock Exchange and the man killed. The other one was already used in DC to target Birch. The guy who had the bomb is the same CIA agent who tried to take Tate right after the bombing. He went silent after the bombing. Not because he was successful, but because he was dead," Alex said so quickly Dalton didn't have time to process it before the girl spoke.

"And Locke has one of the Russian suitcase bombs. Along with a combination of military, former military, and government agents in London, Sydney, Hong Kong, and Zurich."

"Fuck," Grant said softly. It was the same sentiment Dalton had.

"What are their targets?" Dalton asked.

"I think it's the financial institutions," Alex said with a little less confidence. "Roxie . . . um, this is Roxie. This is Dalton and Grant."

"I know," she smiled. "I read your records when I hacked Alex's private message board you all use. Sorry," she grinned in a proud way that Dalton knew meant she wasn't the least bit sorry.

"Well, then I guess Alex has some work to do to make it more private." Dalton glared at Alex.

"I already took care of it." Roxie smiled tightly at the group as she looked back at her laptop.

"You are so awesome." Alex sighed before his face went back to a look of deadly seriousness. "The report Thurmond made on the New York Stock Exchange combined with the failed attempt in China and the attempted hacking of the London Stock Exchange led us to look into it. Here are the men carrying the weapons. All of them are in a city with an international exchange. It can't be a coincidence."

"Alex, send everything to Birch and Humphrey. Text a picture of Locke to us as well. Grant, get hold of Lizzy and Valeria to fill them in. I'll let Jason know. But when are they going to strike?"

"Fourteen hundred hours, but I don't know what time zone," Roxie said, nerves causing her voice to sound slightly strangled and her British accent thicker.

"Everyone is hitting at once?" Grant asked as he sent a text to Lizzy and Valeria.

"Yes," Roxie answered. "They said they were going to move into position."

"UTC," Grant said tightly as he and Dalton cursed.

"What?" Alex asked.

"Coordinated universal time. Dammit, they're attacking in seventeen minutes."

Chaos ensued, but you would never know it. Grant and Dalton were two of a kind. The worse things got, the calmer they appeared. It was how they made life-and-death decisions. Grant sent follow-up texts before checking his weapons while Dalton tossed him a Kevlar vest and strapped one on as he filled Jason in.

"What can I do?" Roxie asked in near panic.

"Call in a bomb threat. Have your friends call them in at every exchange. Anything to get as many people out of the buildings as possible," Dalton ordered as he strapped on his vest and guns.

"Can you freeze trading for the exchanges that are open?" Grant asked as he slipped his phone into his back pocket of his jeans.

"We'll get the word out," Alex told him as he and Roxie stood at the bar top with their laptops open and fingers flying.

"Wall Street is five blocks away. We need to move," Dalton barked as he and Grant ran out the door with an extra gun and vest for Jason in hand.

VALERIA WAS AMAZED at how much talking Lizzy could do without saying a single thing. She had Bertie eating out of her hand about what was going on at SA Tech while never disclosing any important trade secret, not that they knew any.

One thing was clear though, Bertie loved power as much as Sebastian did, and he hated that Sebastian was nipping at his heels. Valeria kept an eye on Rue as he stared at her. Someone was holding a grudge.

Val's phone vibrated, and she looked at her watch. Nine forty-four. This was taking forever and Valeria had already decided Bertie was exactly the same as Sebastian. She didn't know what Lizzy was looking for. Either man would do anything, legal or not, to defeat the other.

Valeria's phone buzzed again. Grant knew they were busy. It buzzed again and Valeria slowly pulled it from the front pocket of her jeans and casually looked down. Shit. Her heart sped up so fast she was sure she was flushed, but instead of leaping up, Valeria rolled her eyes and let out a sigh.

"Look. I got things to do. We've given you enough to

know we're legit. Wire us a million dollars now and my girl here will get you some more information. Here's the account." Valeria leaned forward as Lizzy looked at her. She tapped her phone with her left pointer finger as she used the right to write down an account number. Valeria slouched back in the chair and crossed her arms and resumed looking bored.

"That would be good," Lizzy smiled, encouraging Bertie to pick up the phone. In less than a minute, the wire had been placed, hands had been shaken, and they were out the door.

"What the hell is going on?" Lizzy asked as she headed for the elevator. The door opened instantly and Valeria pushed the button for the lobby.

"I'll tell you in a second." She looked up at the video camera and flicked it off.

The elevator slowed to a stop and the door opened. Turning away from the lobby, Valeria led them out the back door, setting off the fire alarm. "*Mollia Domini* is going to try to blow up the world's biggest stock exchanges."

"When?"

Valeria looked at her watch. "In thirteen minutes."

"What time is it?" Tate asked as she and Humphrey walked toward the Oval Office. "I know our meeting was for 9:45, but I'm moving so slow on these stupid crutches. I thought I was ready for them, but it's irritating my shoulder wound a bit."

"It's just now time for the meeting. Somehow I don't think Birch will care if we're a few minutes late," Humphrey said as they headed through the office full of secretaries, staff, and various people waiting for meetings.

The door to the oval office flung open and a white-faced Birch stood, pain radiating from his face as he held his broken ribs. "Get me the head of the SEC and the president of the New York Stock Exchange!" Birch yelled at his secretary. "And Jess, get me the heads of the New York offices of the FBI, police, and Homeland." Birch looked up and saw them. "We're under attack."

Birch disappeared back into the Oval Office as Humphrey ran and Tate hobbled so fast the pain of the crutches slamming against her upper ribs would make a normal person cry.

"Freeze the markets now! We have credible intelligence there is an imminent terrorist attack ready to strike the exchange in thirteen minutes," Tate heard Birch order into the phone when she got there. "Evacuate the building immediately."

"New York police commissioner, FBI, and Homeland on conference line three," Jessica shouted out.

"Jess, I need the British and Australian prime ministers, the Federal Council of Switzerland, and the chief executive of Hong Kong," Birch shouted back as he picked up the phone.

Birch looked at them then. His face was hardened in the midst of potential disaster. "Tate, Humphrey, be ready to take over any calls. It's *Mollia Domini*. They're taking out the markets with suitcase bombers. Looks like New York is the main target. They're hitting it at peak trading time. If any of these exchanges are damaged, it'll be enough to send the world's markets into chaos." Birch trailed off, imagining a result that would be incomprehensible in terms of damage.

"I have pictures and am sending them now to the heads of state and our agents in New York. They're in your inbox."

Tate nodded as she pulled up the files. Locke. Son of a bitch. He was going to hit New York.

"Now!" Birch yelled. "And don't you fucking dare give me that jurisdiction shit. Everyone clear the area and look for Brandon Locke and his men. The bomb will be in a bag of some sort."

"I have London and Switzerland on two," Jessica called out.

"Here, talk to my chief of staff for the rest of my orders." Birch handed the phone to Humphrey and picked up the secure line. "You need to close your exchanges immediately. We have credible intelligence of a terrorist attack and have sent the names and pictures of the men with the suitcase bombs. Freeze trading and evacuate. The attack it set for twelve minutes from now."

"I've woken up Hong Kong and Australia and have them on a line out here!" Jessica yelled, standing with a phone in her hand and the cord stretched as far as it could.

Birch tossed the phone to Tate as he ran. "Finish it!"

"This is Tate Carlisle, press secretary to the president." Tate answered the questions as fast as they came. Oh God. They had thought they had been prepared for whatever *Mollia Domini* had planned.

24

"JASON!" Dalton called out as they raced down the steps with Secret Service emblazoned across the back of their vests. "Locke is going to bomb the exchange!"

Dalton threw the vest at him and handed him the M-16. People were giving them wide berth, and some were even taking pictures. Dalton stepped into the street and held up his hand. A minivan screeched to a halt and a scared woman clung to the steering wheel.

"Secret Service. I need your vehicle. It's a matter of national security," Dalton yelled, but the woman just shook her head.

"We don't have time for this," Grant told him as he looked around for another ride.

Dalton slammed the butt of the gun through the driver's window. "I said it's a matter of fucking national security!" He reached inside and opened the door as the woman screamed. He used his knife, sliced the seat belt, and dragged her out as he hit the unlock button. Jason jumped into the back and Grant took the front as Dalton sped away. With his hand on the horn and weaving in and out of traffic, it wouldn't take long to get there, but could they find Locke in time?

VALERIA'S ARMS sliced through the air as she sprinted straight down the middle of Broad Street. Lizzy was right behind her. Neither talked. Eleven minutes. Valeria was counting down in her head. They wouldn't make it.

"There!" Lizzy shouted. Two blocks ahead was Wall Street. The cobbled street was cut in half by barricades as a large American flag stretched across the six Corinthian columns starting around two to three stories up from the ground and stretching upward toward the pediment. The sculpture of Integrity, with her arms stretched outward and her hands clenched in fists, came into view right as a minivan slid to a stop before hitting the barricades.

A large mountain of man in Kevlar leapt from the front. "Grant!" Valeria screamed over the traffic at the same time shouting erupted.

"Ten minutes," Lizzy called out from behind her as the men ran toward them.

"We have to get these people out of here," Valeria yelled as Jason went right toward the guards and began talking to them.

"We know Locke," Dalton told them as they stood with their hands on their hips in the middle of Broad Street as hundreds of people came and went. "You two get people out of here. Folks in the other buildings should find a safe place to hunker down or evacuate away from the exchange."

"I'll block the street with the minivan. Good luck." Lizzy placed a quick kiss on Dalton's cheek and then ran toward the minivan.

"Stay safe, lass," Grant whispered to Val. She closed her eyes for one second taking in his voice, the press of his lips on hers, the hardness of a gun being shoved into her hand, and then he was gone. When she opened her eyes, the fear was pressed deep inside her as she surveyed the best way to evacuate thousands of people.

ALEX'S BODY SHOOK, but his fingers did not. "Nine minutes," he said out loud. "I got through to the security at the exchanges. Let's hope they believe my bomb threat. The exchange hasn't frozen trading yet, though."

"Shut it down," Roxie said in the same voice devoid of emotion. "The group is working on the other locations. I almost have London's exchange safely closed and the bomb threat was called in. I fully expect we'll be shut down quickly since they'll have our phones."

"Birch will take care of it," Alex said as he worked his way through the highly protected firewall of the exchange. "This is going to take a while."

"We don't have a while," Roxie reminded him. "Dark Surfer has Australia taken care of. He's called in three threats to different agencies and trading has been frozen. He's moving onto Zurich now."

"Fire Dragon is locking down Hong Kong," Alex said as the message flashed across the top of his computer. "He needs five more minutes."

"Eight minutes," Roxie said as the clock continued to move.

"WHY THE FUCK aren't you evacuating?" Dalton demanded as the guard outside the main entrance refused to let him in without authorization. A couple of the guards moved Dalton and Grant away from the entrance and to the side of the building as a few more guards began to surround them. Jason had taken off the Kevlar and was mingling through the pedestrians as a fire alarm sounded in the building Valeria had ran into. Six minutes.

"Why don't you show us your badge?" the main officer asked with his hand on the butt of his holstered gun.

"Call the president. He ordered us here," Dalton said with clenched teeth. This was the one time he'd kill for identification. The guards laughed and Grant nudged him. When Dalton looked up, Grant was focused beyond the cluster of guards they were standing with at the side of the building. Flashing a badge and walking right through security was none other than Brandon Locke.

His hair had turned lighter, his features leaner, but there was no mistaking that sharp nose and the scar that ran along his cheek. There was no doubt in the way he held himself, the way he walked with purpose, that he was ex-military. And there was no doubt there was a bomb in the bag he carried in his right hand.

A second alarm sounded from behind them and the guards turned to look. It was the building Lizzy had gone into after blocking traffic a block away. But there were still too many people on the street and Locke was almost to the front door.

"I'm calling this in," the officer said, pulling out his walkie.

"Shit," Dalton cursed as he shoved the guard in front of him out of the way and sprinted forward as Grant pushed the guards down and went into the middle of the street.

"Gas leak! Evacuate the area immediately!" Grant yelled a moment before a taser was shot at him. Grant rolled his eyes as he yanked it out of the vest.

"Locke!" Dalton yelled. The man stopped as he walked toward the front doors. In one hand was a duffle bag, and Dalton knew exactly what was inside it. If Locke made it inside and that bomb went off, *Mollia Domini* would win. The exchange would be crippled. The market would crash. Retirements, savings, pensions—all gone.

"Five minutes!" Grant yelled as he shoved people away from the exchange. Guards rushed him and the sound of a helicopter grew so loud that Dalton momentarily looked away from Locke.

"NYPD!" Dalton heard Crew's voice boom out from a speaker on the helicopter. "Evacuate the area immediately!"

Locke looked around, and his eyes caught Dalton's. They stared, and when recognition set in, Locke ran. Dalton hurdled the security blockade as he used every ounce of energy to push himself harder and faster.

Locke's hand was on the door when Dalton tackled him. His shoulder rammed into Locke's side, sending them crashing to the sidewalk. Dalton didn't hear Crew continuing to evacuate the area from the air. He didn't notice the doors to the exchange open as people ran screaming from the building. All he saw was what looked like a car's key fob remote in Locke's left hand and Locke's finger reaching for the red button.

"I'll blow us right now," Locke grunted as Dalton smashed his hand into his stomach.

Dalton grabbed for Locke's hand as Valeria came out of nowhere and slammed her foot into his face. Blood poured from Locke's now crooked nose. "Key fob detonator!" Dalton yelled as Grant and Valeria joined the fight.

VALERIA DIDN'T like the order Dalton had just given her to try to keep Locke alive, but it was an order from Dalton, and she'd follow it. She fought to get Locke in a stranglehold as Dalton and Grant grappled for the detonator. But Locke was a fighter, a dirty one at that. She should have seen it coming, but she didn't. He pulled a knife with his right hand as he kept the key fob closed tightly in his left fist.

"Dalton!" Valeria screamed, but the warning was too late. The blade slid into Dalton's hip. Dalton grunted as Locke twisted the blade. He smiled, his teeth outlined in blood from where she'd broken his nose.

Val had had enough. She would take this son of a bitch out now and be done with it. She didn't care that sirens were approaching. They had less than three minutes left and she refused to let Locke or anyone from *Mollia Domini* win.

"Two minutes!" Crew called from the helicopter hovering above the exchange.

Val bent to brace her arm into place across Locke's throat when pain exploded in the side of her head. Valeria screamed as a man bashed the side of her head with his closed fist. "Miss me?" Manuel's thug dug his hands into her hair and dragged her away from Locke who flashed a victorious smile.

"You didn't think I'd come alone, did you?" He laughed as Valeria struggled. Grant was up with his gun drawn, leaving Dalton to grapple with Locke.

"Get the bomb!" Val ordered to Grant. "I can take care of myself!" Valeria placed her hands over the man's hands on the top of her head from where she sat on the ground. She brought her knees up, planting her feet on the ground and pushed off her right leg. She used the force and momentum to kick with her left. The toes of her sneakers slammed into his forehead as she tried to twist away. Suddenly he let go and Valeria was free. She rolled away from him and leapt up to see Lizzy standing over his unconscious body.

Another man was already closing in on them while Val scanned the area. People were pouring out of all exits at the exchange, screaming. The officers had their hands full with the evacuation to the point they didn't even see Dalton lying across Locke as he tried to pry his fingers open. And another man was raising his hand with a gun aimed right for Grant.

"Grant, watch out!" Valeria yelled from where she threw a punch at one of Locke's men before pulling out her gun and shooting him. The man with the gun aimed at Grant and fired as Grant dove behind one of the steel barrier posts lining the sidewalk. Bullets pinged off the post and into the Kevlar of Grant's shoulders and back.

"I got him," Lizzy yelled over the panic as she closed in on the new man coming at Valeria. Valeria took off toward the man storming at Grant. She was behind him as she fired. The man fell forward to the ground, blood running from his head.

"Forty seconds," Crew yelled over the loudspeaker as he buzzed the area, ordering people to evacuate.

Grant was already up and running toward her as they both hurried to Dalton's side. Valeria stopped next to him and aimed the gun at Locke's head.

Locke just laughed. "It's over. The bomb detonates on its own. You get to go to hell with all these people and me. What a dilemma. You take the bomb, but then I press this button and it explodes in your hand. You fight me for the fob and the bomb explodes anyway because you'll never get it before the timer goes off."

"Get the bomb!" Lizzy yelled as she delivered an

uppercut that sent another Locke goon crashing to the ground.

"Take it and we all die right now, but in another twenty-five seconds we'll all die anyway." Locke gave a bloody, toothy smile of victory as he looked at Dalton to his right.

"I don't think so, Locke."

Locke's head spun to the left as Jason stabbed a knife into Locke's wrist, slicing through the soft tissue it came in contact with. Blood sprayed across Valeria's legs and the fob dropped to the ground. Grant grabbed it as Locke stared in shock at his mutilated hand and up to Jason's cold face.

"Wolski, you bastard. It's too late. You're a dead man."

"Get the fuck out! Fifteen seconds!" Crew shouted as he pulled his helicopter up and started to fly out of the blast zone.

"I've been a dead man since your group killed my wife. But I'll be damned if I let you take another person to hell with you." Jason pulled the gun from his holster and fired.

"Run!" Valeria yelled as Locke stared back at them with open eyes and a trickle of blood running from the bullet hole in the center of his forehead.

Grant grabbed Val's hand and Dalton was already taking off after Lizzy, but Valeria turned at the last minute and saw Jason grab the bomb. "JASON! NO!"

"Eight, seven, six," Dalton was counting down as they ran. Grant tugged her to follow and the last thing Valeria saw was Jason stuffing the bomb in a thick cement flower planter.

"Three, two—" Grant flung Val forward around the corner of the building across the street and covered her body with his as the earth shook. Windows cracked as heat and debris filled the air. Then silence. The only thing she could hear was the ringing in her ears.

Valeria looked around, seeing Dalton and Lizzy farther up the street from them turn and look at the exchange. Val felt Grant flip her over. His mouth was moving, but she didn't hear anything except for the ringing.

Valeria looked over Grant's shoulder at the exchange. She couldn't see it through the smoke and dust. It had to still be standing or *Mollia Domini* would have won, regardless of Locke's death, because if the exchange went down, the markets would be completely wiped out. There would be no more trading, no more stock market, it would be even worse than the 1929 crash. And in today's global economy, if any of the bombs succeeded, then there would be a ripple effect and every market around the world would suffer.

"Val!" Off in the distance, a whisper of her name drew her attention. It was Grant, right next to her, yelling her name.

"I can barely hear you," Valeria yelled.

"Are you hurt?" Grant screamed, even though it still sounded like a slightly louder whisper.

Valeria shook her head, but then it came back to her. "Jason!"

25

BIRCH LOOKED at Tate and Humphrey. It was ten o'clock. The phones began to ring off the hook. It had happened.

"Mr. President," Jessica said quietly from the door to the Oval Office. "Director Kirby is on the phone for you."

Birch picked up the phone with dread. Was his team safe? Did they stop the explosion? "Yes?"

"There was an explosion at the New York Stock Exchange."

"Damage?"

"I don't know yet. I'm on my way up there, and the New York office is calling me in a couple minutes when they arrive on site. We got the call through 9-1-1. There were reports of two Secret Service agents on site. Would you know anything about that?" Kirby asked.

"I do. They're my men. Secure the area. I'm on my way to the site."

Director Kirby paused for a moment. "Are you sure about that?"

"Only terrorism would cause an explosion at such a location. I'm determined to show them the US won't back down. We'll meet there, and I want all the intelligence you have on this."

"Yes, sir."

Birch hung up and looked over at Humphrey. "Did you get hold of them?"

Humphrey shook his head as Tate covered her gasp with her hand. Tate looked down at her phone. "Governor Orson Benning is calling in the New York National Guard and has just declared martial law. He's sending private security to all major targets including water and electric."

"Get my helicopter and get Orson on the phone," Birch yelled as Humphrey called in Marine One.

"It's ringing," Jessica called out as Birch grabbed his secure line.

"This is President Stratton, get me Orson now," he demanded of Orson's secretary in a stone-cold voice as Tate rose.

"I have to get to the press room. Any comments?"

Birch shook his head. "Tell people to remain calm, and I'll address the country as soon as I know something concrete."

"Let me know the second you hear from our team." Tate tried to be strong. She *was* strong. She'd proven it. But the thought of her friends dying was crushing.

"SOMEONE ANSWER THE FUCKING PHONE," Alex cursed as he paced the hotel room. He was trying to contact his friends while Roxie was talking to Fire Dragon and Dark Surfer.

"There were reported explosions in each location, but nothing yet on where those explosions took place," Roxie called out as Alex hung up on Lizzy's voicemail.

"I was in the process of shutting down the market when the president of the exchange froze all trading." Alex angrily hung up when he heard Dalton's voicemail pick up. He dialed Valeria and closed his eyes. The news was reporting the explosion, but nothing was known at this time. "I can't stand this. Let's go."

"Go where?" Roxie asked as she looked up from her laptop.

"To the exchange. I can't sit here wondering if my friends are all dead."

Roxie typed something quickly into her laptop and closed it. "Let's go. They'll email me when they hear anything."

"It's not secure."

Roxie shrugged as she reached out for his hand. "I know someone who will recue me if I get arrested. Let's go see about your friends." Even though she said it reassuringly, there was worry in her voice. The same worry he felt as they hurried to the street and took off running.

"ARE YOU TWO HURT?" Lizzy asked as she limped toward where Grant was helping Valeria from the ground. The back of Grant's vest was torn to shreds from debris and bullets, and he was covered in dust and glass.

"I'm banged up, but Grant took the brunt of it," Valeria yelled a little louder than she needed. "But, Jason. He took the bomb and shoved it in a planter. There was no time—"

She didn't need to finish. They all turned to look at where the large rectangular cement planter had once been. There was nothing but a hole in the ground now. The windows from the exchange were blown out, the stone was covered in black powder, and a fire burned the American flags hanging from the exchange.

Fire trucks, police, and agents were flooding the scene. "We have to find him," Grant said, looking to Dalton.

"They'll try to kick us out," Lizzy told them as they limped, cursed, and hobbled their way toward the center of the explosion.

"You can talk them out of it," Valeria said with confidence.

"I won't leave a man behind." Dalton tightened his jaw as he and Grant pushed past the flood of nearby police rushing toward the scene.

Valeria and Lizzy shared a worried look as they followed. There was smoke, people crying, screams as people looked for friends or family, and the wails of sirens. But Lizzy didn't hear it. Instead, she felt as if the world stopped moving when Dalton and Grant stopped running and dropped to their knees next to the entrance of the exchange.

No. No, please, not Jason. Lizzy stopped behind Dalton and Grant. Valeria reached out and took her hand. As one, they stepped forward.

Jason was lying on the sidewalk against the building. Blood streamed from his neck where a large sharp piece of concrete was embedded. That wasn't his only injury. Blood flowed from his stomach and leg. Grant and Dalton worked in quiet unison to stop the bleeding, but even though Lizzy wasn't a trained paramedic like Grant and Dalton, she knew the result. Jason wasn't going to make it.

Valeria squeezed her hand and dropped it. She moved to wedge herself between the wall and Jason's head and placed her hand on his shoulder. Lizzy hurried to join her and reached for his hand. His face was black from the fire, and he had debris and glass lodged all up and down his body.

"You saved us by putting the bomb in the planter," Valeria told him as she stroked his cheek.

"Hang on, Wolski. That's an order," Dalton commanded as he ripped his belt from his jeans and applied a tourniquet to Jason's thigh where blood was flowing out.

"I'm sorry," Jason whispered softly. "It's an order I can't follow. It's an order I don't want to follow."

"No, Jason," Dalton said harshly. Emotion was choking his voice and he refused to look at Lizzy. He kept his eyes on the wounds as he and Grant worked quickly to stop as much bleeding as possible.

Lizzy squeezed Jason's hand as tears fell silently down her cheeks. "Love each other," Jason whispered, even more faintly this time.

"No!" Dalton yelled. "It's an order, dammit!"

"It's okay, Dalton. I've been trapped in a cage of misery since Michelle. Don't you see? I'm free now. I get to be with my love once again." Jason's lips curved up into a soft smile as his eyes focused heavenward.

Lizzy couldn't hold it together anymore when Dalton and Grant began CPR. She raised Jason's scraped hand to her lips and pressed her lips against the back of his hand. "Thank you, Jason. Be at peace."

Valeria wrapped an arm around Lizzy as EMTs and police surrounded them. Dalton and Grant refused to give in to their grief until Lizzy and Valeria pulled them off. Dalton's eyes were red as anger and grief warred within.

"It's over," Lizzy said softly, rubbing her hand over his cheek and down to his chest. She held him then as the body bag was closed over Jason's body.

"It's not over until I kill them all."

"I'm good with that," Valeria agreed. "But right now we need a plan. And we need to get our teammate home."

Seconds later, they were surrounded by FBI. Their fingers were laced behind their head as they were searched and weapons were seized. Nobody said a thing when they were questioned and handcuffed.

BIRCH HUNG up the phone with the British prime minister and let out a breath. They'd been stopped. No exchange had been brought down. It had been close, but they'd survived. Trading had been frozen and would remain frozen while this threat was dealt with. But catastrophic damage had been avoided.

Governor Orson Benning, on the other hand, was trouble.

"What's the word?" Humphrey asked from his spot on Marine One.

"The exchanges are safe. All assailants were killed. Bombs were either detonated through a remote or by the timer. There was damage to the outside of the buildings and cars, several civilian injuries, and a couple deaths of police officers. The threat has been neutralized. For now."

"There's a reason you couldn't get through to Orson. He just happened to be in New York City today. He's heading down there with the guards to make a statement at the bombing site. He's saying you're weak on terrorism, and he's not going to let his city burn while you do nothing. Martial law has been enacted. A curfew is set. No large public gatherings are being allowed. And he's ordered the reopening of the stock exchange as a show of strength."

"Son of a bitch." Birch slammed his hand on the leather couch. "Get me Alex and Senator Epps."

"STOP!" Grant growled when an EMT went to remove Jason's body. "He's our man, and we're not leaving him."

"Look, right now I'm thinking you might be one of people responsible for this," the agent said. "So, I give zero shits about what you want right now. Not until you start answering questions. The officer over there identified you two as the ones pretending to be Secret Service moments before the explosion. Until you tell me who you are working for, you're coming with us."

"Get Director Kirby on the line," Lizzy said as they watched Jason's body being lifted onto a stretcher.

The agent snorted. "You want me to just ring up the director?"

"Yes. And you tell him you have FBI Agent Elizabeth James in custody and that she's requesting she be released immediately. Then see what he says."

"You're FBI?" the agent said skeptically as the other men around them chuckled as if this were a joke.

"I was. Kirby wants me back. Call him."

"She's legit," a female agent said, holding her phone over for the agent questioning them to see.

"Hey, boss!" the agent called out to a man directing other agents and talking to the police. "This woman is a former agent and says she wants us to call Director Kirby. She's with the two men pretending to be secret service."

The boss put a phone to his ear as he walked toward them. He was in his late fifties, and Lizzy knew he had been running the New York office for the past eight years. He was a tough as nails agent, but a reasonable person. He wore the standard-issue dark suit with an American flag on the lapel. His dark brown hair had gray around the temples, but otherwise you would have pegged him to be a decade younger than he was.

"Yes, sir." He lowered his phone and looked right at her. "I'm Special Agent in Charge Cromwell. What's your name?"

"Elizabeth James."

He repeated it into the phone and then nodded. "And you guys are my two Secret Service agents?"

Dalton and Grant nodded.

"And who are you?" Cromwell asked, pinning Valeria with a stare.

"She's with me," Lizzy said in her best agent voice.

"FBI?"

"DEA," Valeria answered with the same no-nonsense agent voice.

"Yes, sir. I'll hold them here."

"I want to go with my fallen partner," Dalton requested with a nod to where Jason's body was being loaded into an ambulance.

Cromwell spoke into the phone with Kirby and then hung up. "You may go with your partner. I don't know who you are, but the president has ordered your release. The rest of you stay here. I have questions for you, and Director Kirby will be arriving shortly."

Dalton turned to Grant, and with a single hard look, Dalton conveyed his instructions to him. "Be careful," Dalton whispered to Lizzy before kissing her quickly on the cheek.

"We'll see you back in DC," she told him, sounding more

confident than she felt. Right now she wasn't sure exactly what was going to happen.

"What were you doing here?" Agent Cromwell asked.

"I'll only talk to Kirby," Lizzy told him as her team all stepped back and took a seat on the sidewalk in unison.

Cromwell stared down at him until his phone rang. "Cromwell," he answered and then suddenly stood up straighter. "Mr. President." Cromwell's eyes shot to them sitting on the sidewalk as he nodded. "I'm sorry, did you say National Guard? What the fu—? Sorry, sir."

Lizzy, Valeria, and Grant looked at each other. National Guard? Cromwell continued to nod. "I want to make sure I understand my orders. You want me to stop the governor from visiting the bombing site and withhold all information about the investigation from him?"

"That's interesting," Lizzy whispered as Val and Grant nodded their agreement.

"Yes, Ms. James is here. One moment." Cromwell walked over to her and handed her the phone. "The president wants to speak to you."

Lizzy stood up and took the phone into her hand. She put it to her ear. "This is Elizabeth," she said as she walked down the street far enough so that Cromwell wouldn't be able to hear her conversation.

"I got hold of Alex. He's minutes away. He has information with him that connects Governor Benning to *Mollia Domini*. I want this information to get to Cromwell, but he can't know where it came from. I want to see Orson in handcuffs in front of the camera crew he's bringing along."

"What's going on, Birch?" Lizzy asked, dropping her voice.

"Orson is on his way there with the New York National

Guard. He's declared martial law as well as declaring me a terrorist sympathizer and demanding the immediate reopening of the exchange. Alex found illegal payments from Manuel Hernandez, along with emails outlining a conspiracy to have me overthrown through a military coup. CBL Services Group and Brandon Locke play into his plan as CBL will be taking over security in place of the feds."

"Well, you won't have to worry about Locke. He's dead." Lizzy paused. "And so is Jason."

Birch was quiet for a long moment. "How?"

"He shot Locke so he couldn't detonate the bomb, and then with seconds remaining on the timer, he took the bomb and stuffed it into a large cement planter. It helped minimize the damage. Because of his actions the people running from the exchange's side doors were saved and the building itself was saved. There's damage, but it's superficial. Dalton is with his body."

"I'll make sure I put in an order for Jason and Dalton to clear the medical examiner's office ASAP and arrive home with full military honors," Birch sighed.

"He told us he was finally free to be with Michelle again." Lizzy turned her back to the FBI and wiped the tears forming in her eyes.

"They will both be honored. I swear to it." Birch paused again and took a deep breath. "I've also gotten a phone call from Sebastian and a message from Bertie Geofferies asking when the stock exchange will reopen. The president of the exchange was smart enough to defer to me for the time being, but those two are putting immense pressure on him to reopen as soon as the building is cleared."

Lizzy pushed the hurt and pain of loss back down inside of her and focused on the now. "I know why. Their artificial intelligence software must be ready. The best time to test it is when the market is headed toward a big movement. And it's going to most likely plummet if it's reopened too soon."

"The question is, did they know about the attack?" Birch asked, finally addressing the possibility that his best friend could be the head of *Mollia Domini.*

"I don't know, but I have a plan."

"The operation is in your hands. Take them down by any means necessary. Now."

Lizzy took a deep breath. "Consider it done."

26

"THIS IS REAL?" Agent Cromwell asked as he looked at the stack of papers Roxie had shoved in his hands before running off.

"Governor Benning is guilty of treason," Lizzy said matter-of-factly as her team surrounded Cromwell and handed him back the papers after reviewing them. No other agents were allowed near them. They were too busy keeping Orson away from the active crime scene. "You have the authority to arrest him. Verify the information, personally, right now and then see what Director Kirby has to say. I would say it would make your career, but I've heard about you from other agents. You're not the kind to care about that."

"No, but I am the kind to care about treason." Cromwell said in his graveled, no-nonsense voice. "I'm guessing you're not going to tell me how I was suddenly handed this?"

"Nope. And since you don't know the person who handed it to you, you can honestly testify to it being from an anonymous source," Valeria pointed out.

"I haven't figured you out yet. I've run background on

you all. You're active military, you're a disgraced DEA agent who works as a bartender, and you're a disgraced FBI agent who owns a bar while working for SA Tech. Yet you have access to extremely sensitive information and the president wants to talk to you."

"Does it matter?" Lizzy asked with a shrug.

"You of all people should know I can't let this go." Cromwell thought about it. "I got it. You work for SA Tech. Sebastian Abel's company. The same Sebastian who just so happens to be friends with the president."

Lizzy smiled but didn't say anything.

"You're not going to say anything, are you?"

"I'm a civilian now. There's nothing to say. I don't have the power or the authorization to do anything. But when I see a wrong, I try to right it. It's in my FBI blood after all."

Cromwell looked at her, but before he could ask more questions a helicopter landed a block away, and Director Kirby and his staff hurried toward them. Conrad Kirby had obtained his job as director because of his connections with the late President Mitchell, but Dalton had discovered Kirby and Senator Epps were actually trying to investigate *Mollia Domini*. Well, Kirby and Epps had investigated as best they could while confined to legal restraints Lizzy and her team didn't necessarily follow. Now, standing next to Agent Cromwell, they appeared to be two peas in an FBI pod. Kirby was a decade older but had the same crew cut as Cromwell. The main difference was the mustache Kirby sported.

"Agent Cromwell, what do you have?" Kirby looked to the right and solemnly nodded his head at her. "Lizzy. I was surprised to hear you were here."

Cromwell noticed the informality but didn't say anything. Instead, he briefed Kirby and handed him the papers Roxie had given him. Kirby's eyes widened, and Lizzy knew he was putting it all together. The missing bomb he and Senator Epps were looking for, Phylicia's death, Sandra's disappearance, and Orson Benning initiating the beginnings of a military coup. He looked at Lizzy and then back to Cromwell. "Did she give these to you?"

"No, sir. I don't know who the person was. An attractive young woman with glasses and multiple ear piercings gave them to me."

"The president is close behind me. We need to show him this and then act. I've had reports of Benning waiting to get here to hold a press conference. If this pans out, we'll arrest him for treason. In the meantime, get a judge to give us a warrant for Manuel Hernandez. Do it all yourself. I don't want any of this leaking out."

"Yes, sir." Cromwell shot off with his phone to his ear.

"Now, would you like to tell me what's going on?" Kirby asked as he grabbed Lizzy's arm and pulled her away from her team. Lizzy smiled as Grant and Valeria simply followed.

"We were just in the right place at the right time and were able to help evacuate the area."

"Bullshit."

Lizzy shrugged. "We've given our statements. You know we didn't plant the bomb. It was a person named Brandon Locke. Never heard of him, but Cromwell knew who I was talking about. I believe we've done our civic duty. I need to get back home. I have a bar to run after all, and you know how those FBI and DEA trainees get when they don't get their drinks on their nights off." Lizzy looked to Grant and Valeria as they heard another helicopter approaching. "Let's go."

"James," Kirby called in a warning voice.

"If you have any questions, you know where to find me," Lizzy yelled back with a wave of her hand. "Birch is arriving. We can't be seen with him. It was enough that he asked to talk to me, but there can't be any photos of us together," she said softly to her team.

"Alex is waiting for us. Dude, his hacker girl is hot," Grant whistled.

Valeria smacked him on the back of the head. "Dude?"

"It's contagious," Lizzy smiled. "I need to tell you what Birch told me. We have orders. But to pull off my plan, I need to get back to Quantico."

"Then let's go," Valeria stated, pulling out her phone and calling Crew.

"You can call someone, but you can't call me? Dude . . . Roxie and I have been worried sick," Alex called out, running toward them as Valeria told Crew to pick them up at the top of Sebastian's hotel. "Where's Dalton and Jason?"

Their faces must have told him the answer. "No," Alex whispered.

"Jason saved us. Dalton is escorting his body back to DC," Lizzy told him as Roxie took Alex's hand in hers.

"What can I do?" she asked in a soft British voice.

"If I turn a phone on that has a GPS tracker on it, can you both trace who is receiving the GPS coordinates?" Lizzy asked as they began their trek toward Sebastian's hotel.

"Sure. Think of it this way," Roxie said as Grant slung his arm around Alex and began talking to him, "if someone can access the phone to see where it is, then we can use the phone to access who is snooping around on it. You just need to know what you're doing."

"And you know what you're doing?" Valeria asked. "You're like, twenty."

"Twenty-two, and I've been doing reverse hacks since primary school." Roxie winked and Valeria grinned.

"I like her. And she doesn't say 'dude.'" Valeria grinned before slapping Alex's back. "Come here, dude." Val wrapped her arms around Alex as the others walked on. "We're family, and it hurts when we lose our family. But we need you now. Do you think you can help us bring the rest of these bastards down?"

"You bet I can."

BIRCH STEPPED off Marine One like a man possessed. He had wrapped his ribs and would be damned if he'd even flinch because of the pain. Right now the country was about to learn he wasn't a president who bent to pressure. Tate had called, and the press release was ready. Flint was also working on a piece that would be released shortly after he decimated Governor Orson Benning.

Kirby approached him as Humphrey kept anyone else from getting close. Humphrey motioned to his Secret Service team to keep people back, and they formed a large circular barrier around him, Humphrey, and Kirby. "Have you been briefed on Orson?"

"Fill me in," Birch ordered, hoping the information Alex had found actually made it through the wheels of justice.

Kirby told him of the information and even added that Agent Cromwell of the New York office already had a warrant for both Orson and Manuel Hernandez's arrest. "I wanted to ask you first, but it's a clear case of treason on Orson's part. We have Hernandez on bribing a public official, wire fraud, and money laundering. Of course, being in Mexico has problems. We can ask for extradition."

"Do it, but let's give Orson enough rope to hang himself. Let him start talking, and you'll know the right time to arrest him. Let Cromwell do it. You and I can stand together during my speech. Then I want to see you and your good friend, Senator Epps, in my office tonight at eight."

"Epps?" Kirby feigned confusion.

"Yes, Epps. I know you two were looking for the bomb stolen from the FBI lab in Quantico. Subsequently, I think we found it when I was having dinner." Birch looked toward the exchange and shook his head. "If you think Orson is the only one trying to bring me down, you're naïve. There were coordinated attacks all over the world today that were stopped by good intel. That lets us know more's at play than only one missing bomb. I'm ready to read you and Epps in because I need your help to bring the whole ring down."

Kirby was quiet for a moment. "You have your own intelligence? Geez, Lizzy *is* working with you, isn't she?"

"Lizzy who?"

"Lizzy fucking James." Kirby looked around. "She was just here."

"I know Lizzy James, but only through her father. Lance James and my father were war buddies. That's beside the point, though. The point is you knew something was off, and you didn't come to me. Why?"

"I didn't know who to trust," Kirby admitted.

"Well, I didn't either. Now it's time to take a leap of faith and bring you two into the fold. Are you ready to take them down, Kirby?"

Kirby looked around him with a sad face. "If I'd been doing a better job, I would have caught this bastard before he got to you and your team. Damn right I'm ready to take them down."

"Then let Orson through and get ready to go."

He smashed his fist on the table as Roland read the reports to him. His blood stirred, and by the end of the report, it was boiling. They had all failed! "Where the fuck is Sandra?"

"I-I don't know," Roland stuttered. "But since she's not here and there was obviously someone giving the authorities inside information, I can only assume she was flipped."

"What about Governor Benning?"

"He's moving forward with the plans. He's declared martial law, has called in the state guards and CBL Services, and is about to give a press conference."

He turned up the television as Benning stood in front of the bombing site at the New York Stock Exchange. He was six feet, but looked seven by the way he carried himself. Orson's football muscles had softened as he approached sixty. Orson's black hair was fading as gray now sprinkled through it. He liked Orson because he didn't give a shit about politics. Orson gave a shit about himself. Always had as a kid growing up in the Bronx. Orson hustled and didn't care if he crossed the lines to get what he wanted: power. And that meant Orson was pretty easy to predict and control.

The news station zoomed in on Orson closing his eyes and bowing his head in a moment of silence for the asshole who had been killed, minimizing the impact of the bomb. Because of that bastard, the exchange was still standing and his plans were in the shitter. Although he did always have a Plan B. And right now Orson was enacting it.

With a mix of sorrow and anger in his eyes, Orson opened his eyes and looked directly out to the first responders and lines of New York National Guardsmen who had been brought in to guarantee his plan went into effect. "I've failed you. I swore I would protect you, and I allowed this unspeakable act of terror to occur."

Orson shook his head with disgust. "I allowed it to happen because I fell in line with politics, and I knew better to do that. I knew when President"—Orson sneered the word as if it had a bad taste to even say it—"Stratton ordered me not to act on intelligence of a terror attack, instead saying the feds would handle it. Well, I should have known better. After all, the only person able to look after New York is a New Yorker."

The crowd cheered, and he smiled as Orson seemed to grow even taller as he felt the power the people were ready to hand over to him. "That's why I am taking back our city, our exchange, and our state from the feds. New York will no longer be accountable to a sham of a president who purposely kept you, my New York brothers and sisters, in the dark, allowing terrorists to damage our beloved city. The New York Guard will be here to keep us safe as I kick out all the federal agents. I refuse to comply with their corrupt orders! The president"—Orson again sneered, looking off camera to where he bet Stratton stood—"no longer has any power over the citizens of New York. To show the terrorists of the world, including the president, it takes more than a failed attempt to scare us, I demand the exchange be reopened immediately!"

"Amazing," Roland murmured on the video conference screen as he watched the speech. He agreed. Orson was a natural. He'd need to be watched, though. If someone was able to manipulate others so quickly, he wasn't naïve enough to think Orson wouldn't try to take over his spot on the top. It was a delicate balance trying to find men and women who craved power, but who weren't powerful enough to take his.

He watched as the crowd cheered, and then a man a couple years younger than Orson in a dark suit and wearing an American flag pin slowly walked over to Orson, grabbed his left arm, and cranked it behind his back. His right hand was cuffed to his left. Even Orson didn't react until he felt the bite of the handcuffs locking into place.

"What the fuck do you think you're doing?" Orson screamed. The camera zoomed in on them and the cuffs.

"I'm Special Agent Cromwell of the New York office of the FBI and you, Orson Benning, are under arrest for treason against the United States, sedition, wire fraud, bribery, and abuse of power in relation to your actual and active participation in the assembly of a group that the president of the United States notified Congress of his declaration of open war against. You have the right to remain silent—"

He stared at the screen as Orson was dragged away in handcuffs. "Assembly of a group? Declaration of war? What does that mean?" Roland asked as he stared off camera at his own television.

"Stratton knows about us."

BIRCH WATCHED Orson rant against federal authority and protest that they had no right to arrest him. He was governor after all. Well, was. Birch looked out to where the National Guard moved with their weapons toward Orson. The entire New York FBI office blocked their path, and Birch knew it was time to stop the escalation.

Birch stepped up onto a pile of debris as the news reporters yelled questions and the Guardsmen looked confused on whose orders to follow. "This morning I have declared open war against a group who is secretly trying to overthrow not only the presidency, but also the rights of citizens all over the world. This group has killed world leaders, plotted these bombings, conspired with the world's deadliest drug lord, and manipulated you through the use of the media. This group reaches from Hollywood actors, news anchors, and to the presidents of banks. From princes to presidents. From FBI agents to senior members of the Hill. They're behind my attempted assassination, this bombing, and much more.

"Today I notified Congress of a group known as *Mollia Domini* and my intent to rid this world of these power-hungry parasites who care nothing for your lives, rather only how they can help themselves. Today they wanted your money and the power that came with controlling it. In coordinated attacks against multiple major exchanges around the world, they were going to take it. They were going to take your livelihoods, your pensions, and your hard work. But today I say, no more hiding in the shadows. No more playing the puppetmaster behind the scenes. This isn't the type of war we are used to fighting, but make no mistake, this is a war."

There was no clapping as Birch looked around. There was confusion, murmurs, and looks of fear. "The founding fathers of our great nation divided the power among us. They had learned from history that the power should stay with the people and so have I." Birch looked directly into the camera. "I will not march out in our colors so you can shoot me down like wars of the past. You will never see me coming. I will not fight fair. I will take everything from those trying to tear our country apart. I will expose those in the media who tell lies in order to manipulate the public."

Birch looked behind the cameras to the journalists. "There will be a list emailed out by my press secretary along with a statement and evidence of every media manipulator, and you'll recognize quite a few *trusted* names. In fact, some of you are standing right here. You might want to think what your next article or report says before that email is sent. It's time to do your job—report the truth. Director Kirby and I have a plan and all I can say is"—Birch looked directly into the camera again—"we're coming for you."

27

THE NEXT MORNING'S sun shone bright as Grant slipped his arm around Valeria. He watched the C-17 land at Andrews Air Force Base, the tires leaving a thin sheen of rubber on the well-used runway. Grant looked to where Valeria held Lizzy's hand and Lizzy held Tate's. Birch and Humphrey filled in the end of the line, facing the back of the plane. Behind them were Alex, Roxie, Director Kirby, and Senator Epps, as well as over fifty wounded veterans Jason and Michelle had helped over the years, all in dress uniforms of their military branches. Off to the side, the members of Andrews Air Force Base lined up ten rows deep, dressed in their finest.

The back of the plane lowered into a ramp as the Honor Guard moved forward. Grant straightened his maroon beret with the silver pin of the USAF Pararescue attached. Valeria looked at him sadly before he strode in even steps toward the plane with President Stratton, dressed in his Army blues.

Grant, in his Air Force dress, stopped at the base of the ramp. Two members of the Honor Guard lined up on each side of the ramp, facing each other. Grant stepped into the third spot on one side and Birch filled the third spot on the other. Grant looked up and met Dalton's wounded eyes. Someone had brought him a dress uniform.

Grant held his salute for Jason, while the rhythmic sounds of marching boots echoed in the early morning peace as the wounded veterans formed a row slightly behind each side of the Honor Guard. Grant and the rest of the Honor Guard moved up the ramp and saluted. They reached down, and with heavy hearts, lifted Jason's flag-draped coffin. Three by three, they carried him down the ramp and past the soldiers who were now living full lives, thanks to Jason and Michelle. Lizzy, Tate, Valeria, Alex, and Humphrey watched with tears as Jason's body was loaded into the back of a hearse.

In silence, the men and women who had gathered overnight to bury Jason moved to the caravan. Grant and Dalton sat with their fellow PJs as the rest of the team rode to Jason and Michelle's farm under the anonymity of blackened windows. Secret Service cleared traffic as curious onlookers pulled over on their morning commutes to watch the procession. Media was not invited, although Tate would be releasing selected photos in a press release honoring Jason at a later time.

IN TOO SHORT A TIME, Dalton was back in the woods looking at Michelle's grave. Next to her, Jason's coffin rested as the minister talked about Jason and the good he and Michelle did. They were united in love on earth as they were now in heaven. The flag was removed, folded, and handed to Birch. Jason and Michelle had been all each other had. By the way

Birch clung to the flag, Dalton knew his memory would live on.

In silence, those who had served with Jason, or who had been helped by the couple, lined up behind Dalton and Grant. Dalton stepped up to the coffin, saluted it, and unhooked the silver USAF Pararescue pin in the shape of a parachute with a guardian angel holding the world safely in her hands in the center and placed it on the coffin. *That others may live* was engraved on the pin. Jason had lived and died by their motto. Dalton closed his hand into a fist and slammed it onto the pin, embedding it into the coffin. With a deep breath, he turned and silently joined Lizzy as Grant set his PJ pin next to Dalton's and with a hard hit, sank it into the top of the coffin. PJs, Seals, Marines, Rangers, Army, Navy . . . they all showed up as pin after pin was hammered in long straight lines down the length of the coffin until only one person remained.

Birch may have been in military dress uniform, but it was his own presidential pin he pulled from his lapel and placed in the middle of the coffin. Birch bowed his head and then with a final echoing sound, hammered the gold pin. The center was enclosed in a ring of fifty stars and emblazoned with a golden eagle clutching an olive branch in the right talon and thirteen arrows in the left, symbolizing peace and war. As Birch saluted, everyone rose. The sound of the twenty-one-gun salute echoed across the woods as Jason was laid to rest.

BIRCH SAT in the chair between the two couches in the Oval Office as Senator Epps and Director Kirby sat down on either side. It had been a long morning, honoring Jason, and he was in pain, but important matters needed to be addressed. Tate had sent out a press release and Birch had talked to the White House press corps who had thinned greatly since Tate had released the evidence that *Mollia Domini* had paid off reporters. But now, it was time to fight. Lizzy and her team were beginning their plan while it was time for Birch to play politics.

"I never knew you had men helping you," Epps said with a sigh. "Retired military volunteering to protect our country. I've submitted Jason and Michelle for congressional honors. Who are the others? I believe I have met a couple in my house."

"Thank you for honoring Jason and Michelle, but I'm not disclosing the volunteers. Neither Congress nor the office of the president pays them, so I'm not required to disclose anything. Suffice it to say, their lives are, and will continue to be, on the line for some time."

Kirby nodded. He knew most of the team by now. But there was no evidence to prove he was correct, so he'd kept his mouth shut. "Orson is raising holy hell."

"I don't care. He's a small fish. After he's been exposed, no one will listen to him. We're after the big fish now. What I need is the FBI working with the locals so there's no confusion that federal law still rules. Yet we're in no way trying to infringe on anyone's rights. I've talked to the heads of the exchanges that were hit and everyone is in agreement to keep the exchange closed until the head of *Mollia Domini* is captured or killed." Birch leaned back in the chair as Epps looked worriedly at him.

"But how long will that take?"

"There's no saying, but I would guess very soon. It won't be closed any longer than it was after 9/11, which I know wreaked havoc on the markets. But it's so much better to open when we're stable than to have the panic caused now with sell-offs, no matter what Bertie Geofferies or Sebastian Abel preaches to the media."

"Mr. President," Kirby said with worry, "I hate to point this out, but you're not allowed to authorize a private military of retired agents to wage a legal war. Any evidence collected would be a bitch to take to a judge. And anyone who kills under those circumstances would technically be guilty of murder."

"I haven't authorized them to do anything. They're a volunteer group of concerned citizens who know they are bound to the laws of this country." Birch could practically hear Humphrey snort, but there was no denying the team existed. Not after New York.

Kirby looked annoyed at the loophole, but the only thing he could do about it was to arrest them if he ever got evidence they'd committed a crime. "How about if I send someone with them?"

"Or how about you give Elizabeth James her job back, only this time she reports directly to you?"

"She won't be able to work at SA Tech anymore," Epps pointed out.

"I think she'll be okay with that." Birch grinned. He knew she'd already drained his account and got another million dollars from Bertie Geofferies in his desperation to beat out Sebastian. "And maybe she'll want to take a nice teaching position at the academy after this is all over. You know, since she's still trying to run her father's bar."

"One of these days I'll learn what she's already done for this country and will probably need to buy her a beer. Until then, I'll have her reinstated immediately," Kirby said, pulling out his phone.

"What do you need of me?" Epps asked. He'd been a big

help making sure Birch's declaration of war against *Mollia Domini* would be as well received as possible.

"I need you to keep Congress under control. My office will be here for you and my door open to any member of Congress who has a problem. But I need you to try to pull rank against some of the people we have evidence against."

Humphrey pulled out a packet and handed it to each of them. They opened it and started to read Thurmond's affidavit. "Jesus," Kirby said, looking up at them, "the secretary of state?"

"And many more. There's your evidence. All nice and legal, wrapped in a little bow." Birch stood as Epps shook his head.

"Branson Ames is alive?"

"He is. And he's ready to come home and testify as soon as it's safe. Take this information, gentlemen, and unify our country against those wanting to tear it apart."

Birch shook their hands and wished like hell he could be with his team at that moment. But it was all in their hands now.

LIZZY HUNG up the phone and announced, "I've been reinstated, and Kirby got the DEA to hire you back, secretly of course." Lizzy grinned at Valeria. "Kirby is coming along with a team of handpicked agents, so we'll be ready to go shortly. Kirby is meeting us here in forty-five minutes."

The group relaxed as Lizzy poured them a beer. Roxie was having a blast serving the patrons of Lancy's with Alex. Dalton and Lizzy were behind the bar, standing shoulder-to-shoulder pouring beers. Valeria was sitting on a barstool resting her back against Grant, who was standing behind her with his arms around her. It was yet another calm before the storm.

Buzz and Snip happily took their seats as Crew and Flint slid into the next two spots. Crew turned to Valeria and Grant and raised his beer in silent salute.

Buzz shook his head. "It's a sad day when a Marine's matchmaking skills have been undercut by a pair from the Chair Force," Buzz said teasingly, making fun of Grant and Dalton being part of the Air Force.

"What did two old jarheads expect?" Dalton grinned back.

"Two grandsons and neither could land a date," Snip complained.

Crew and Flint rolled their eyes at each other as Grant bent his head and whispered something into Valeria's ear. The smile she sent Grant could only be described as wicked. She slid from the chair, and the two of them hurried from the bar.

"Be back in forty minutes!" Lizzy called after them, earning the bird from Valeria and a chuckle from Grant.

"I am so jealous right now," Dalton whispered as he pressed against Lizzy while reaching for a beer mug.

"The closet is soundproof," Lizzy whispered back.

"Alex! Come watch the bar. We need to restock the shelves."

Lizzy handed Roxie a tray filled with beer mugs and shot glasses as Alex walked around the bar. "I just restocked the shelves at the beginning of the week."

"You know Buzz and Snip," Lizzy said with a smirk. "Always drinking the stock when we're not looking."

Alex shrugged and Lizzy met Dalton in the storeroom. It was their secure meeting place. Thanks to Alex, it was soundproof and constantly swept for bugs, but none of that mattered as Dalton pressed her against the locked door with a ravenous kiss. This wasn't the time for lovemaking. Knowing what they were walking into sent complex emotions flying out the door. They were operating on basal feelings, and right now seduction and gentleness weren't on the brain. Hard, primal passion was.

They didn't talk. They didn't espouse words of love. Their tongues battled and their bodies took what the other was offering.

VALERIA STROKED her fingers in a slow circle over Grant's chest as she lay in his arms. Grant softly ran his hand over her hair and down her bare back. She looked out the window of her small bedroom at the early night sky. Complete darkness was still hours away, but the evening held the hints of night as the shadows lengthened. Not too much longer and they'd be walking into the shadows one last time.

"I know you'll get defensive, but I have to say it," Grant said softly as he ran his hand over her head and down her back again. "Dalton and I are trained in combat warfare. It's our job to fight our way into enemy territory, achieve our objective, and then fight our way out. You and Lizzy are not."

Valeria opened her mouth to argue, but Grant used his finger to close her jaw. "Hold on, lass. Let me finish."

Valeria let out a loud breath of annoyance but didn't say anything.

"You know Dalton loves Lizzy. While I'm not one to talk about my feelings, you're important to me, Valeria. I don't know what I'd do if something happened to you. You've captivated me since the moment you climbed into my helicopter under fire. I'll do anything to get back to you.

That's the reason I'm asking you to consider staying here with Lizzy, or at least not going in to fight with us. Let us focus on the objective and getting back to the women who hold our hearts."

Valeria felt Grant hold his breath. Normally she would rip into him, but this time she didn't. Why? Because she felt the same way. "I was going to ask you to stay with the helicopter and let Lizzy and me handle it."

"You . . ." Grant stopped himself and then laughed. "What a pair we make, lass."

Valeria smiled against his chest before swinging her leg over his and straddling him. She sat up and looked at him as his hands cupped her breasts and ran his thumbs over her beaded nipples. "Aye, we sure are," she playfully mocked before lifting her hips and sliding him deep inside her.

28

To say the director of the FBI, the administrator of the DEA, and the attorney general caused a commotion as they strode into Lancy's was an understatement. Even Lizzy was shocked by the show of authority. She'd expected Kirby, but Janet Salinger, the head of the DEA, and William Knoll, Attorney General of the United States, were enough to have the recruits practically falling out of their chairs.

"It's like the holy trinity of federal law enforcement," Valeria whispered as she watched them in full buddy-buddy mode, shaking hands with recruits and smiling as if a war hadn't just been declared.

Knoll chuckled to a group surrounding them. "No, we were just here for a meeting about the DEA and FBI training facilities. Nothing exciting, but making sure you all are getting everything you need during training before sending you out to fight for justice."

"He's good," Valeria said as her lips turned up in an amused smile.

Janet Salinger was something of a hero to Valeria. She'd just been appointed the administrator of the DEA and had fought tooth and nail up the ranks. She wasn't a politician. She was an experienced agent.

"Are you Valeria McGregor?" Janet asked, taking a seat at the bar, letting Knoll and Kirby handle the trainees.

"Yes, ma'am," Valeria said, showing her the respect she'd earned. Janet's dark brown skin glowed with the excitement of the upcoming fight. Her black hair was slicked back around her face into a bun. Instead of wearing a suit like Kirby and Knoll, she was in jeans, a black T-shirt, and a pair of combat boots. Valeria had feared Janet would never live up to her reputation, but so far she exceeded it.

"I have something for you." Janet set a badge and gun onto the polished bar top along with a piece of paper and pushed it toward Val. "That's an order signed by Mexico, granting the DEA and FBI joint task force on drugs access into the country with the objective of taking Manuel Hernandez and Roland Westwood into custody."

"How did you get this?" Valeria asked, amazed. She'd tried to work with local Mexican officials many times with no success.

"There's a rumor that Manuel wants to run for president." Janet smiled in such a way Valeria knew how that rumor started. "The current president is happy to cooperate. Do you know where they are in Mexico?"

"No, but we have a plan to find out."

"Welcome back, Valeria. You never should have been fired in the first place. Know your old office has been cleaned. The job to run it is open if you're interested." Janet set her elbows on the bar top and looked at Val as if she were measuring her up.

"I'll think about it. Right now I have another job to do first."

Janet smiled approvingly. "Good. Then let's get this party

started."

"You're coming along?"

"Sure am. So is Kirby and Knoll. There's no way any of this will fall apart in the judicial system. Not with us as witnesses. I'm with your team. Kirby and Knoll will be with Delta team."

"Okay, let's do it."

THE BAR MUST HAVE THOUGHT they were crazy. There was no other explanation for the attorney general, the director of the FBI, the administrator of the DEA, Lizzy, Dalton, Valeria, Grant, Alex, and Roxie to be crammed into the small storage room.

Everyone was shoulder to shoulder around the edge of the room as Lizzy, Dalton, Valeria, and Grant stood in the center of the room.

"Okay, here's the game plan," Lizzy said, holding up a cell phone she'd retrieved from a vodka case. "This phone belonged to Dan March. I'm sure there's a tracking app on it. There's never been a body found. *Mollia Domini* will come if we turn this on. And that's what I'm hoping."

"You want them to come to us, so we have home field advantage?" Kirby asked.

"Yes and no," Lizzy began. "I have a good idea where Roland Westwood and Manuel Hernandez are, based on previous tracking. There's a compound via tunnels from the US into Mexico. I want the phone to be turned on and Alex and Roxie to track the GPS signal being sent from the phone. I want to know who's retrieving it. I'm betting it's someone in Mexico. Then I want that phone mined for all intelligence while we go into Mexico via the same tunnels I think Manuel's men will come out."

"It's a diversion," Janet said, smiling. She was in her late forties but hadn't developed the politician softness that Kirby had. She still looked as if she could handle herself in a shootout, especially with the three guns Lizzy had been able to spot on her so far.

"Yes," Lizzy answered. "I need the bees to leave the hive."

"Where do you want us?" Kirby asked.

"San Diego."

TATE RESTED her head on Birch's shoulder. They sat on the couch in the Treaty Room in the middle of the night as Lizzy and her team flew to California. The White House was quiet at this time of early morning, especially in the residence. Crew was sleeping in a nearby chair. He'd been asked to keep an eye on her and Birch while the group of agents and Lizzy's team took a military plane. They'd be arriving in an hour.

She and Birch had thought about going to bed, but they couldn't. Not when their friends were walking into the lion's den. Instead, they found themselves sitting in the Treaty Room with the televisions on silent, waiting to see if there was a leak in the handpicked team sent to collect Manuel Hernandez and Roland Westwood.

Birch rubbed his hand over her shoulder as he kept her pressed tight against him. "How are you feeling?"

"Anxious. What happens if—?"

"Shhh. We don't talk about what-ifs. We're prepared, and they will handle anything that comes their way."

"I don't think I could stand another flag being handed to us." Tate looked to where Jason's flag had been placed in a shadow frame and hung on the wall.

"I know. Right now we must simply have faith that good people doing hard work will win. It's never easy to stand up against the hate and the division that a group like *Mollia Domini* thrives on achieving. They want to pit us against each other to tear our country and democracy apart so we don't see what they're doing in the shadows. We'll be doing their job for them. Chaos creates opportunity for the ambitious. It's exactly what they want to happen to us. It's easier to overtake half the people than a united country demanding their leaders check their power and do what's right for their citizens. No, *Mollia Domini* wants that division so they can tell their oblivious victims what they want to hear. Give me your freedoms and I'll make the others pay. That was their plan. To kill the strong leaders, to tear the country apart by having them pitted against each other, and then swoop in as the savior. It's the dictatorship playbook." Birch kissed the top of her head reassuringly.

"But they've already lost. They lost the second your speech was given. The second people started questioning the bias. They lost the second people took a hard look at who was screaming hate, and instead looked past it to all to the quiet goodness of the people trying to do what was right. That was when *Mollia Domini* lost. They saw our field team even though they never laid eyes on them. Good will always win. Because I have faith that, at our core, we all want to not only be good, but do good."

Tate lifted her face to his. "I hope so. I almost lost you to the hate once. I won't be able to stand it if they come after you again."

"Even if they don't, they'll never succeed. Will you come with me?" Birch asked as he sat up straighter.

Tate nodded and took hold of her crutches to stand.

"Where are you two going?" Crew asked sleepily when

Birch grunted as he stood. His ribs were still tender, but improving each day.

"We'll be right back. Don't worry, we're not leaving the residence."

Crew nodded before lying back against the cushion of the chair. His feet were propped on the matching ottoman as he drifted back to sleep.

Tate used her crutches to maneuver out of the room, Birch held the door, and then walked side by side with her down the hall. They made their way to the solarium and then out the door onto the promenade. She breathed in the heaviness of the night air. The dew that came about before the sun made everything seem fresh and clean as they walked to the baluster and looked out over the fountain on the South Lawn and at the Washington Monument, lit up against the dark sky.

"Soon we're going to be caught up in the whirlwind of the mission. Once again, *Mollia Domini* will be all we're talking about, either in victory or defeat. Right now, right here, I have you beside me." Birch stepped up behind Tate and set aside her crutches.

Tate leaned against the baluster and smiled. "I'm glad we have a moment together alone. I love you, Birch. I've missed not being at your side more, but with all this craziness—" Tate took a deep breath and let some of the tension go. She felt powerless as her friends headed straight into danger.

Birch leaned forward and brushed his lips against hers before taking them fully in his. Tate sighed. She was home in Birch's embrace. "Thank you for loving me despite me being president. We'll never have a normal relationship."

"You're worth it, Birch. It's not the amount of time we have together but what we do with it. And I know one thing

I can't wait to get back to doing," Tate leaned up and kissed the man she loved.

GRANT SMILED DOWN AT VALERIA. She was asleep in the plane but had slumped over in her seat and curled into his side. She was snoring softly and drooling on him, but it was the best feeling in the world.

This woman who had shot her way into his life was suddenly at the center of it. He pulled her closer to him and shut his eyes. They were almost to their destination, but his mind was on Valeria instead of the jump they would have to make. The thought of Valeria being injured caused his heart to seize. How could he tell her he loved her? How could he explain it when he didn't understand it himself? It had hit hard and fast, but he wouldn't change it for anything. It motivated every move he made. Tonight he could end *Mollia Domini* and tomorrow he could ask Valeria to marry him. But until *Mollia Domini* was caught, there was no point saying things that might distract them from the mission at hand.

"Ten minutes to jump," the pilot called over the speaker.

Valeria shot up and wiped her mouth. Then she looked at his black shirt and squinted. "Sorry about that," she said, wiping at the wet spot. She looked at all the agents Kirby had brought with them to Quantico. They'd taken off from the Quantico MCAF, a small airstrip on the base, in a small cargo plane. There was a wall cutting the plane in half. The front half was crammed with seats and through the airtight door was the cargo area.

Grant grabbed her hand and brought it to his lips. "Be safe tonight. I'm depending on you to have my six."

"I thought you'd have my six," Valeria teased as they

stood up and made their way to the back of the small cargo plane. Lizzy and Valeria had made a stand when Dalton and Grant tried to talk them out of going. Surprisingly, it was Janet Salinger who had been the most difficult. She'd wanted to go in first, but finally they all agreed Dalton and Grant had the most experience breaching buildings. Then Lizzy and Valeria, with Janet covering the back. It has been a hard sell, but finally they'd all agreed.

Dalton closed the door to the cargo area once everyone was in then locked it shut. Each person grabbed a parachute and started pulling it on. Valeria tugged her parachute into position and Grant checked it before she checked his. "How are you doing, Salinger? Feeling rusty after sitting behind a desk for so long?"

"Bite me," she snapped even though she had a grin on her face.

"You all ready?" Dalton asked as he strapped the helmet onto his head. The helmets were not only bulletproof, but they also had night vision cameras attached to them.

"I've been ready since before you were in diapers," Janet called out. Valeria snorted, Lizzy chuckled, and Dalton and Grant shot worried looks at each other. Janet didn't become the head of the DEA by riding a desk, and she was reminding them of that.

"Okay," Lizzy called, bringing them all around. Alex and Roxie joined them even though they weren't jumping. "We jump and rendezvous here," she said, pointing to a map. "The mountains, right here, are very rocky. Grant and Dalton will be here, near the door. Janet, I want you across the way with the rifle, and more importantly, the camera. Everything needs to be recorded for the courts."

"You've got it," Janet said, double-checking her rifle

straps and holding the gun tight against her body in preparation for the jump.

"Then Val and I will take these points here to be able to lay cover fire if Dalton or Grant become exposed. Any questions?" Lizzy asked, holding out the map to let everyone get one last look.

"I think we're good," Alex said seriously, causing Janet to look confused. "And dude, I got the best idea for the ambush."

"Alex is so smart." Roxie looked up at Alex with adoration, and he blushed.

"I thought Kirby had this handled," Lizzy said, not sounding happy.

"But I came up with an even better plan. A boat."

"A boat?" Dalton asked.

"Yeah, we'll turn on the phone once it's on a boat. It'll look like Dan's coming into port. It funnels them into one area to get onto the boat and it'll keep civilians safe. I can do all I need to do from the boat as long as it has a stable internet connection."

Everyone was quiet for a moment. "Dude, great plan," Dalton jested, smacking Alex's back. Lizzy smacked them both and rolled her eyes.

"But it is a good plan. We'll see you on the other side." Lizzy grabbed Alex into a brotherly hug before Kirby came over to open the door. The plane had steadily been decreasing its altitude to near thirteen thousand feet. It was time to jump.

"Come on, kids. Let's let them get to work. Keep in touch, James," Kirby yelled over the sound of the engine as he pushed Alex and Roxie back toward the seats. He checked the door, wrapped his arm around a cargo net, and pushed the cargo hold button.

Wind raced in as the back of the plane opened. It might have been a warm summer night, but not at thirteen thousand feet. Here the wind had a bite to it as they stepped forward. No longer alone, Lizzy still was depending only on her team. It didn't matter five FBI agents handpicked by her and Kirby were up front. They weren't part of the team that got them this far. They weren't her family. The people she was jumping out of a plane with were. Except Janet. However, if Janet ever wanted to leave the DEA, Lizzy would make a place for her on the team.

"Now!" Kirby yelled.

Grant jumped. His body was yanked from the plane by the rushing air as he disappeared into the night. Dalton grabbed her before Lizzy could jump. "If we get through this, we're getting married." He kissed her then as her mouth hung open in surprise. The kiss was hard, fast, and then nothing but the wind dancing along her still moist lips. Dalton had jumped.

"Holy shit, you're getting married," Valeria said as she turned her back to the night air. "I better be your maid of honor." Valeria opened her arms, laughed, and jumped backward into the night.

"Are you crying?" Lizzy asked Janet as they moved to the edge of the cargo ramp.

"That was the most romantic proposal I've ever seen. If only someone had been shooting at you right then. You better say yes," Janet ordered before jumping.

Lizzy shook her head and jumped. The air fought her body, disrupting it as she pulled her arms to her side to speed up her freefall. The bastard had jumped before she could give him her answer. For that she was going to make him wait.

29

ALEX LEANED over the rail of the boat and threw up for a third time. Whose bright idea was it to get on a boat? Roxie rubbed his back, and his humiliation was complete. He'd wanted to be a hero. He wanted to be Dalton or Grant. Instead, even Humphrey was more macho than he was. What hero got seasick the second they left shore?

"Maybe we should move back onto land?" Roxie suggested.

"No," Alex said, wiping his mouth and taking a sip of water. "It's a good plan."

He took a deep breath and looked around the boat. It was a confiscated drug smuggling boat the DEA had lent them. The deck of the small million-dollar yacht had an outdoor couch that was actually storage space. Two agents were going to be hiding there in order to surround whoever came for Dan's phone. The Coast Guard was out of sight, but fully armed and ready to move in to surround the yacht as soon as they were given a signal. Inside in the large saloon on the main level would be Kirby with three agents and the phone. One agent in the empty refrigerator, one in the bathroom, and Kirby sitting at the kitchen table with an agent that freakishly resembled Dan March. Lizzy had helped with supplying the right clothes and haircut from the last time she'd seen him, which no one bothered to fill in Kirby or anyone else about.

Alex and Roxie would be hidden in one of the bedrooms while Knoll would be operating the cameras in the main bedroom. The whole living room was rigged with cameras and bugs. Audio and video of the apprehension would be taken. Knoll, as attorney general, lectured the agents nonstop over the last hour of the flight about what to say and what not to do.

Alex walked on wobbly legs toward the living room. AG Knoll had been handpicked by Birch just two weeks before. He'd been confirmed three days ago, and now he was in on the biggest takedown in history. Birch had told Alex that Knoll was a former JAG lawyer before becoming a prosecutor. He was levelheaded and didn't scare easily. Alex didn't know about Knoll, but he was scared shitless. The AG was dressed in a freaking suit, sitting with his legs crossed and flicking a piece of lint off his tie. Alex guessed he really didn't scare.

Roxie slid her hand into his, and Alex realized he was shaking. God, he was embarrassing himself. Roxie looked nervous, but she wasn't puking over the rail like he was. Alex took a deep breath and felt his stomach roll. He swallowed hard as everyone turned to look at them.

"Are you ready, son?" Kirby asked him.

Alex nodded. He didn't trust himself to speak when his stomach was pitching a fit.

"One minute," Roxie said cheerfully as she took out her phone and cranked up some heavy metal. Kirby looked assaulted, Knoll bounced his leather-clad foot to the music, and the agents were a mix of confused and amused.

Alex and Roxie opened their computers side by side in the small built-in booth in the kitchen area. They sat shoulder to shoulder and someone placed a trashcan next to Alex with a smirk. Alex would have been insulted, but the fact is, he would probably need that trashcan.

Alex hooked the phone up to his computer and nodded. Kirby leaned over the table and turned the phone on. No one spoke as the guitar wailed and the bass strummed. The phone's screen popped up, and Alex went to work breaking into it.

"Got it," Alex said as he pulled up the phone's GPS app.

"I see it. I'm inputting the information now," Roxie said, chomping on a piece of gum. Her entire being was focused on her computer.

"We've got action," Alex said as his fingers flew over the keys of his laptop. His program tore apart the app. Instead of seeing what a normal person saw, he saw numbers, data, and code. Code that gave him the unique signature of the person currently accessing the GPS in Dan's phone.

"Come on," Alex muttered as he followed the digital crumbs the intruder left.

"It's a Mexican IP address," Roxie said, her eyes never leaving the screen.

"Dude." The high Alex felt as he outsmarted the person on the other end of the internet rushed through him and pushed the nausea down. "Duuuude . . . come on, come on. Yes!"

"What?" Kirby asked but Alex didn't answer.

"I'm closing in on it." Roxie said.

"Verifying." Alex double checked the location and pulled up a satellite image of the location.

"Got it," Roxie said. "Are you ready?"

"Go," Alex ordered, knowing they had found them. Roxie read off the GPS coordinates. "It's a match. We found them, and it's right where Lizzy and Dalton thought they would be."

"Where?" Kirby asked as he and everyone else squeezed in to look at Alex's laptop. "Is it Manuel's main compound?"

"No. It's on the northwest side of Laguna Salada."

Kirby looked at the map. "Pull up images for within a quarter mile of the border. There has to be some structure we're missing."

"There's a small solar field here that feeds electricity to this cell phone tower." Roxie pointed to the screen.

"Enlarge it," Kirby said, moving to stand behind them.

Alex zoomed in and cocked his head. "There are tire marks leading from the main road to the solar field, but no cars can be seen."

"There," Roxie said excitedly. "Zoom in closer."

Alex did so and saw the back end of cars hiding under the solar panels. "There's a structure under the solar panels."

Kirby slapped his back and Alex grabbed the trashcan and puked.

"Sorry," Kirby cringed. "You two did good. Give the coordinates to the drone."

Roxie sent them off to Grant who was carrying the Raven drone. He would assemble it and fly it from his location. Soon a feed came online as the drone was launched.

"Here we go," Kirby said, crossing his arms over his chest and watching.

HE LOOKED into the television where he projected the videoconference. "What the hell am I looking at?"

"It's the location of Dan March's cell phone, señor."

He sat up on his couch with surprise. He'd been woken in the middle of the night by Manuel, and that normally didn't bode well. The past two days had been shit, and he was plotting his next move. He'd put this whole plot into motion, and he sure as hell wasn't going to let Birch Stratton ruin it for him, no matter how many people he had working with him now. He shook his head. He'd been cut off from the president, and it worried him.

"Dan March? That bastard. Where the fuck is he?"

"Ten miles west of San Diego, heading into port."

Right now he needed Dan. He had thought he was dead, but the son of a bitch must have survived and slowly made his way back from the South China Sea on a boat. "Go get him. Give him whatever he needs—men, food, weapons. I don't know how the president found out about us, but we need to shut him up and fast. Send him to DC with orders to take Birch out once and for all."

"I'll send my men now."

He disconnected from the video call and ran his hands over his face. Where had everything gone wrong? Well, at least one thing he was sure of. He didn't become as rich and powerful as he did by giving up when things got tough. No, he would fight this to the bitter end. Presidents came and went, but power . . . you held on to that. You accumulated that over time. And he'd accumulated a lot of power. Enough power to take down a sitting president, that was for sure.

~

"So, DO YOU LOVE HER?" Dalton asked Grant as they lay on the ground of the mountain, hidden by rocks.

Grant didn't answer. Below them was the entrance to the tunnels. Grant maneuvered the drone to the coordinates Alex had given them, but so far he didn't see any movement.

"Stop pretending you can only do one thing at a time. I've seen you lay cover fire as you carried out a patient. You can damn well talk to me while you play your video game," Dalton ribbed.

"Of course I bloody well love her," Grant said, zooming in on the solar panels.

"Have you told her?"

"No. I've been a wee bit busy. But when I do, it'll be more romantic than your proposal." Grant grunted. "There's no movement."

"Do you feel that?" Dalton asked.

Grant pressed his hand to the rock and closed his eye. "There's a vibration."

"Get ready," Dalton said quietly into his coms. "Is everyone in position?"

"Yes," came the soft replies.

A moment later the door below them opened and six men rushed out speaking quickly in Spanish. Grant grabbed Dalton's ankles and Dalton reached down to the door before it shut and wedged a piece of cardboard along the top of the doorjamb. The door looked closed, but there was enough of a buffer to prevent the lock from engaging.

No one seemed to notice as they tore the camouflaged tarps from the helicopter. The pilot climbed into the helicopter and the five men stepped into the back as the engine was turned on and the blades began to spin.

"There's only room for one more person on the return

trip," Grant said after pulling Dalton back up and hiding behind the rock.

"That makes sense. They think they're picking up Dan. But where did they come from?"

"There must be a structure under the solar panels." Grant and Dalton rolled onto their stomachs and hid their heads as the helicopter took off. From the air, their camo would hide them well enough.

They listened to the helicopter take off and fly west toward San Diego before moving. Grant moved the drone to see the cars beneath the structure and confirmed people were there. Grant dropped to the ground outside the door and propped it open with a rock. Dalton hurried to the various cars covered by the tarps and slashed all the tires as Lizzy, Janet, and Valeria made their way to the door.

"Six men left with the intention of coming back with seven. Taking the helicopter tells me they're interested in speed and getting Dan March back here immediately. We don't know how many are left behind, but if Manuel is here, there will be some tough fighting ahead of us," Grant told them as Dalton jogged over to join them.

"The middle SUV is ours. I took off the distributor cap." He held up the small object that would prevent the car from starting and put it into his pocket.

"Manuel always has four men with him," Valeria cut in. "Two like to act tough and shoot anything that moves, but they're easy targets since they can't hit a target to save their lives. They'll just spray the area with a rifle. It's the two quiet ones you need to worry about. One is good with knives. He's the one with a beard. The tallest is a crack shot. Go after those two first."

"We need either Manuel or Roland alive. Preferably both," Lizzy told them. "If this is indeed where Sebastian was taken, and if Sebastian is telling the truth, then Roland may very well be here and can lead us to the head of *Mollia Domini*."

"Got it," Janice said, looking at the body cam she was wearing. "Ready for us to turn this on?"

"Let's go," Dalton said as she and Lizzy turned their body cams on. Dalton and Grant slipped into the tunnel. Grant felt Valeria's hand tap his shoulder letting him know she had his back. Grant looked at Dalton and then to the lights. The tunnel had electricity.

"There could be cameras," Grant whispered.

Dalton nodded and halted the group with a quick hand signal. He reached up and inspected the wiring. He pulled out his knife, and with a quick slice the lights went out. Grant lowered his night-vision goggles and felt Valeria's tap again. She was ready. He tapped Dalton and they were off.

The tunnel smelled of earth and was noticeably cooler than outside. The walls were reinforced with wood as thin wires connected the exposed bulbs that hung along the wall by nails. What was more interesting were the metal railroad tracks down the middle of the tunnel. It was probably used to move heavy amounts of drugs into the US. When he looked back, he noticed Janet aiming her camera at them. Valeria was three feet behind him, and Lizzy was similarly behind Dalton. Both had their weapons drawn.

Grant looked ahead. They moved quickly and quietly farther down the tunnel. The tunnel seemed to go on and on before it began to widen. Railroad carts were off to the side. A forklift was ready to be used. Shovels, crates, and old pallets were stacked against the wall. Ten yards ahead of them was a door that matched the door on the outside of the mountain.

The tunnel was over half a mile long and let out on the

other side of the border. The distance lined up with the cell tower he saw from the mountains on the US side. Grant motioned for the women to take cover behind the forklift as he and Dalton got to work with the explosives. Explosive breaching wasn't the first thing they wanted to do. It was dangerous, and it took knowing the precise amount of C4 to use. Too little and the door wouldn't open, but Manuel would know they were there. Too much and the whole tunnel could collapse on them.

Dalton and Grant fell to the ground and set up the detonating cord, blasting caps, and C4 along a wooden lath. Grant used his teeth to tear the specialized tape to bind everything together. Carefully, they lifted it to the door. As Dalton held it, Grant taped it to the metal. Lizzy, Valeria, and Janet pushed a heavy railway cart to the right of door. Grant wanted to yell at them for not staying put, but he knew exactly what they were doing, and it was the right call. Grant stepped back behind the nearby forklift to the left of the door and felt Valeria grab his arm behind him as Dalton primed the det cord and lit it. Dalton headed for the rail cart feet from the door where Lizzy and Janet stood pressed against the wall.

Instead of hiding, they readied their weapons. They looked down briefly as the C4 exploded and then they charged forward. The rush of battle filled Grant as he and Dalton raced through the opening with guns raised.

30

VALERIA PUSHED past the smoke and saw they were in a storage area. Drugs wrapped in bricks were packed five feet high on pallets. On the far side of the square underground room, a door was thrown open.

Dalton shot and a man dropped, revealing a set of stairs. Valeria could hear the footsteps above as people reacted to the explosion. Lizzy and Val took cover behind a pallet of heroin five feet from the door as Dalton and Grant took each side of the door.

Dalton looked to Grant, who gave a nod and then went low. He fired as Dalton tossed a flash grenade up the stairs. The men flattened themselves against the wall, covered their ears, and closed their eyes. Valeria did the same as she felt the sound from the grenade shake her body like a clap of thunder. She took a deep breath and pushed aside the nerves. She used the fear to propel herself up the stairs behind Dalton and Grant.

They were pinned at the top of the stairs. Dalton was low and Grant was high as they fired into the main part of the living area. The ceilings were low, only seven or eight feet, but it was above ground. The solar panels were essentially the roof. The floor was polished cement and there was a large black leather sectional couch, a polished table in a white kitchen, and behind that were closed doors, probably leading to bedrooms.

Valeria looked around. There was a window behind them, but too high up for her to reach from the stair landing. If Manuel had any sense, he'd be trying an escape, and she couldn't let that happen. Valeria turned among the smoke and smell of gunfire and shot out the window.

"Lizzy, help me up!"

Lizzy looked toward the window and back to Valeria and cupped her hands.

"What are you doing?" Grant yelled.

"Clearing the outside. I'll come around in through the back and trap them."

Before Grant could argue, Valeria put her foot in Lizzy's hand and was boosted up and out of the window. The morning sun was beginning to rise as the dark dampness of the tunnel seemed far away.

Valeria whirled at the sound behind her and saw Janet drop to the ground next to her. Janet didn't say anything, just continued scanning the area. Four cars were lined up to their right near the front door of the compound. Valeria closed her eyes and focused on the sounds between the bullets. The sound of glass shattering told her Manuel was coming right to her.

Valeria ran crouched over to the nearest car. She opened the gas tank and tore a strip off her shirt. She stuffed it down into the gas tank and then lit the end dangling out. There was no way she'd let Manuel escape.

"Come on," she whispered to Janet as they both ran to the front door of the house. The house was painted desert tan with only small narrow windows above her head. No wonder they had trouble seeing it.

At the sound of heavy footsteps running toward them, Valeria raised her weapon and pressed her right side against the house. Janet dropped to her knee just to Valeria's left and aimed for the men running toward them. In less than a split second, Valeria and Janet saw who was in front, decided it wasn't Manuel, and fired. The two men dropped as Val aimed her gun around the corner. Manuel darted behind a solar tower support as a volley of gunfire erupted from the house.

"Manuel Hernandez, DEA, put your weapon down and come out with your hands up," Valeria yelled a second before the fire reached the gas tank. The car exploded, shooting up and breaking some of the solar panels and rocking the rest of them. Valeria made her move. She ran to where Manuel was hiding right as Manuel stepped out with his knife.

"Watch out!" Janet screamed but it was too late. The knife sliced and Valeria screamed in pain.

GRANT COUNTED FIVE MEN. Three of his team were left in the building. It should be easy, but the enemy was hiding behind the polished concrete island and an overturned natural wood dining table. An explosion shook the house, sending the solar panels rocking above them. Above all the noise, Grant heard a scream.

"Val!"

"Focus, Grant," Dalton ordered as he fired a round of shots into the dining table.

"We need to make a move," Grant said as he looked around the room. "Cover me, and I'll run for the couch."

Grant didn't wait for Dalton to agree because he knew he wouldn't. The chance of being shot was high, but something needed to be done or Manuel and Roland would escape while they were pinned down in the stairwell.

Grant focused on where he wanted to run and kept low as he darted around the furniture. His shoulder was already sore from the shots Locke fired into his vest in New York, and he wasn't surprised when he felt bullets slam into him once again.

Grant dove for cover behind the couch. He slid on the polished concrete floors and slammed his shoulder and head into the leather couch. Adrenaline was pumping as he hunkered down and felt the soreness, shortness of breath, and blood. Not all the shots had been stopped by the vest. Blood bubbled from a bullet wound on the outside of his upper arm before disappearing under the dark camo he wore, but he felt the hot sticky liquid running a path down his arm.

Grant held up his hand signaling to Dalton to lay cover before pulling out two handguns and taking a deep breath. Lizzy had taken Grant's place by the doorjamb and the two opened fire on the two locations on opposite sides of the room. Grant crouched and then exploded. He leapt onto the couch and launched himself up and over the back of it. He sailed through the air and over the table where two men were hiding. Grant's momentum slowed when a bullet ripped into his leg from behind the counter on the other side of the room at the same time a scream came from the same spot. Grant dropped like a weight to the ground, rolling with guns in hand as he fired.

The two men behind the table hadn't even turned all the way around when the bullets tore into their heads.

Suddenly there was silence as Grant, Dalton, and Lizzy looked around.

Dalton ran across the room with Lizzy right behind him. "Are you hurt?"

"Nah, just a couple holes." Grant looked down at the blood dripping out the cuff of his sleeve and down at the dark hole in his hip.

"We need to dress that," Dalton said, pulling out his first-aid kit.

"No time. Find Roland and Manuel. I'm fine." Grant took a deep breath and pushed himself against the wall to stand. His arm was numb, but his hip was on fire, a burning feeling so hot he swore his blood was going to boil. "See, I'm fine."

"You're white and sweat is pouring off your face," Lizzy pointed out.

"Yet I can still shoot a gun, so let's go."

Grant turned to the two doors behind them. "Dalton and I will take this one. Can you get that one?" he asked her.

Lizzy didn't bother answering. Instead she stepped up to the door and waited for Dalton to get into position. Grant held up an open palm with his pointer finger sticking out. "One," he silently mouthed before a second finger joined the countdown. On the silent three, Dalton and Lizzy kicked in the doors.

A man's scream came from the door Dalton had breached as Grant cursed with each step he took. Leaning against the doorjamb on his good side, he swept the area while Dalton bent over the bed and grabbed a pair of very nice loafers. Attached to the loafers were expensive trousers. And in those trousers was Roland Westwood.

"The other room is clear. Window broken. And it's much nicer than this one. I'm guessing that was Manuel's room," Lizzy said as a smile grew on her face watching Dalton trying to wrangle a slippery Roland who was trying to flail out of his grasp.

"Then where is Manuel?" Grant asked.

"Where's Valeria?" Lizzy asked as they both turned to look out front where the explosion had been.

THE KNIFE TORE through her shirt and sliced her shoulder open. "Shit!" Valeria screamed as the pain shot through her. Manuel was already moving. He was running toward the car farthest from the fireball threatening to ignite the second car.

Gunfire sounded as Janet took aim and peppered the car with bullets. Valeria ignored the pain and sprinted after Manuel, who paused momentarily, trying to decide which direction to run now that his two bodyguards were dead. He spun to face her, and the gun he pulled out had Valeria leaping behind the metal base of a solar panel for protection.

"Manuel Hernandez," Janet called out. "We're DEA agents. You're under arrest by the authority of the US and Mexican governments. Put down your gun and lie on the ground."

Valeria yelled it out in Spanish even though she knew Manuel spoke perfect English. She wasn't going to have him suddenly claim he didn't know what was happening because he didn't understand what they were saying.

Manuel responded by firing a shot at her. It pinged off the metal base. Janet began to fire and Valeria ran. It would be much easier if they didn't want him alive. Valeria pumped her arms as she pushed herself faster. Right before she jumped, Manuel turned and fired.

GRANT SHOVED OPEN the front door right in time to see Manuel raise his gun and fire it at Valeria. The momentum of the bullet counteracted her forward movement and sent her flying back.

"NO!" Grant yelled, running straight at Manuel, firing. Manuel turned to run, but then Valeria rolled over onto her hands and knees behind Manuel. She raised her gun and fired. Manuel's knee buckled as he fell to the ground. In a flurry of Spanish and Gaelic, Valeria cursed as she slowly pulled herself upright and tugged at the Velcro holding on her Kevlar vest. With a gasp, she dragged in air as the vest dangled open at the sides.

"Motherfucker!!" she yelled in three different languages as Manuel turned and raised his gun. Valeria slammed her foot into his face, sending him flying backward and crying out in pain.

He struggled through the pain, trying to find the gun he'd dropped as Valeria kicked it out of the way. Janet raced forward with her gun drawn, reciting his rights. Grant hobbled forward. He needed to see that she was safe. He needed to touch her, to hold her.

"You bitch! I should have killed you the last time I had you!" Manuel surged up, grabbing her legs and pulling her to the ground. The impact of her hand hitting the ground was unexpected and sent the gun skittering away. Her back was to his chest as he wrapped his arms around her waist, clawing for her secondary weapon.

"You already tried what, twice, to kill me? What makes you think you can succeed this time? Locking me in a barrel for days and you still couldn't kill me." Valeria raised her right arm across her face and slammed her elbow back into Manuel's face. She rolled off him as soon as his grip loosened and sprang to her feet, pulling her second gun.

"Make one move toward her, and I'll blow your fucking head off. We have Roland. You're expendable now." Grant's hard tone caused Manuel to pause and look up. Janet and Grant had him completely covered. He wasn't getting out of this alive unless he surrendered.

Valeria was standing slightly behind him as Janet stepped forward with cuffs in her hands. "Put your hands on your head," she ordered, but when Manuel moved his hands, it wasn't to his head.

"Gun!" Valeria yelled as Manuel pulled up the back of his shirt and reached for the gun, located in the small of his back. It happened too fast to stop. Manuel pulled the gun and swung it toward Janet. A trio of gunshots erupted as Manuel was hit from all directions.

Silence. Only the sound of Manuel's quivering body hitting the ground was heard. Valeria slowly moved forward and kicked the gun from his hand. Janet hurried over and pressed her fingers to his neck. "Dead."

31

Janet blew out a breath, and Valeria looked surprised to see Grant limping. He had tried to hide it, but he was losing blood, and the pain was growing. "What happened?" Valeria asked, running toward him. "Are you hurt?"

"Nothing major," Grant smiled even though his lips were thinned with pain.

"Nothing major? You're leaving a fucking blood trail!" Valeria was immediately under his arm giving him something to lean on. "Where were you shot?"

"Biceps and hip," Grant grunted as they made their way inside. "I can see you're hurt, too."

Valeria looked down at her shoulder. Blood had soaked her shirt. When she looked up and smiled at him, Grant forgot all about the pain. "I couldn't let you have all the fun."

Janet led them into the house where Roland was cuffed and sitting on the couch, waiting for them. All he was missing was a big red bow.

Dalton's eyes quickly assessed the damage. Grant could tell he was worried, but he wasn't about to stop now. Not when the mission was so close to the end. Lizzy nodded to

Janet who moved to have a clear view of Roland's crumpled and dusty suit-clad body. It looked as if he'd put up a fight after Dalton dragged him out from under the bed as one eye was beginning to swell.

Janet read him his rights as she leaned against the wall, keeping her body cam pointed right at Roland.

Lizzy sat on the coffee table in front of Roland and leaned forward, putting her elbows on her knees. "Roland, you've fucked up."

"You can't come into Mexico and assault me like this," Roland said, trying to put on his elitist airs.

"I can when I have a joint warrant from the US and Mexico. Also, you attacked a federal agent." Ah, so it was Lizzy who gave him the shiner. Grant looked at her knuckles and saw her right hand was slightly red.

Roland froze and shook his head. "My lawyers will eat you for breakfast."

"I don't think so. Now, you sit here and listen to me. Then you can talk or not talk. Okay?" Lizzy asked. Roland looked skeptical, but nodded. "Manuel is outside. Sebastian Abel is in DC. What do you think they're saying right now about you and your role in *Mollia Domini*? An organization that has attempted to assassinate the president and failed to blow up the world's exchanges."

"You've been talking to Manuel and Sebastian?" Roland asked, suddenly looking nervous.

"Sure have," Valeria said, crossing her arms over her chest.

Roland's eyes darted around the room. Lizzy snapped her fingers, drawing his attention back to her. "Right now is when you decide whether to live or die. You know the penalty for treason can be death, right? If you tell us everything from how you were recruited, to what you've done on behalf of the organization, to a list of active participants in *Mollia Domini* right now, then I'll get the attorney general on the phone and ask him to spare your life."

Roland was quiet for a second. "Maybe I should—"

"Maybe you should answer the question." Dalton crossed his arms over his chest. "Live or die?"

"If I talk, he'll kill me," Roland said quietly as all the ego and bluster was torn from him. His body deflated. His head hung, his shoulder caved inward.

"We can protect you," Lizzy promised. "But first you have to prove you deserve it."

Roland nodded his head slowly and sat silently for a moment. Then he began to tell everything. "It started three years ago during President Mitchell's campaign. I was contacted by Mrs. Mitchell. They needed money to win. She promised me a seat at the table if they won. I'd have the president's ear. When I shuffled around some money to make it look like legitimate campaign donations, I was invited to sit at the president's table at fundraisers and campaign rallies. He endorsed me and my bank as examples of the future." Roland ran his shaky cuffed hands over his face and dropped them into his lap.

"Then his chief of staff approached me about a loan for the campaign. It would have to be hidden because it was illegal. I made it happen, and a week later I got an invitation to the Tech Summit Ball. I wasn't going to go. What did I care about tech? But I was strongly encouraged to go."

Roland took a deep breath. "It was there I learned about *Mollia Domini*. I was sitting at a table with Sebastian Abel, Bertie Geofferies, his prick of a son, Rue, Sandra Cummings, and George and Helena Stanworth. Their talk turned to how the country was really run from behind the scenes.

They talked about President Mitchell's hands were tied by public opinion, laws, and regulations. George mentioned that public opinion could be changed. The public did what he told them. He told them what movie was the must-see movie. He told them what book was the next bestseller. He told them what to spend their money on. And most importantly, he told them what to be upset about."

Roland looked up at them. "Don't you see? Stanworth ran the media, and through the media he ran the world."

Lizzy nodded. They'd seen that firsthand with numerous celebrities and news anchors pushing their own agenda of lies. "So, what happened then?"

"Sebastian asked if anything could be done to help free up Mitchell. He had numerous policy ideas that would be beneficial to both Sebastian and Bertie and would get major pushback if the public knew."

"Then what?" Lizzy asked. She may have looked relaxed, but Grant could see the tension in her body.

"Bertie suggested Sebastian help him from the background. Use his influence over Stratton to get things done. Apparently Sebastian had already taken his concerns to Stratton, who shot him down, claiming what he wanted to do was illegal. 'AI should never be used to manipulate the market. Supporting bad people just because they'd let Americans come in and use up all the resources as payment wasn't right.' Stuff like that. Sebastian was going to give up."

"But . . ." Lizzy prompted.

"But Bertie said, why did they need Stratton when they had all the power they needed at the table? They could form their own group to run things behind the scenes. To be the ones to pull the strings."

"And Sebastian?" Lizzy asked, leaning back giving Roland room.

"He was called away from the table, and Mrs. Mitchell took his seat. While he was gone, Bertie talked about it more. Sandra would be the secretary of state if Mitchell won. She was already a powerful congresswoman. She said she knew of some people who wouldn't mind crossing the line. That crazy colonel of hers, for starters. I didn't know she meant murder. I thought she'd just take a tougher stance on handing out foreign aid or sanctions. But then she started having the opposition killed. I swear, I didn't know that was going to happen."

"Go back to the dinner. Sandra said she was in. Then what?" Lizzy asked, trying to refocus him.

"Then the Stanworths jumped in. They said if there was something in it for them, they could swing the media for Mitchell. Mrs. Mitchell promised them everything they wanted. Tax breaks for Hollywood studios, unlimited access to her husband, exclusive interviews, promotion of his movies . . . you name it, she said they would have it. Bertie thanked her, and Mrs. Mitchell smiled and left the table. He turned to us and grinned. *That's what fifty million will buy you—the presidency.*"

"Bertie funded the Mitchell campaign?" Lizzy asked.

Roland nodded. "I handled the money myself. But then Bertie asked me if I knew someone who was good at cleaning money before we began to move it around. I told him about Manuel. I, um, helped clean his drug money for years. A deal was made for me reach out to Manuel and see if he had interest in partially funding and laundering the money to finance our group. He did, and as a result, Mitchell withdrew border patrol agents and ordered investigations against Manuel closed once he was in office. Bertie would make a *business* payment for one of his companies to Manuel, who would clean it, and I would help launder it to get it into the hands of whoever needed it."

"Like the five million Sandra intended to give to the rebel leader in Syria," Lizzy stated rather than asked.

Roland nodded. "I know there were other people involved, but Bertie handled it all. We each had one or two people under us we gave orders to, and then we ran everything through Bertie. It was to protect our identities."

"What about Sebastian?" Lizzy asked it casually, but Grant knew this wasn't a casual question.

"He came back to the table, and Bertie stopped us from talking. I could tell Sebastian knew he was being excluded from something. He asked me about it later, but I'd been ordered not to say anything about the group. I was told to see if Sebastian could be brought up to snuff after Stratton became president. I inquired about donations to help with the African leader we wanted to get out of office. He was later assassinated, but I told Sebastian we needed money to arm the rebels. He wouldn't do it, so Bertie froze him out again. But Sebastian never really goes away. He knew something was going on, and when Manuel's accounts were frozen and Bertie didn't want to put in personal money, he said to bring in Sebastian and let him put his neck on the line. Bertie believed Stratton wouldn't jail his best friend. Suddenly, Sebastian was useful, but he was brought in wearing blinders. There was this party the other night and Sebastian was there. I took him down here. He talked with me and Manuel. And he donated some money to our cause."

Grant looked to Dalton and Val, who were very tight-lipped. They weren't reacting at all. "And what did he think about working with Bertie?"

Roland shrugged. "He didn't know who he was working

for. I told him he had to prove himself first. I told him it was a secret club of the most powerful people in the world. I'm sure he put two and two together, though."

"Who else is in the group? Besides Prince Noah, since he was conveniently killed off." Lizzy kept her eyes on Roland giving him just enough to not suspect she didn't already know the answer.

"There's a long list, but I don't have it. Bertie does. He's paranoid about being hacked so everything is written down."

"Where?"

"I don't know where he keeps it. But it's a notebook disguised inside an old book—brown leather, gold lettering. I can't remember which book." Roland started to sound tired and argumentative. "Will you call the AG now?"

"We'll have more questions for you, Roland. But you did well. You'll live."

"Manuel will kill me. And if he doesn't, Bertie will. I'm a dead man."

"We won't let them touch you," Dalton swore. "Come with me. We'll leave through the tunnels and Manuel won't know you're still alive."

"You promise?"

Dalton nodded. "These two will go with us to make sure you aren't seen while these two ladies," he said nodding to Janet and Lizzy, "will stay here to make sure Manuel is taken someplace else."

"Thank you," he said softly, hanging his head as he stood up. "I really didn't want anyone killed. It just spiraled out of control, and then Bertie shot Helena and George right in front of me. I knew he'd kill me if I ever talked."

"I promise you, we'll get Bertie. But what about Rue?" Lizzy asked as Roland started walking away.

Ronald turned slowly around. "He's the worst of them all. He has no real power, so he constantly tries to prove he does. He went crazy when his dad announced Vivian was pregnant. I'm pretty sure Rue tied up the Stanworth loose end."

"Christine?" Lizzy asked.

Roland nodded. "She knew about these dead hit men Bertie had had Sandra and George send on errands. By the time I got back to LA, Christine was dead. When I saw Rue, he was bragging about the power one has when they take a life. I put two and two together this time and have been staying the fuck away from him."

Grant closed in behind Roland with his arm around Valeria as Dalton walked Roland down the stairs and into the tunnels. They had their answer. Bertie Geofferies was behind it all.

LIZZY AND JANET silently turned off their body cams. She was shaking after that interrogation. She had hoped she could scare Roland into a confession, but she'd never dreamed he would know so much. And Sebastian . . . he wanted to participate, but didn't. Then he did jump in but told her about it. She didn't understand him at all. What stood out though was that Sebastian knew about *Mollia Domini* before anyone else and told no one. He even figured out who was in charge. Instead of telling her or even Birch, he chose to remain silent. Why?

"I'll call Knoll and Kirby and let them know what happened. Good work, James."

Lizzy smiled in return and called Humphrey. It was too risky to call Birch.

"Lizzy?"

The slightly high and nasally voice made her smile. It had been hard seeing Val and Grant bleeding. Way harder than it should have been. It brought her own mortality into question, and when you were in her line of work you couldn't think about that. "Bertie Geofferies is the head of the organization. His son, Rue, is also involved, as well as Mrs. Mitchell. It appears she was active in its organization. Since her husband died, she has no real role besides trying to shape Birch's staff to keep those she and Bertie had recruited in power."

"Evidence?"

"Taped confession of Roland Westwood."

"A former first lady whose husband died in office . . . it better be ironclad or we'll be the worst kind of villains."

"It is."

"What about Sebastian?" Humphrey asked.

"I'm still trying to work that out. He definitely knew about the group and knew Bertie was in charge of it. Yet he helped us . . . kind of. However, he was also poised to take over the group if we had failed to bring down the entire inner circle. I don't know yet what to make of him. We're on our way back home with Roland. We're driving to San Diego to meet up with Kirby and Knoll. We'll be there in two or so hours. Then we'll catch a flight back to DC. We'll be there tonight."

"Good job, Lizzy. Your father would be proud."

Humphrey hung up and Lizzy took a deep breath. It was time to end this. Her father deserved as much.

32

VALERIA HISSED as Dalton cleaned her wound and stitched it together. It was nothing compared to the curses Grant wielded when Dalton checked to make sure the bullets had passed through and cleaned him up.

They had made it to the airfield in San Diego very quickly. Valeria wasn't surprised when Janet said she'd drive and drove them faster than Lizzy did. As soon as they hit the airfield, they were ushered on board where they found Alex with a black eye, Roxie clinging to him and looking as if he were her hero, and two of Manuel's men in custody.

"What happened?" Lizzy had asked, rushing toward Alex to look at his eye.

"My hero," Roxie had answered instead. "He jumped on one of the men when they broke into the bedroom we were hiding in. Alex distracted him long enough for Mr. Kirby to shoot him."

Alex noticed the blood soaking Val's and Grant's clothes and threw up. Apparently not for the first time that night.

"Ouch," Val snapped as Dalton knotted the last stitch.

"Stop being a baby," he teased, and Val gave him the finger.

Janet had Kirby and Knoll huddled in a corner of the plane, showing them her camera feed, but no one in the group felt like going over and answering questions. Kirby had lost a man and another was at the hospital in San Diego with a bullet wound. That bullet hadn't been nice enough to come out and had been lodged inside the agent, requiring surgery. Instead of a debriefing, Lizzy crawled into Dalton's lap, and he wrapped his arms around her. "You better still marry me," Lizzy whispered a moment before Dalton kissed her.

Grant wrapped his good arm over Valeria's shoulder and pulled her against his side. She sighed with contentment. He lowered his lips and placed them gently against her temple. "I love you, Val."

He said it so softly that Valeria wasn't sure she heard him, but she didn't need to hear him. She knew he loved her, and she knew she loved him. When she had seen him bleeding, it had about ended her. If something would've happened and she hadn't been able to tell him what he'd come to mean to her, she'd be shattered. "I love you, too, you stubborn Scot."

She tilted her head and looked into his eyes, as green as the wilds of Scotland, and kissed him. "Don't ever get shot again, promise?"

Grant tossed back his head and laughed. Others turned to stare before going back to what they were doing. Valeria rested her head on his broad shoulder and smiled. "Only if you promise not to get stabbed again, lass."

"Deal." Valeria sealed the promise with a kiss and closed her eyes. The madness would reignite when they returned to DC, but for right now it was just her and the man she loved.

"THEY'VE LANDED," Humphrey said, storming into the Oval Office. Birch looked at his watch. A little after six o'clock. People were starting to leave for the day.

"Have Dalton take Roland and Kirby to the holding area Jason set up. Tell him to have Kirby turn it into a legit site that only he and two or three of his most trusted agents know about. It's where we're going to hold everyone until they testify."

Humphrey was already sending out the order. "What about the others?"

"Let's meet at the FBI training center in Quantico at nine tonight. Classes will be out and the grounds are highly restricted. If seen, we can pass it off as a meeting about upgrading the facilities, and I was touring it."

"And Sebastian?"

"Have him meet us there at ten. I need to have a word with him."

The door opened and Tate hurried through on her crutches. "What is it? Is there a problem?"

Birch shook his head and kissed her quickly before Jessica got up from behind her desk and closed the door, giving them privacy. "Sorry, sweetheart. I've been in meetings all day. It's been hard, but I've had to continue governing the entire country even as we're handling this threat. But that threat will soon be over."

Tate swatted at him. "I know that, you told me that in a rush before I was shoved out the door for your meeting with the ambassador. Is everyone coming home? Is everyone safe? Do we know who is behind it all?"

"No, yes, yes."

"Birch Stratton!" Tate wanted to stomp her foot if she could, so she slammed her crutch down instead. She'd been working nonstop since the bombing. She would have liked to say she had a moment to check on her friends, but she hadn't. She'd been fielding constant questions about when the stock market would reopen, what the motivation for the bombing was, who was the mysterious hero who sacrificed himself to save others, and so on. She'd just finished all the responses for the evening news and was being flooded with questions for the late night news programs.

"Sorry, sweetheart." Birch looked grim for a moment. "We lost an agent and another is in the hospital, expected to make a full recovery. Grant was shot twice, but Dalton was able to stitch him up. Valeria sustained a knife wound that she described as a 'wee little scratch.'" Tate smiled as Birch tried to imitate Valeria's voice. "Manuel Hernandez is dead. We handed the body over to the Mexican president to claim a successful mission against drugs. Mexican authorities have raided all of Manuel's compounds and will share with us everything they find. Roland Westwood is in custody and has already talked."

Tate sucked in a breath. "Sebastian?" She knew how nervous he was about his best friend's involvement.

"No, Bertie Geofferies, with recruiting assistance from the former first lady." Tate grimaced at that news. It would be easier taking down the richest man in the world than a former first lady who recently lost her husband to cancer. And here she thought her job couldn't get any harder.

"However, Sebastian knew more than he let on. We're all

meeting in Quantico tonight at nine, you included. Then I'm meeting with Sebastian at ten."

Tate nodded her head. "I'm getting tons of questions about the stock market and the investigation."

"Tell them we foresee the opening of the stock market shortly, but have no current statement due to the ongoing investigation. Tell them I have complete faith in the FBI to eventually track down those responsible for this cowardly act."

"Sneaky," Tate said, grinning. "Lull Geofferies into a false sense of security and then strike."

"Exactly. Let's hope it works."

LIZZY CHECKED in at the bar while Valeria and Grant put on fresh clothes. Janet and AG Knoll had taken a separate car with Alex and Roxie ahead of everyone else to make sure the room was clean and to set up the camera equipment. Dalton and Kirby had taken Roland and would also meet them there.

It was strange being back at the bar filled with laughing Marines after the long night in Mexico. Snip and Buzz didn't ask questions, but did comment on how tired she looked. But the end was in sight. Revenge for her father's death was at hand. One more big fish and then the rest would fall like dominos.

Lizzy, Grant, and Valeria met behind the bar and drove the short distance to the FBI training center in silence. They arrived as four other SUVs pulled up. One with Dalton and Kirby, and one with Birch, Tate, Humphrey, and some older guy with an old-time leather medical bag. The other two SUVs were filled with Secret

Service agents who swarmed Birch the second his door opened.

The three of them went on ahead, knowing Birch would ditch his agents once inside the conference room. Sure enough, a couple minutes later only Birch, Tate, Humphrey, and the older man walked into the small conference room.

"I am so glad to see y'all!" Tate's southern belle voice slipped out when she was emotional, and it made Lizzy and Valeria smile as they hugged her.

"Valeria, Grant, this is Dr. Wilson. He's here to check you two out after we talk."

Val and Grant shook his hand. "Thanks, Doc," Grant said with a grimace. His pain level was obviously high.

"I'll set up in one of the nearby rooms. Come see me as soon as you're finished here."

Dr. Wilson handed Grant what looked to be a lollipop. "Take a couple of licks on this now, but no more than half. You can have the other half after you finish your meeting," he said of the painkilling lollipop. "It's faster than morphine, and I can better control the dosage so you can still focus. So, no more than half. Got it?"

"Got it," Grant tore open the lollipop and stuck it into his mouth with a sigh. "Thank you again, Doc."

Dr. Wilson made his way out the door as the rest of the group hugged Tate, Birch, and Humphrey. Janet, Kirby, and Knoll looked on with interest. Knoll shook his head. "You have a fucking secret group of soldiers carrying out missions for you, don't you?"

"Soldiers get paid, right?" Lizzy asked with a smile. "Because Birch hasn't paid me anything. In fact, he told me straight out he wouldn't do anything to help us."

Knoll rolled his eyes. "Volunteers, is that what you're going with?"

"Concerned citizens," Lizzy said innocently.

"What they are doesn't matter. When they went on the mission to Mexico, they were government agents with long records of service."

"And those two," Knoll said, looking to Grant and Dalton.

"Military rescue," Humphrey responded, tossing what looked to be orders sending Major Cage and his pilot, Grant Macay, to evacuate an injured American agent.

"Okay, it'll pass if they're real." Knoll sighed as he looked at the papers. Lizzy hid a smile as Humphrey sent a wink to Alex and Roxie.

But Dalton looked confused. "Major?" he mouthed to Humphrey who came over to them as Janet began talking.

"I might have fibbed when I said you were kicked out of the Air Force. You've been receiving pay the entire time and listed as reassigned to DC from the second I pulled you out of the jail in England."

Lizzy didn't know what Dalton's reaction to be, but laughter wasn't it. He thumped Humphrey on the back, sending his glasses sliding down his nose. "Good one, Humphrey. You got me there."

Birch nodded his head approvingly at Dalton, who nodded back. "Okay, Janet, show us what you've got."

THE TAPE from Mexico was shown, followed by the footage from the boat. Alex and Roxie had been in the corner with earphones on, working on their laptops the entire time. They were probably texting each other. Lizzy went back to Knoll's talk about what their options were to charge Gene, Thurmond, and Roland.

"But where is Sandra Cummings?" Knoll suddenly asked.

Dalton's breathing changed, but nothing else did. Sandra had hung herself in a secret prison. It's not like they could publicize that.

"We don't know. We're trying to find her. Sometimes she uses an alias. We'll find her," Birch promised. "First, what do we need in order to bring Bertie Geofferies down?"

"Who do you want more? Geofferies or Mrs. Mitchell?" Knoll asked. "Whichever one you want more, turn the other."

"Valeria," Birch said, turning to her. "Bring me Mrs. Mitchell later tonight."

"You've got it."

"Of course, a confession would be good, too," Knoll smirked.

"I know how to get one," Lizzy said slowly.

"How?" Birch asked suspiciously.

"I need Sebastian."

Birch's lips thinned. He was thinking the same thing she was, but could Sebastian be trusted?

BIRCH SIGHED as the room cleared. Valeria and Grant were with Dr. Wilson. The feds had headed back to DC. Alex and Roxie still hadn't come out of their corner. Dalton and Lizzy were talking quietly as Tate hobbled up to him. "I want to go with Valeria. I know women like Mrs. Mitchell. I can reason with her."

"She'll eat you alive."

"I can handle her."

"Okay. Go see how Val is, and bring me what you can." Birch watched as Tate turned to leave, but Alex stopped her.

"How about all of Mrs. Mitchell's emails trying to recruit people to *Mollia Domini* with promises of power and the access to the president?" Alex asked as he turned his laptop around.

"Good job, you two," Tate said, reading over the emails. "Send those to me." Tate leaned up and kissed Birch's cheek. "Love you."

"Love you, too, and be safe."

"Can Lizzy and I have the room?" Birch asked as Humphrey and Dalton looked at each other, and with a shrug headed out with Alex and Roxie. "Send in Sebastian when he gets here." Birch waited for the door to close. "Do you really think you can handle Sebastian?"

"We're about to find out," Lizzy said instead of answering. Sebastian was early. Birch should have guessed that.

Sebastian strolled in as if nothing was wrong in the world. As if he hadn't lied to the president of the United States. As if he hadn't sided with *Mollia Domini*, even if it was just keeping his mouth shut instead of reporting them. Anger raged through Birch and Lizzy. When Sebastian held out his hand, Birch slammed his fist into Sebastian's stomach. Pain shot through Birch from his own injuries, causing his vision to blur. But he refused to show the pain as Sebastian hunched over.

"What the fuck?" he asked, gasping.

Birch grabbed Alex's laptop and pulled up the clip Alex had ready for him. Roland's image came on screen as his voice filled the room. "Sebastian knew something was going on—"

Birch watched as his friend's face tightened until the end of the clip. Birch closed the laptop and crossed his arms over his chest. A lifetime of friendship, over like that.

"Congratulations," Sebastian said. "You caught Roland and you found out Bertie Geofferies is the head of the organization. I'm assuming you'll arrest him tonight."

"You kept it from me," Birch growled. "You knew the whole fucking time and you kept it from me."

Sebastian shook his head. "I had a hunch. That's different from knowing and certainly different from proving. And I gave you everything you needed to look into him to find out if he was the head."

"You only did once it was clear Bertie was freezing you out of the organization."

Sebastian shrugged. "It's business. I knew he wouldn't want his biggest competitor in the game as soon as I said you wouldn't bend to my power. I was useless. But I got the last laugh, didn't I? I'm not the traitor, Birch. I gave you money, access to my properties, my tech expert, and everything you needed to catch the bad guys."

"I'm sure when this blows up and as Bertie is being hauled off in handcuffs, you'll be on television telling how you and your best friend worked together to bring down this organization." Birch took a deep breath, trying to calm his temper.

"While you might not think it, Birch, I have always had your back."

"You just did it in the most self-serving way," Lizzy added.

"Business is business. You don't climb the ladder like I have from the bottom without knocking some people off to get ahead."

"What if Bertie had included you from the beginning?" Birch asked quietly.

"It had nothing to do with them then, Birch. It was President Mitchell then. I would never do anything to hurt you. I may be a self-serving ass, but I'd never turn against you."

"Prove it," Birch said simply.

"How?" Sebastian asked, getting ready to negotiate.

"Wear a wire with me," Lizzy said. "We'll meet with Bertie, and you'll tell him you caught me spying on your AI for him."

Sebastian's eyes widened. "You—?"

Lizzy smiled. "It's business." She shrugged.

"And," Birch said sternly, "that AI software is to be destroyed."

Sebastian whirled on Birch. "That's worth billions."

"What is our friendship worth?"

Sebastian looked ready to explode. "Is that what it takes to prove to you that I never intended to hurt you? That I have been your friend and will continue to be your friend?"

"It's a start. Furthermore, you'll help me write limitations of AI use and testify against Bertie."

Sebastian suddenly looked ten years younger as he slouched. He let the hardness fade from his face as he held out his hand. "Deal. And for what it's worth, I'm sorry."

"You're sorry you were caught. I'll believe you're sorry when your actions demonstrate it."

"No matter what, you're still my best friend—my brother."

Birch smirked and shook Sebastian's hand. "Shit, I'm the only friend you have."

"I'll meet you at SA Tech in the morning," Lizzy said as Sebastian turned to leave. He nodded and left the room. "Do you trust him?"

"I do. We have a history. But what I said was true. He's only sorry he was caught. Sebastian will do the right thing. Not because it's right, but because it's the smart play for him right now. But it'll be the right move anyway. And in his own way, he did help bring down Bertie."

Lizzy walked out of the room with Birch. "Which was the biggest self-serving play of all. With Bertie out of the way, Sebastian becomes the most powerful man in America. Even more powerful than you."

"So he does."

33

TATE STARED EMOTIONLESSLY at the car driving Mrs. Mitchell and Valeria to the secret holding facility. In the morning, she would be blindfolded and moved to a secure location to meet with her lawyers. She would be testifying against Bertie Geofferies for treason. The first case to be tried in decades, but Birch was insisting on it. The others were testifying in exchange for lesser charges, but they would still be facing jail time.

Tate slid into the backseat of the SUV driven by her newly assigned Secret Service agent, Ashley Palmer. Tate had handpicked her and so far so good. She hadn't tried to kill her, so that was a plus.

Mrs. Mitchell had accused Tate of trying to ruin her and her husband's legacy. She had accused Tate of wanting to be the official first lady. Maybe she had been right. She did want that, but not because of the title. That she would happily hand back. She wanted it because it meant she'd be with Birch. All of this had taught her the world could be a dark place. But when you found light in the goodness and love of another person, it was there you should focus.

Otherwise the shadows would suck you in and never let you go.

"To the White House?" Agent Palmer asked.

"Yes, please."

"So help me, if you screw Birch over one more time, I'll kill you myself," Lizzy told Sebastian as she purposefully taped the wire over as much chest hair as possible.

"Has anyone told you're sexy when you're mad?"

"I'm pretty sure you've mentioned it before. Whoops, that's not where I want the wire." Lizzy ripped the tape off, and Sebastian grimaced in pain.

She used new tape over some more of his chest hair and patted it down tight. Sebastian could flirt his way into getting his way almost every time, but not with her. It didn't matter that his pecs were sculpted muscle, or that the ridges of his abs begged to be touched. Sebastian lived in the gray area of life, and Lizzy didn't trust anyone who lived there.

"Ready?"

Sebastian nodded. "The question is: are you? I know Bertie way better than you do, so you better be one hell of an actress or it'll be you who blows this."

"Do your worst."

Sebastian gave a killer smile. "I plan to."

Lizzy didn't have to fake the scream when Sebastian grabbed her arm so hard she fell. Sebastian didn't stop as he dragged her off the elevator and down the hall toward Bertie's office. Lizzy also didn't have to fake the cuss words and threats that came out of her mouth as she scrambled to get back on her feet.

The people in the office stood stunned at the aggressive display, and no one bothered to step forward as Sebastian flung open the office door and literally shoved Lizzy to the floor at Bertie's feet.

Sebastian stepped forward and threw a punch connecting with Bertie's face, sending him falling against his desk. Rue jumped forward, and as Lizzy screamed for Sebastian to stop, he broke Rue's nose. Rue fell back onto the couch, clutching his face.

"I give a million fucking dollars to your little club and this is how you return the favor?" Sebastian pointed to Lizzy. "You bribe one of my employees into becoming a fucking spy so you can be the first person to implement AI in the stock market?"

"I don't know what you're talking about," Bertie sputtered as he rubbed his face.

"Roland came begging me for money since Manuel's accounts were frozen. Said it was for that club you talked about starting at the Tech Ball three years ago. The one you wouldn't let me join. The one Roland, Sandra Cummings, and the Stanworths were a part of. Don't play fucking dumb, Bertie, it's beneath you."

Bertie slowly smiled. "You're such a sore loser. You always have been. You just couldn't stand the fact you weren't included when Mrs. Mitchell approached me about this. You know, she told me all about your friend Stratton being picked for VP. He was supposed to be locked out of the government, but then Winston Mitchell went toes up. Did it bother you that we shut you out like we did your friend? Does it bother you we took that money from you, and you'll never make it in the inner circle? How does it feel that I took your trusted employee and bought the bitch with my first offer? You should pay your employees better, Sebastian. Soon I'll be sitting here with billions more than you. The stock market is opening soon, and my AI is ready to go. Is yours?" Bertie laughed as he leaned against his desk and crossed his arms.

Lizzy stood up slowly, ready to leap on Sebastian if he let his temper win out. He looked ready to blow the whole operation to get even with Bertie.

"Is that what this whole stupid group is about? What was the idiotic name you chose for it?" Sebastian pretended to think about it. "*Mollia Domini*, that's it. So *Mollia Domini* isn't about change like you preached at the Tech Ball, is it? It's about making you money and keeping me in second place. Is that it? You did all of this to best me, since you knew I was coming for you? You're pathetic, Bertie."

Bertie's face flushed with anger as he stepped forward. "You know what's pathetic, Sebastian? The fact that you fell for it. Manuel made sure the money you sent for your resorts paid for the same bomb that almost killed Stratton. So I would run if I were you, Sebastian. Because while we hid it, we made sure eventually they'd find the connection. Then you openly gave Roland a million dollars, who will claim you personally put a hit on Stratton since the bomb failed. A hit my assassin will be carrying out shortly."

"You have an assassin?" Lizzy gasped as she stumbled back in faux fear.

"Yes, my dear. He'll be arriving shortly from overseas. Rue, handle this." Bertie waved his hand in her direction. Rue stood from the couch and stalked toward her. She put a chair between them as Bertie and Sebastian ignored them. Their sole focus was on each other.

Sebastian's jaw tightened. "I'll tell them it was you."

Bertie laughed. "No one will believe you. Not when all the evidence points back to you. Dance, puppet."

"Wait!" Lizzy screamed as Rue lunged. She darted around the chair to stand next to Sebastian, who didn't even bother to look at her.

"Ready to beg for your life?" Rue taunted.

"Dan March!" she shouted.

Rue and Bertie froze.

"Excuse me?" Bertie asked slowly.

"Your assassin. Is it my ex-boyfriend? I swear I've caught glimpses of him since he was supposed to be dead. Please, tell me I'm not crazy," Lizzy begged. Sebastian finally looked at her with curiosity.

Bertie gleefully smiled. "So, Dan has been keeping tabs on you? Maybe I should save you for him to handle?"

"I'm sorry," Lizzy said, blubbering as Rue approached her. "Dan's not coming." Her blubbering stopped, and she winked at Sebastian before taking Rue down with an uppercut that sent his head snapping up and his eyes rolling back. Before Bertie could scream, Lizzy turned to him. "Bertie Geofferies, FBI. You're under arrest for treason."

Bertie tried to run, but Sebastian snatched him by the neck and squeezed. "Going somewhere?"

Lizzy slipped a zip tie from her pocket and tied his hands behind his back. "Dance, puppet," she whispered, shoving him toward the office door.

"Call my lawyer, Stan Detrick," Bertie told his secretary with authority as he was pushed through the hall of his office. If he thought Stan Detrick would be able to wrangle him off the hook, he was badly mistaken. Stan wasn't in his office at the moment. Roland said Bertie kept everything written down, and as agents swarmed the scene, arresting Rue and tearing apart every inch of the room, Lizzy knew it was only a matter of time before the book Roland described was found.

The elevator doors opened, and Lizzy handed Bertie off to Special Agent in Charge Cromwell. She stood in the background as Cromwell pushed Bertie forward. Reporters were being held back at the bottom of the steps leading into Bertie's building. The second elevator opened and a pissed-off Rue was shoved forward. Right as the front door opened, Sebastian called out. "By the way, Bertie, your wife's pregnant with Trip's baby."

Cameras flashed at Bertie's look of outrage as he was dragged through the door and to the waiting car with Rue threatening everyone he could, including his stepmother and her unborn child. Lizzy shook her head and looked to where Sebastian had an amused smile on his face.

"You just had to do that, didn't you?"

"You bet your ass I did." Sebastian turned to her and held out his hand. "Well, Lizzy, it's been a pleasure working with you. I look forward to working with you again."

"I wish I could say the same," Lizzy said with a slow grin.

"See, I'm not such a bad guy. Am I?"

"That's still undecided. But know I'll be keeping an eye on you."

"Just as I keep an eye on the world." He winked and sauntered off.

Son of a bitch. "It was you the whole time, wasn't it?" Lizzy called out.

Sebastian turned with a look of exaggerated innocence. "Whatever do you mean?" he asked, walking back to her and stopping inches from her. His body radiated casualness that only came from a man who knew his own power. He looked down and smiled knowingly at her. Her stomach flipped and blood rushed to her cheeks at his devouring look.

"You were the biggest puppetmaster of them all," she said as the realization set in. "You knew what Bertie was up to, and either for amusement or because you really were mad about being excluded, you turned the tables on him. You gave him the strings to pull, not the other way around. You didn't have me spy for you, you were giving me a string to follow. You gave Trip a string to Vivian. You introduced Manuel to Roland. You were pulling the strings the entire time."

Sebastian leaned down slowly with a predatory tilt of his lips that flashed a hit of white teeth. He cupped her face with his hand and ran his thumb lightly over her bottom lip leaving a trail of tingling heat. "If that were true, then I'd have you in my bed right now, and Birch would have never been in danger."

"Even the great Sebastian Abel can't control everything."

"We'll see," he said before slowly placing his lips against hers for a kiss so brief she thought she'd imagined the caress of his lips. Sebastian dropped his hand, sent her a wink, and sauntered off down the hall. Lizzy watched as he slipped his hand into his pocket, pulled out his phone, and pressed a button before putting his phone back in his pocket. A second later her cellphone buzzed.

President Stratton Helps the FBI Bring Down Terror Ring Lead
by Billionaire Bertie Geofferies.
An exposé by Flint Scott

LIZZY READ the headline twice before looking up to see Sebastian walk out the side door. The door closed, and Lizzy finally took a breath. Looking down, she read the article that laid out Bertie's desire for more power and his AI to take billions from the people after the planned attacks on the exchanges.

Flint told about a secret group of agents and military personnel handpicked by the president to chase down the powerful and elite members of *Mollia Domini*. Birch would be declared a hero now. The article read of his heroism at standing up to people who were trying to destroy the office of the presidency, of protecting civilians from the lies they were being told, of Tate's sacrifice to save Birch's life during the explosion, and of the secret group's daring and life-risking missions . . . all without naming or identifying a single person on her team.

Two things were clear. Sebastian was the ultimate puppetmaster, and he'd done everything he could to keep Birch and innocent people safe. The remorse and pain exhibited in the article, talking about the loss of life and Birch's injuries from the bombing, weren't Flint's words. They were Sebastian's. The article even stated *the country would be a worse place if President Stratton weren't in it*, the exact same thing Sebastian had said when he had found out about the bombing at the restaurant. Son of a bitch, Flint had been a string Sebastian had planted for them to use. Lizzy shook her head and went back to reading.

The article continued with those whose lives were given in sacrifice to protect Americans' rights. A long part of it focused on Jason and Michelle Wolski, bringing tears to her eyes as the article showed a picture of Birch saluting Jason's flag-draped coffin in front of lines of the wounded soldiers he and Michelle had helped.

The article ended with thanks given to those nameless heroes who helped protect the country and information that witnesses were already lined up to testify against Bertie Geofferies.

Looking at the door Sebastian had left through, Lizzy had to wonder, who was Sebastian Abel?

IT HAD BEEN forty-five minutes since Flint's article had rocked the world. Tate had left immediately upon seeing it. There was something she had to see done, and she was the only person who could do it.

Tate balanced on her crutches as she raised her hand to knock on the cheery yellow door to the small ranch house on the quiet suburban street. The house was surrounded with brightly blooming flowers, a swing for an infant, and a little red wagon sitting on the sidewalk.

The door opened and a woman in her late fifties opened the door with a baby on her hip.

"Mrs. Bristol, I'm Tate Carlisle, and I was friends with your daughter, Sheila, and son-in-law, Joel Davidson." Tate saw the women's smile slip. "We need to talk. I have information about your daughter's death and how your son-in-law helped bring down the ring currently being arrested for treason against the government."

Mrs. Bristol looked down at her grandson and back to Tate. "Joel killed Sheila. That's what the police told us."

"Ma'am, your son-in-law died a hero, and I believe you have the right to know what really happened the night your daughter died."

With tears streaming down her face, Mrs. Bristol stepped back, and Tate hobbled inside.

34

"I SWEAR," Roland Westwood promised before lowering his hand and taking a seat in the packed courtroom. The trial against Bertie Geofferies was going into the fourth week, but Roland was the last witness to be called for the state.

Jeff Sargent, Branson Ames, Gene Rankin, Thurmond Culpepper, FBI Director Kirby, Senator Epps, and the former first lady were some of the people who had testified. Lawyers were advising Bertie to take a plea deal since Gene pointed to Stan Detrick, Bertie's lawyer who had suddenly come back from a vacation looking pale and tired, as the one who threatened his family. On the third day of the trial, the state produced evidence of Stan buying the burner phone he'd given to Gene. It got worse when Sandra's dead body was found hanging in Bertie's house in Bulgaria with papers scattered around her. Papers that connected Bertie and Rue to the Stanworth deaths and *Mollia Domini*.

In the six months since Bertie had been arrested, Birch had pardoned Gene, honored Jeff Sargent and Joel Davidson, and posthumously awarded Brock, Jason, and

Michelle the Presidential Medal of Freedom after giving the young officer who had saved Tate a medal as well.

"Ugh, turn it off," Valeria complained as she looked up from her laptop.

Lizzy rolled her eyes. "Don't you want to see this?"

"See it? We lived it."

"Fine," Lizzy said, turning off the television over the bar. "How is your lesson plan going for the new class of trainees starting off the New Year?"

"I swear, if one more trainee calls me ma'am, I'm going to fucking snap," Valeria swore. Janet had offered her a job as a higher-up in the DEA, but Val had turned it down. While it hadn't been talked about, the group was sticking together. They were family after all. So instead of more shootouts, Val was now training the next generation of DEA agents at their academy in Quantico . . . for now.

"Don't worry, girlie, you're still younger than we are," Buzz laughed from his usual seat next to Snip.

"Hey, where's your grandson? He promised to teach me how to fly a helicopter," Lizzy asked Buzz. Lizzy had taken to running the bar full-time and teaching one interrogation class at the FBI's academy in the newly built Lance James wing, thanks to an anonymous donor.

"Crew's on call. He's taking the president and that sweet little Tate somewhere." Buzz wiggled his bushy eyebrows and Lizzy tossed a meaningful look to Valeria, who was already smiling.

Birch and Tate were trying to keep their relationship as normal as possible. They didn't answer questions about it to the media during "office hours," only when caught out on dates. After Flint's exposé, the public was dying for a White House wedding. Instead, they were dating and working hard on cleaning up the mess Bertie had left behind.

The exchanges were recovering, the economy stabilizing, and Birch was moving on to his own domestic and foreign policies. Life was moving forward.

"When are those usurpers coming home?" Snip asked about Dalton and Grant. Buzz and Snip still hadn't forgiven them for taking the women they'd picked out for their grandsons.

"They arrived last night," Lizzy told them with a smile as she looked at the diamond ring on her finger. They were getting married in June, and Val was going to be her maid of honor. They'd been planning the wedding while Dalton and Grant had been stationed in Alaska for the past month, training their replacements in Arctic rescue and survival. Right before leaving, they were sent to help rescue a downed spy plane in Russia's Arctic zone before the Russians found them. After bringing the pilot home and destroying the spy plane so the Russians couldn't get any information from it, Dalton and Grant had officially been honorably discharged from the Air Force.

"They're meeting with the bank in charge of liquidating Jason and Michelle's estate right now," Valeria explained.

"What for?" Snip asked.

"You know how important Jason was to them and they want to buy the grounds to make sure the wounded veterans continue to have a place to recover. They want Jason and Michelle's legacy to live on," Lizzy said with a touch of sadness. The Wolskis had been victims in all of this, and the pain still continued as the veterans who had depended on Jason and Michelle's camp fell through the cracks.

The door to the bar flew open and Dalton and Grant stomped inside. "Speak of the usurpers," Snip teased.

"What's the matter?" Lizzy asked as they watched the men angrily yank off their coats. Their eyes were narrowed, their jaws were clenched, and their movements jerky in their anger.

"The bank sold Jason's land already," Dalton answered as he let out a frustrated sigh.

"What? They knew you wanted to buy it," Lizzy said worriedly.

"We didn't have enough cash to hold it before we left for Alaska. We were told the property wasn't going to be put on the market for a couple of months since the estate was still in probate," Grant explained before he kissed Valeria's head and took a seat next to her at the bar.

"So we scrapped and saved everything we had and went with the good faith deposit today, only to be told the bank sold it for all cash two weeks ago," Dalton finished.

"Dude, that sucks," Alex said from where he was working on his computer. He was probably chatting with Roxie who had to go back to England for her last year at university.

"I'm so sorry." Lizzy took Dalton into a hug and kissed him gently. "This won't stop us from doing what's right. We'll start looking for properties tomorrow. We'll find something."

Dalton squeezed her tight and took a deep breath. "I know something perfect will come along. I have you by my side, what else do I need?"

Birch held Tate's nude body against his as they drifted off to sleep. He looked down and smiled at the new ring she wore on her hand. He'd never imagined he'd be married again, let alone to someone as wonderful as Tate. Even though he knew she'd say yes when he had Crew fly them out to Camp David, it still seemed like a shock when she nodded her head up and down and threw her arms around him. With shaky hands, he had slipped the diamond ring onto her finger.

The second they'd made it back to the White House, word had spread that Tate was wearing a very important ring on her finger. In less than five minutes, Humphrey was knocking on the door with a list of dignitaries who must be invited to the wedding. Tate had laughed and used her foot to close the door on him.

At that moment, Humphrey was probably downstairs planning their whole wedding and they'd only arrived back to DC four hours before. A knock sounded at the door and Birch groaned. "Go away, Humphrey!"

Tate's brow wrinkled in her sleep as if she too were annoyed by the interruption.

"I'm sorry, but it's important," came Humphrey's excited voice.

"Give me a minute," Birch called, waking Tate up in the process.

"What is it?" she mumbled.

"Humphrey is at the door."

"I told you I am not picking out the china pattern right this second," Tate yelled.

"I still think you should go with the navy blue one, but that's beside the point. This is important."

Tate shoved off the covers, and they slipped on some clothes before opening the door.

"What the—?" Birch started to say, but was cut off.

"Hey, congrats," Lizzy said, kissing Tate's cheek and pushing into the room.

"Again, I better be the maid of honor," Val said with a wink.

"Aye, there's nothing better than hooking up with the bridal party at a wedding. Congratulations, you two," Grant said with a broad grin as he shook Birch's hand.

"It's better hooking up when that person is your fiancée, but someone is moving slow," Dalton teased Grant.

"I think I'm going to ask Roxie to marry me," Alex said, taking a seat on the bed.

"Dude! You're like a baby," Lizzy exclaimed before slapping a hand over her mouth. "Dammit! I said it, didn't I?"

Everyone laughed, and Lizzy flicked off Alex.

"While we love seeing you all, what's so important you had to come at two in the morning?" Birch asked.

"It's the best time to come in unnoticed," Lizzy pointed out.

"But we have news," Crew said, smiling.

"Bertie Geofferies took a plea deal an hour ago. He pled guilty to treason the second the prosecutor announced they'd found the book with all his notes in it. The book was found in his shower in his Hamptons house. One of the marble tiles was actually a hidden compartment. Inside was the leather book Roland described, full of names, amounts, crimes . . . by the way, I've stricken the French prime minister from your wedding list as he'll soon be in jail." Humphrey huffed as if insulted that a potential wedding guest would dare be named in Bertie's little book.

"What was the deal?" Birch asked. Was it truly finally over?

"Life at an undisclosed location. I was thinking of the secret prison in Saipan."

Birch thought for a second. "Do it. I want him far away from the media or any of his cohorts that will be arrested from this fallout." Birch took a breath then, realizing why Dalton was popping a bottle of champagne. "It's over."

"That's right," Humphrey said, grinning as he handed Tate and Birch a glass. "Everyone who was part of *Mollia Domini* are either dead or now in jail."

Tate squealed as she jumped into Birch's arms. "It's finally over! I can't believe it. We did it. Justice has been served."

Dalton kissed Lizzy, and Grant brought Val close to his side. Everyone smiled and laughed as the last of the web unraveled.

EPILOGUE

THREE MONTHS LATER . . .

THE CHERRY BLOSSOMS were at their peak on April 2nd, the day of her wedding. Tate Carlisle looked out the window of the residence at the White House and at the crowd surrounding the fence. They were all there to see her and celebrate her wedding to Birch. But the memories of the last time so many from the media gathered on the grounds made the moment temporarily bitter before fading away.

News of the wedding date was leaked via one Sebastian Abel two days before when asked about backing out as a keynote speaker at a tech conference. "I'm attending a wedding," he had said.

That was enough for reporters to dig around and discover the president's schedule had been cleared for the next week. People had started arriving within the hour to surround the White House. While her office refused to furnish any details, Tate did announce she'd make a statement that day. She looked in the mirror once more.

"For love of all that's holy, hurry up. You look perfect."

Tate laughed at Valeria sitting in a pink dress and looking as pissed as a wet hen. She wasn't about to forgive Tate for the pink anytime soon, even though she looked beautiful.

"You better not be a bitch at my wedding or so help me, I'll shoot you," Lizzy warned teasingly.

"Have I told you I love you both?" Tate asked, smiling and tearing up at the same time.

"We'll love you more if you get a move on. The limo is waiting to take us to Marine One so we can all travel incognito," Val said, looking at her watch.

"I'm ready," Tate said with a feeling of complete happiness. "I'll meet you in the limo."

"Finally," Val teased as Lizzy grabbed their bags and headed for the garage. "And by the way, you look great."

"Thank you, Val."

"Hey, that's what maids of honor are for."

Tate was alone then, and she made her way down the red-carpeted stairs of the residence and toward the front door. The staff lined the hallway clapping and some even wiped tears from their eyes. Cheers from the crowds went up as Tate walked out front. She waved and caught sight of a little girl using her cell phone to record the moment. Tate walked forward, making Secret Service nervous, but Tate headed right toward the girl who waved frantically.

"Miss Carlisle, I'm Samantha Young of Jefferson Middle School's newspaper. Can I ask you a question?" Smiling, Tate walked to the gate as BBN reporters and other national papers tried to get her attention.

"What's your question, Miss Young?"

"How do you feel about the media now that it's been exposed to have been corrupted by *Molly Dominate*?"

Tate couldn't stop the smile at the girl trying so hard. "I feel we've all been given a second chance to be the best people we can be. And with a reporter like you growing up, I have faith the next generation will succeed where others have failed."

"One more question?" Samantha asked nervously. Tate nodded as the other reporters shouted their questions. "Is this the happiest day of your life?'"

"It sure is. Thank you, everyone. I have a wedding to attend."

THE LAWN at Camp David was full of celebration as Tate and Birch smiled happily at each other and cut their wedding cake. Her brother, Tucker, had walked Tate down the aisle of the rustic Evergreen Chapel. Humphrey and Sebastian had served as groomsmen, and Lizzy hadn't even had to punch Sebastian as he escorted her back down the aisle.

Lizzy smiled as the music began to play and the happy couple took to the dance floor. However, her eyes narrowed at the small band on Valeria's hand. She never wore rings. "Psst," Lizzy hissed, waving them over.

Val looked at her with curiosity as she and Grant grabbed their drinks before coming to stand with them.

"What the hell is on your hand?" Lizzy asked as Val suddenly looked nervous.

"Nothing," she said, holding up her other hand.

"Not that hand." Lizzy grabbed her left hand and turned her hand palm up. Hiding there was a diamond in the center of a band made up of interlacing trinity knots. "You're—"

"Shh!" Val admonished as Dalton shook Grant's hand

with an excited smile. "I was hiding that. We don't want to distract from Tate and Birch's big day."

Lizzy flung her arms around Val. "Congratulations. I couldn't be happier for you."

"Thanks. Grant asked me three days ago by the river in Quantico. He surprised me with a romantic dinner and boat ride."

"I hear congratulations are in order," the deep voice said, drawing Lizzy and everyone else to turn around.

"Sebastian," Val acknowledged carefully. Sebastian had been noticeably low-key since Bertie's arrest. He'd helped Senator Epps author a bill to limit the realm in which AI could be used, and he'd been meeting with Birch regularly, but not asking for anything. Instead, he was being a friend. Lizzy didn't know what to make of it after learning how much of a role Sebastian really had in bringing *Mollia Domini* down. And she wasn't going to pretend he did it all because it was the right thing to do. While that may have played into his actions, Sebastian had profited greatly from Bertie's downfall.

"I heard you tried to buy Jason's property," Sebastian said to Dalton and Grant.

"How do you know that?" Dalton asked suspiciously.

"I own the bank in charge of liquidating the Wolskis' assets. What did you want with it?"

"We wanted to keep it going, to honor Jason and Michelle," Dalton answered.

"Aye, but someone bought it," Grant said accusingly.

Sebastian looked to Lizzy and Valeria and then back to Dalton and Grant. "How was that going to work with you all getting married?"

"We would figure it out," Dalton said defensively. "But we were never given the chance."

Sebastian nodded his head. "I bought it."

"What?" Lizzy gasped as she saw Dalton flex his hand into a fist.

"I bought this, too," he said, handing an envelope to Dalton.

Dalton opened it and scanned it. "It's a deed made out to the Wolski Veteran Foundation for one hundred acres near Quantico," Dalton said, turning the page. "And this is a deed to the Jason's property, also in the name of Wolski Veteran Foundation."

Dalton looked confused. "There's one more page," Sebastian said casually.

Dalton turned to it. He read it and then his eyes shot up to Sebastian's as he handed it to Grant.

"We're the president and vice president of the Wolski Veteran Foundation?" Grant asked without looking up. "With a $10,000,000 endowment?"

"Why?" Dalton asked Sebastian.

"Because sometimes even I can do the right thing," he said, turning to wink at Lizzy. "A full staff has been hired for their camp and the new smaller camp that you two can run near Quantico. You can keep or fire anyone you want. This is your nonprofit to keep their memory alive and to help as many veterans as possible."

"Just like that?" Grant asked, pulling Valeria to his side as if Sebastian would demand her as payment.

Sebastian grinned in such a way that Lizzy knew he thought the same. "Just like that. Besides, you never know if we'll get to work together again. Better to keep close in case Birch needs us."

With a wink to Lizzy, Sebastian sauntered into the crowd. Birch and Tate's dance finished as they clapped for the happy couple. When Birch and Tate joined them,

Humphrey hurried over with handfuls of drinks and handed them out like a proud papa. With champagne flutes filled, they raised their glasses.

"To President and First Lady Stratton," Humphrey said happily.

"To Jason and Michelle," Dalton said, showing Birch the papers.

"To Brock," Val said as Grant put his arm around her.

"To Joel and Sheila," Tate said with a finality that said their deaths had been avenged.

Lizzy leaned over and kissed Humphrey's cheek. "Thank you, Humphrey."

Humphrey turned scarlet as he stuttered, "What was that for?"

"For plucking me from the dark."

Valeria kissed his other cheek. "For rescuing me from the shadows."

Tate kissed his forehead. "For helping me see the light."

Birch held up his glass and tapped it against Tate's as the group of friends toasted each other and their friendship, laid the past to rest, celebrated the present, and swore to face any conflict that might arise standing shoulder to shoulder. "To a bright future."

THE END

Bluegrass Series

Bluegrass State of Mind

Risky Shot

Dead Heat

Bluegrass Brothers

Bluegrass Undercover

Rising Storm

Secret Santa: A Bluegrass Series Novella

Acquiring Trouble

Relentless Pursuit

Secrets Collide

Final Vow

Bluegrass Singles

All Hung Up

Bluegrass Dawn

The Perfect Gift

The Keeneston Roses

Forever Bluegrass Series

Forever Entangled

Forever Hidden

Forever Betrayed

Forever Driven

Forever Secret

Forever Surprised

Forever Concealed

Forever Devoted - coming January 30, 2018

Women of Power Series

Chosen for Power

Built for Power

Fashioned for Power

Destined for Power

Web of Lies Series

Whispered Lies

Rogue Lies

Shattered Lies

ABOUT THE AUTHOR

Kathleen Brooks is a New York Times, Wall Street Journal, and USA Today bestselling author. Kathleen's stories are romantic suspense featuring strong female heroines, humor, and happily-ever-afters. Her Bluegrass Series and follow-up Bluegrass Brothers Series feature small town charm with quirky characters that have captured the hearts of readers around the world.

Kathleen is an animal lover who supports rescue organizations and other non-profit organizations such as Friends and Vets Helping Pets whose goals are to protect and save our four-legged family members.

Email Notice of New Releases
kathleen-brooks.com/new-release-notifications
Kathleen's Website
www.kathleen-brooks.com
Facebook Page
www.facebook.com/KathleenBrooksAuthor
Twitter
www.twitter.com/BluegrassBrooks
Goodreads
www.goodreads.com

68438618R00205

Made in the USA
San Bernardino, CA
03 February 2018